Rachael Anderson

HEA Publishing, LLC

ISBN: 978-1490986371

Published by HEA Publishing

For Jeff.
I love you.

Other books by Rachael Anderson

Novels

The Reluctant Bachelorette
Divinely Designed
Luck of the Draw
Minor Adjustments

Anthologies

All I Want: Three Christmas Romances
*The Timeless Romance Anthology: Summer Wedding
Collection*

One
♡ ♡ ♡

One person tried Seth Tuttle's patience like no other. The beautiful, sweet, and totally frustrating, Lanna Carver. She was the closest thing he had to a sister, and for the most part, Seth adored her. But when she raised her chin in that defiant, I've-made-up-my-mind-and-you're-not-going-to-talk-me-out-of-it way, Seth might as well beat his head against the nearest brick wall.

Or white painted cinderblock, in this instance.

"You want to do *what*?" Seth raked his fingers through his short hair as he paced across Lanna's worn carpeted floor.

Lanna sat on the armrest of her faded sofa and clasped her fingers together, her large blue eyes wide and innocent. "It's called a bachelor auction, and *I* don't want to do it. Milly does."

"But you're going along with it."

1

She threw up her hands. "I'm out of fundraising ideas, okay? Milly swears this will earn enough to keep the afterschool program going for at least another year. So yeah, I'm going along with it. I'm even helping as much as I can because we need the money. Evidently the Seattle area is filled with single women, and many of them would pay well for a date with a handsome, wealthy, and charming bachelor." She paused. "Like you."

She didn't even blink when she said it. There was no twitching of her lips or hint of a smile either. Lanna was serious. She actually wanted Seth to be one of the bachelors.

He groaned. "You've got to be kidding me."

"It's for a good cause, Seth. Those underprivileged kids need our tutoring program, especially the ones struggling with English. They're so far behind."

It was a problem for which Seth had a solution, if only Lanna would see reason and accept it. "Which is why I've offered—more than once—to fund your little program. Remember? Have you even told Milly about my offer? Because I *know* she'd accept the money."

Lanna rubbed her hands across the top of her jeans and lifted her chin. "How many times do I have to tell you that it's not your job to fund my projects? I'm trying to *run* a charity—not be one. Milly and I can do this on our own. I *want* us to do it on our own."

"Why?"

"Because."

Seth felt the stirrings of frustration that came with any conversation revolving around money and Lanna. He didn't get it, or her. Dropping down next to her on the sofa, he placed his hand over hers. "That's my point. You don't have to do it on your own."

Lanna's expression turned pleading as she covered his hand with her other one. "Listen, Seth, I appreciate the offer, I do. But ever since Mike died, you've been trying to take care of me and solve all of my problems. That needs to end. I want and need you in my life as a brother figure, not a benefactor."

She sounded so confident, but Seth knew from experience that Lanna needed looking out for—not that anyone would know based on her appearance. The girl definitely knew how to dress well, even though her clothes came from some off-price department store like TJMaxx. But one look at her dumpy third-floor studio apartment in a slummy part of town and anyone would know the truth: Lanna was barely scraping by.

Seth, on the other hand, had more money than he knew what to do with. Yet would Lanna accept his help? No. Oh, he'd tried. Many, many times. But it always came back to bite him. The worst being when he'd attempted to anonymously pay for her rent one month. The next day, she showed up on his doorstep, cash in hand, to pay him back. Then she yelled at him about wasted gas money and for making her late to work.

Sometimes Seth wondered if Mike, his former best friend and Lanna's brother, had known what he'd asked of Seth in that dreary hospital room all those years before.

"Seth, take care of Lanna," Mike had whispered from the bed. "Please."

Seth had readily agreed. Of course he'd look after Lanna. He'd already planned on it. Problem was, Mike didn't exact a similar promise from his sister. Something along the lines of "Lanna, please let Seth help you out every once in a while" would have been helpful.

Looking back, Seth often wondered if Mike had any idea how difficult his sister would end up being. Probably. Seth wouldn't be surprised if his old friend was looking down from heaven right now and laughing.

Seth squeezed Lanna's hand, as if the pressure would somehow make her see reason. "But that's what I'm trying to do. If Mike were still here and offering the same thing, you know you'd accept the money from him."

Lanna pulled her hand free and stood, staring down at him. With her petite build, standing above him while he sat was the only time she could ever tower over him, which she apparently felt the need to do at the moment. Her arms folded as a determined look flashed across her face. "But Mike's not here, is he? And any day you could be taken from me as well, especially with all the crazy stunts you like to pull. I need to know for myself that I'm capable of doing things all on my own. Why can't you understand that?"

Seth rolled his eyes and flopped back on the couch. Going up against Lanna was like taking on a brutal workout. It exhausted him. "I'm not going anywhere, Lanna."

"You can't guarantee that."

Seth didn't understand why they were even talking about this. "This isn't even about you anyway. I'm not trying to pay your rent or the balance on your credit card. I'm trying to pay for a *charity*. You say you don't want my help, but yet you still want me to be one of the bachelors and auction myself off like some kind of animal."

Her expression softened, and the corners of her mouth tugged up into a teasing smile. "Of course I do. You're handsome, smart, and have that confident swagger most girls find irresistible. You'd get top dollar."

Seth closed his eyes in frustration. It was no use. Arguing with Lanna was like arguing with a two-ton boulder. She wouldn't budge.

"It's in three weeks," Lanna continued. "And it's going to be really nice. Milly's dad is friends with the owner of the Bellevue Hotel, so we're having it there. We're only inviting a select group of women, so we'll have complete control over who comes. It will be classy, I promise."

How like Lanna to refuse to give an inch while still expecting Seth to capitulate. Well, that wasn't going to happen—not today, anyway.

Seth stood and squared his shoulders, looking down on her instead of the other way around. "Why is it that Milly doesn't have a problem taking handouts from people, but you do? Doesn't the owner of that hotel contribute to your cause?"

"Yes, he has been very generous. But that's just it. He contributes because he *believes* in our cause and the good it will do for our community. You, on the other hand, only want to donate to ease your conscience about me, which isn't okay. I refuse to take any money from you when your heart's not in it. I will, however, happily add your name to the list of bachelors." Her expression turned hopeful, almost pleading.

Seth raked his fingers through his hair again and resumed his pacing, wishing he could shake some sense into her. "Sorry, but that's not the kind of help I'm offering. No way am I going to parade around in front of a bunch of desperate women and be forced to go out with the highest bidder. It's the money on the table here—not me. Take it or leave it."

Lanna's expression fell slightly, and her smile took on a strained quality. But she kept her head high. "I'll leave it, thanks."

Knowing he'd be tempted to strangle her if this continued much longer, Seth turned on his heel and walked to the door. With one last look over his shoulder, he said, "If you change your mind—"

"I won't."

His jaw clenched, and Seth closed the door behind him with a hard tug. Walking past the elevator, he opened the door to the stairwell and took the stairs two at a time, needing to burn off some of his frustration. Lanna had her sights fixed on one thing and one thing only: to prove to the world she didn't need any help from anyone—least of all from him.

Well, no more. Seth was sick of it. Whether Lanna liked it or not, she would get his help. He was just as determined, if not more so, than Lanna. After all, he'd made a promise to Mike, and Seth always kept his promises.

Seth emerged outside and filled his lungs with Seattle's cool and humid January air before searching the street for his car. What he needed now was some good hard exercise to shake this off and figure out what to do next. Thank goodness he and his buddies had a basketball game lined up in an hour. He could throw a few elbows, make a few baskets, and clear his mind from all thoughts of Lanna Carver.

For now.

Two

♡ ♡ ♡

Grace Warren waved goodbye to her last patient of the day and walked into the break room to get her things. It had been a long and emotionally exhausting day. One of her patients became frustrated with the slow progress of rehab and had ignored her advice, went to the gym on his own, and reinjured his shoulder lifting too much weight. Now they were back to where they'd started—possibly worse.

Typically, Grace loved her job as a physical therapist. There was no greater reward than seeing someone who came to her broken walk away fixed. But every now and then she'd get patients who thought they knew better, like her patient today. Or worse, those who didn't have the desire or willpower to put forth the necessary effort—sort of like her brother, Alec.

But Grace didn't want to think about Alec or her other patients right now. She wanted to go home, take a soothing hot shower, put on her favorite yoga pants, and curl up on the couch to watch her favorite TV series. A new episode had aired two days before, and she wanted to catch up. Tonight was all hers.

"Oh good, you haven't left yet." Cameron, another therapist in the clinic, poked his head through the door and gave it a shake, forcing his dark hair away from his eyes. If he'd just trim it a little shorter, he wouldn't have to shake his head all the time, but Cameron preferred his hair slightly longer, the way he'd worn it throughout high school and college based on all the pictures he had scattered around his office. Sometimes Grace wondered if that was his way of trying to stay connected with the past—a feeling Grace completely understood. How often had she wished she could rewind time and go back to the day when things were easier, simpler, happier.

"I'm heading out now," Grace said, slinging her bag over her shoulder. "You caught me just in time. Was there something you needed?" Cameron often picked Grace's brain when it came to some of his patients. She spent a lot of her spare time researching, attending seminars, and learning the newest techniques. Over time, she'd gained the reputation of being one of the best in her field—something Cameron used to his advantage.

"No, I, uh, actually need a favor." His expression turned sheepish. "A big favor."

Grace raised an eyebrow. It was Friday night, and if Cameron needed a big favor, it probably meant something non-work related. Which also meant the comfy couch and TV show would likely get pushed back yet again. But Cameron was a friend, and if he needed a favor, she couldn't say no. "Sure, what's up?"

Cameron let out a breath as he turned a chair around and sat on it backwards, resting his arms on the back of it and allowing his hair to fall forward once again. Another head shake came, making Grace draw her lips into her mouth so she wouldn't smile. His head shake, combined with his crooked nose, always made her want to laugh—especially considering his name literally meant "crooked nose." Grace wondered if his parents named him that because he was born with a crooked nose, or if his nose was destined to become crooked *because* of the name Cameron.

Some might think it crazy that Grace—a scientist—would even care what a person's name meant, but it had all started as a high-school science experiment. Grace had set out to prove that the meaning behind a name didn't actually *mean* anything, but she'd been surprised by the results. Most people actually epitomized their names, and over the years, she'd used that knowledge as a sort of personality test—especially when it came to the guys she'd dated or the people she worked with. One quick internet search, and Grace knew a little something about someone.

"It's a long story," Cameron said, bringing Grace back to the present. "But the gist of it is that I've agreed to be a contestant in a bachelor auction and—"

"Wait—what? Did you just say 'bachelor auction?' But what about Talia?" Grace said, naming his girlfriend of four months now. "Or did you two . . . ?" She let the sentence hang there, too scared of the answer. Talia was sweet and smart—the best girl Cameron had ever dated. Grace didn't want to hear that he'd done something stupid like break up with her.

Cameron held up a hand. "We're still together, so don't worry. This is more of a favor to an old college friend who's trying to raise money for some afterschool tutoring program for underprivileged kids."

"Oh." Grace sank down on the seat opposite him, wishing she could kick off her sneakers and put up her feet. They ached so badly. "What do you need my help for?"

"I need you to bid on me."

"Excuse me?" A laugh escaped, mostly because Cameron had never looked quite so vulnerable. It didn't jibe with his normally semi-cocky attitude.

"Talia was going to come and bid on me, but something came up, and she can't make it. Please, Grace? I don't want to get stuck going out with some random, desperate, and probably weird girl. And Talia doesn't want me going out with anyone else, period. You can spend whatever you need, and I'll pay you back."

Grace sighed, mentally saying so long to a much needed night of relaxation. If only she had it in her to just say no. "Okay, fine, I'll go. Just tell me when and where, and I'll be there."

"Eight o'clock at the Bellevue Hotel."

Her eyes widened. "Wow, that's, uh, pretty posh."

Cameron nodded then stood and walked to the door, stopping with his hand on the frame. "Oh, and it's a black tie thing, so make sure you wear a nice dress."

With that, he was gone, leaving Grace blinking after him with her mouth hanging slightly open. Did he really just say "nice"? Because black tie was not *nice*. Black tie was *fancy*. How did Cameron not know that? What's more, how did he not understand that most girls don't have that kind of dress hanging in the back of their closets on the off chance they'd need it one day?

Grace let out a breath and rubbed her temples, feeling a headache coming on. Cameron was going to pay for this—literally. Not only would she wait until the last second to bid on him, but she would double the highest bid.

Three

♡ ♡ ♡

Grace stepped from her car into the chilly late January air and lifted her skirt, careful to keep it clear of the asphalt as she walked toward the impressive entrance of the Bellevue Hotel in downtown Seattle. Thank goodness she'd been able to locate a dress-rental place that agreed to stay open a little later for her. Located on the other side of town, Grace had made it there with only minutes to spare and had tried on a couple of dresses—one of which happened to be the light blue, almost aqua, floor-length gown she now wore. Although suited more for spring than January with its capped sleeves, it fit the best, and Grace wasn't in a position to be picky.

She'd handed over her credit card, bit back a wince at the exorbitant rental fee, and quickly decided to triple the highest bid for Cameron.

Head held high, Grace handed her wool coat over to a porter then followed the signs to the Olympic room. A short line of elegantly dressed women waited to give their name at the door, making Grace hesitate. Clearly this was an invitation-only event, and—thanks to Cameron—she'd arrived empty handed.

Well, if she couldn't get in, that was that. At least she could tell Cameron she'd tried and there would still be time for that bath and her favorite show.

Grace moved to the front of the line and smiled at a petite woman wearing a red evening gown, with her light-brown hair pulled back into a twist.

"I'm here as a guest of one of the bachelors," Grace said. "Cameron Williams?"

"Oh, you must be Talia." The woman gave an answering smile as she held out her hand. "I'm Lanna Carver, Cameron's friend from college. Thank you so much for coming."

Grace took Lanna's hand and gave it a quick shake. "Actually, Talia couldn't make it tonight, so Cameron asked me to come in her place. I hope that's okay. My name is Grace Warren."

"Oh, of course," said Lanna. "Any friend of Cameron's is always welcome." Lanna handed her a white paddle, along with a brochure. "This is your number for the auction and a brochure with a listing of all the bachelors. I hope you find one who piques your interest."

"Thanks."

"No problem," said Lanna. "Be sure to sample all the desserts while you're here. The food is to die for."

"Will do." Grace smiled again and walked into a beautiful room. Elegant tray ceilings complimented the large rectangular chandeliers, under which dozens of women mingled. Even with her silk gown and simple up-do, Grace felt underdressed in comparison to the rest. She clung to her skirt as she made her way to the dessert table, her stomach grumbling since she'd skipped dinner—also thanks to

Cameron. The list kept adding up. If the desserts didn't look so appetizing, she probably would have considered quadrupling her bid.

Grace loaded up the small plate with a few tarts, a macadamia cookie, and a mint brownie. It was her reward, she rationalized, for agreeing to do this.

As she munched on the goodies, Grace took a moment to look over the crowd, noting the array of dresses—everything from the cliché mini black dress to long, flowing evening gowns. One woman even went all out, with a short chiffon train trailing behind. The room was filled with blondes, brunettes, and red-heads all dressed their best to impress men like Cameron Williams—a man with a crooked nose who perpetually shook his head to keep the hair out of his eyes and enjoyed talking about himself a little too much.

As Grace continued to people watch, a tall, willowy woman mounted the stairs to a platform at the front of the room and introduced herself as Milly Lebaron. As she spoke, the rest of the women moved closer, their dresses combining to form colorful patterns that sparkled beneath the dim lighting. Milly welcomed everyone and gave a short presentation on the afterschool program, explaining what the money would be used for. She thanked several benefactors, including the owner of the hotel, then explained how the auction would work.

Finally, Milly gestured for the first bachelor to join her on the platform. A handsome man of average height stepped next to her, turning slightly to the side with his thumb hooked into the pocket of his tux jacket. He was introduced as Ty McPherson, and Grace immediately sized him up by his name alone. She'd once dated a Ty and knew the meaning of his name well. Stubborn—as in a pain in the neck.

Don't do it, girls, Grace thought. *If his personality fits his name, you'll be wasting your money.*

"We'll start the bidding off at one hundred," Milly announced. A woman immediately raised her paddle.

Grace bit her lip, lingering at the back of the crowd, away from the others. Exhaustion seeped through her body, making her wish the auction were over already. Her gaze travelled longingly to the side of the room where several chairs stood against one wall. Empty chairs. Did she dare take a seat while she waited, or would that be rude?

"Going once, going twice, sold to the woman wearing the lovely emerald dress!"

Grace's gaze snapped back to Milly. How much had the stubborn Ty been sold for? And how many bachelors would be auctioned off that night?

Grace opened the brochure Lanna had given her and started flipping through the pages. Each bachelor had a quarter page dedicated to them, along with a picture, brief bio, and what kind of date a woman could expect from him. Grace flipped to the end, where Cameron's face stared at her from the last page. Since Ty's bio had appeared at the front of the brochure, Grace assumed the bachelors would appear in the order listed, which meant Grace would be here for a while.

Great. She'd be quadrupling the bid for sure now.

Grace scanned through Cameron's bio, picking up words like *physical therapist, healer, athlete,* etc. When she came to the type of date a woman would expect from him, she slowed down and read the paragraph.

If you read my bio, you'll know I'm a fan of the great outdoors. The woman who wins a date with me will get a day filled with high adventure and surprises around every corner. From the moment I pick you up, I'll take you away from normal, everyday life and into a world where your dream date becomes a reality. Whether it's parasailing across the Seattle skies, taking a romantic horseback ride down the beach, or ziplining to a beautiful, private location for dinner, the day will be one you'll never forget. Guaranteed.

Quickly, Grace covered her mouth to muffle the laughter threatening to burst. No wonder Cameron was petrified of someone else bidding for him. He'd actually have to put some thought, effort, and money into a date. Cameron was more of a "Let's grab dinner, hit a club, or catch the latest sports game on TV" type of guy—at least based on his experiences with Talia and past girlfriends. High adventure and surprises around every corner? Not likely.

Grace shook her head, thinking that maybe quadrupling his bid would be letting him off easy. Maybe she shouldn't bid on him at all.

"Sold to the woman in black!"

Once again, Grace had missed the amount the latest bachelor had gone for. She needed to pay better attention and forced her eyes to follow the movements of the next bachelor coming on stage. Tall, with wavy dark blond hair and light eyes, he was incredibly attractive. Grace's interest was piqued.

"Welcome, Jake Peters."

Jake. As in supplanter. As in would do whatever it took to get to the top, like the Jake in her freshman biology class who'd swept her off her feet then stolen her idea for the final project. Grace had been forced to come up with a new idea on the spot and had ended up with a B because of it.

Her eyes narrowed. Okay, not so attractive anymore.

Grace shifted her weight from one foot to the other and eyed the chairs once more. But if she sat down now, she might be tempted to rest her head against the back of the chair and fall asleep. As much as she wished she could do just that, her conscience would never allow it. She'd made a promise to Cameron, after all.

Carefully, Grace shifted her weight once again and kicked off one of her black heels, followed by the other. If she was going to stand here for another hour, she would do it without her feet screaming.

"Can't you drive a little faster?" Seth urged his friend, Garrett, who took the speed limit very seriously, especially when it came to driving within city limits. "I'm late."

"I told you we didn't have time to play one more game," Garrett said, referring to the two-on-two pick-up game of basketball they'd just played. "But would you listen? No. Come to think of it, you never listen to me."

Seth frowned at the traffic light as it changed from green to yellow, causing Garrett to slow the car to a stop once again. They were so close. He could see The Bellevue at the end of the street, but it still seemed so far away. "I wasn't about to walk away as a loser—especially not to them. We should never have lost to them."

"Well, now we're losers twice over, and you're late to a bachelor auction, which I still can't believe you're going to."

"Lanna gave me no choice."

Garrett snorted. When the light finally changed, he moved the car forward at an almost painfully slow speed. It seemed like hours before he finally pulled into the parking lot. For a guy who could elbow his way to the basket with the best of them, Garrett drove like a snail. A really sluggish snail.

As soon as Garrett pulled up to the front entrance, Seth leapt from the car.

"What about your tux?" Garrett gestured to the garment bag in the back seat. "I thought this was black tie."

Seth grabbed a hoodie from the front seat and pulled it over his head, hoping it would mask the smell of sweat. He didn't have time to change. "They'll have to take me as I am. Maybe if you'd driven faster . . ."

Garrett rolled his eyes. "Whatever, dude, I drove the speed limit. This one's all on you."

"I just hope they let me in."

"It might be a good thing if they don't."

Seth shut the car door and jogged inside, following the signs to the auction room. The doors were closed, and a porter sat at nearby table. Ignoring him, Seth went straight to the doors and pulled one open.

"Hey, you can't go in there," the porter called.

Seth ducked into the back of the room, hoping the porter would prefer not to make a scene and leave him alone. But the man caught up and stopped Seth with a hand on his arm. "Sir," he whispered, "This is an invitation-only event. You're not allowed in here."

"I'm friends with Lanna Carver. She's expecting me." Okay, so that was only partly true, but Seth was desperate.

The porter looked skeptical, but finally nodded and relinquished Seth's arm. Breathing a sigh of relief, Seth made his way to the back of the crowd, next to a woman wearing a shimmering blue dress.

"Two hundred to the woman in red," Milly announced from the podium.

Good, Seth wasn't too late. He sidled closer to the woman in blue. "How many more bachelors are there?" he said quietly.

Startled green eyes blinked at him. "What?"

"How many more guys are left?" Seth gestured to the bachelor on stage.

The woman's gaze shifted back to the man standing on the platform. "Why?"

"Three hundred from the woman in green," Milly continued, accepting more bids.

"Because I want to know, that's why," Seth said. It was a simple question. Why wouldn't she answer it?

The woman looked him up and down the way she'd size up a crazy person, probably taking in his sweat pants and hoodie and wondering what mental hospital he'd escaped from.

"Going once, going twice . . ." Milly's voice rang out.

The woman next to him quickly averted her gaze and raised her paddle, indicating a bid.

"Five hundred from the woman in blue," said Milly. "Do I have five-fifty?"

Not wanting to chance it, Seth went to raise his hand, only to realize that he didn't have a paddle. He looked around frantically, spying one on a table not too far away. He grabbed it and held it up.

"Five-fifty to the"—Milly's voice drifted off as she squinted at Seth—"um, person in the back," she finally finished.

"What are you doing?" hissed the woman in blue. "That's not your number, and you can't bid on Cameron."

"Why not?" Seth looked around to see if anyone else planned to bid. He couldn't leave it at five-fifty. That wasn't nearly enough.

"Six hundred, anyone?" Milly's voice echoed through the room.

When no one raised a paddle, Seth elbowed the woman in blue, who stared at him as if he'd grown two heads. "Bid again," he whispered.

"Excuse me?"

"Going once, going twice . . ."

"Bid again!"

She raised her paddle.

"Six hundred to the woman in blue," said Milly. "Six-fifty, anyone? For the date of your dreams?"

Seth raised his paddle once more. "Twenty thousand," he called out.

A hush fell over the crowd as every woman in the room turned to stare at him, including the woman in blue. But Seth didn't care. He only cared about Milly's reaction. Would she accept the bid or have him dragged from the room?

A slow smile made its way to her face as recognition dawned. "Twenty thousand to the man at the back." She playfully elbowed the bachelor standing next to her, whose face had drained of color. "Wow, aren't you a wanted commodity," she teased. "Do I have any other bids?"

The bachelor's eyes flickered from Seth to the woman in blue, who turned her palms up in question, as if asking what she should do. The bachelor shook his head slightly, and Seth got the impression he'd just messed up whatever plan the two had going on.

"Going once, going twice—sold to the man in sweats at the back!" Milly pronounced.

Seth's mouth turned up in a self-satisfied smile as he gave himself a mental pat on the back. No way could Lanna turn down the money now, not when Milly had accepted his bid. It felt as though he'd crested Everest, even with all the women in the room staring and whispering at his expense. Apparently they didn't understand that he'd one-upped the most stubborn woman of them all.

The woman in blue faced him, her arms folded as she studied him. A few dark curls escaped the knot at the nape of her neck, hanging next to her dangling pearl earrings and giving her a casual elegance which Seth liked. With her light-green eyes and arched eyebrows, she looked beautiful beneath the dim lighting in the room. He held out his hand for her to shake. "The name's Seth."

She ignored his hand, gesturing to his clothing instead. "This is a black tie event. You're wearing sweats."

"You don't say."

Her eyes continued to search his face—well, more like probe—as though she could see into his mind and thoughts. She held up the brochure she carried, showing Seth the face of the bachelor he'd just bid twenty grand for. He took it from her to get a closer look.

"What do you plan to do about the incredibly expensive date you won?" she asked.

Seth scanned through Cameron's bio, a smile tugging at the corners of his mouth. He returned the brochure back to her and tapped the page. "Experience an unforgettable day of high adventure, apparently. Sorry if I, uh, took that away from you."

She looked completely unfazed, as though this strange situation happened all the time. "You know he's not gay, right?"

"I made that assumption, yes," Seth said, wondering what was going through that pretty head of hers. "Why? Are you hoping I'll hand the date off to you since I'm clearly not gay either?"

"Aren't you?"

The way she said it made Seth's jaw work back and forth. She looked so confident, so unshakable, reminding him of someone who got under his skin on a regular basis— Lanna. Except the two women looked nothing alike. Lanna was petite and fair, whereas this woman was taller, with darker hair and a darker complexion. But that expression— that impassivity—exactly the same. Maybe Lanna had given her lessons.

Yet for whatever reason, it bothered Seth that this woman might think he preferred men to women. "No, I'm not."

"Then you won't mind if I do borrow that date from you. I'm sure Cameron would prefer me over you anyway."

If she didn't look so sure of herself, Seth would have said, "Have it, it's yours." But something in the way she said it made Seth bristle. "Yes, I would mind, actually. I happen to like ziplining, parasailing, and . . . romantic horseback rides."

"And Cameron, apparently."

Seth took a step forward, leaning close so his eyes were only inches from hers. "Like I told you, I'm not gay."

"Oh yeah? Prove it. Give me the da—"

Seth immediately dipped his head slightly and covered her mouth with his. Her lips were warm and soft, and she smelled faintly of citrus. For a second, it seemed like she responded, but then she planted her palms against his chest and shoved him away.

"What are you doing!" she hissed, looking a lot less assured than she had moments before.

Seth's mouth drew into a smile. "You said you wanted proof, so I gave it to you. Is that enough, or would you like more?" He took a step closer.

Her fists clenched at her side, but she stood her ground, glaring up at him. She opened her mouth to say something then snapped it shut. Lifting her skirts, she turned on her heel and stormed away, only to stop, turn back, and pick up a pair of black heels lying on the ground where she'd stood.

Seth couldn't help but chuckle as she strode away once more, head held high, her bearing stiff and full of pride. Seth felt as though he'd won a battle—well, two battles actually. Milly had accepted his bid after all.

Seth's eyes followed the woman in blue as she disappeared through the door. Then he turned and scanned the room, his gaze landing on the dessert table. He started forward. Tonight was a night for celebrating, and he'd start with those delicious-looking brownies.

Small fingers clenched around his arm, stopping his progress. "We need to talk," Lanna said, her voice quiet but firm. "In the hall."

Slowly, Seth turned around and bit back a groan. He knew he'd have to answer to Lanna at some point, but he'd hoped to get some sustenance in him first. Facing her on an empty stomach was like giving himself a handicap. "Can't we talk by the dessert table? I haven't had dinner yet, and I'm starving."

"In the hall. Now," she repeated, this time with more steel in her voice.

Seth let out a sigh, said a mental goodbye to the desserts, and allowed Lanna to lead him out of the room and around the corner to a secluded alcove. She let go of his arm and turned on him. "I can't believe you did that. How could you? You just made a mockery of this entire night."

Seth blinked, confused. Where had Lanna been during the final bid? In a bubble? "No, what I did was make your afterschool program an additional twenty grand. I get that you're mad at me about the money, but I didn't make a mockery of your auction."

"You bid on another guy, Seth!"

Oh, well there was that. For whatever reason, her words struck Seth's funny bone, making him grin. "Didn't you see the date that guy offered? How could I pass on something like that?"

"Stop it! This isn't funny!" Her foot stomped on the carpeted ground with a soft thud. Based on the way her eyes misted over and how she looked away, Seth could see that she really didn't think it was funny. He'd never seen Lanna cry before. It immediately wiped the grin from his face.

Seth reached for her arm, but she pulled it free, still not looking at him.

"You wouldn't take the money any other way," he said softly. "So I did what I had to do to finally get you to accept my help. You and I both know that Mike would want me to do this."

Her eyes turned back to him, harder now than ever before. "No, he wouldn't. Don't you get it? You can't force your help on people. Life doesn't work like that. All you can do is offer, and if I say no, you have to walk away and leave it be. You can't do this to me anymore, Seth. You can't." Her voice broke at the end.

Seth suddenly felt as if he were two inches tall, even next to her petite body. He wanted to draw her into a hug and assure her that he'd come here tonight because he cared about her and not for any other reason. But if she'd slapped his arm away earlier, she certainly wouldn't let him hug her now.

"Okay," he said. "Lesson learned. I promise to only make offers from here on out. There. Happy?" Seth certainly didn't feel happy.

She sniffed and nodded, not looking remotely happy either—or triumphant, for that matter. "I know Milly accepted your bid, but we're not taking that money."

Whoa—what? Seth blinked, feeling as though she'd tricked him. In his mind, they'd each surrendered some of their pride and made a compromise. She finally agreed to take his money, and he promised to never pull a stunt like this again. Done.

But not really, because Lanna was incapable of compromising.

Seth lifted his chin. "Good luck telling that to Milly and the reporter I caught taking notes and snapping a few pictures. Oh and the parents with kids in your program who will read about tonight's success in tomorrow's paper. Good luck with that."

Lanna bit her lower lip, her eyelids blinking rapidly.

"For Pete's sake, Lanna, take the stupid money," Seth begged. "You need it. Those kids need it. If for no other reason, take it for them."

Tears leaked from the corners of her eyes as she stood there, shaking her head and looking almost as miserable as she'd looked the day of her brother's funeral. Seth's heart wrenched at the sight.

"Fine," Lanna finally said, tears drizzling down her cheeks. "You win. I'll take the money."

With that, she walked away, the same way the girl in blue had done earlier. Only this time, Seth didn't feel triumphant at all. He felt like he'd broken something special, something that could never be put back together the same way it had been before. He'd broken Lanna's spirit.

Four

♡ ♡ ♡

Still wearing her dress, Grace drew her legs beneath her and settled against the back of her comfy microfiber couch as she stared at her laptop, waiting for the website, WhatsInAName.com, to load. When it did, her fingers quickly tapped out the name *Seth*.

Grace had never known another Seth before—at least not well enough to research the name. But now she did. Only thirty minutes before, someone with that name had challenged her, caught her off guard, and caused her to run away—something she never did.

It was the kiss that had done it. That warm, soft, and completely inappropriate kiss. To make matters worse, for one brief moment, Grace had actually enjoyed the sensation of that man's lips against hers—*enjoyed*. She'd even kissed him back, though it made her cringe to admit it. What had she been thinking? Especially after he'd just outbid her for Cameron—*Cameron*!

It didn't matter how handsome Seth was, with those piercing blue eyes and dark hair, Grace should have done more than shoved him away. She should have slapped him then stood her ground and told Seth exactly where he could put those lips in the future—anywhere but on her. Then she should have slapped him again.

Even now, she still couldn't shake the horrible, anxious feeling that crawled across her skin like a colony of ants.

Grace glared at Seth's name on the screen, hating it more than ever. What had prompted him to go to the auction anyway? Wouldn't it have been easier—and far less humiliating—for him to simply donate the money? It didn't make sense.

Realizing she hadn't clicked the search button, Grace quickly did so, waiting for the results. What would it mean? Arrogant? Jerk? Self-serving? All of the above? It had to.

The page finally loaded, and two results appeared—one with the Hebrew meaning, the other with the Egyptian mythology meaning. Grace clicked on the Hebrew version first.

Third son of Adam and Eve. Means "placed" or "appointed."

Grace frowned. Placed? Appointed? That sounded way too positive, like someone destined to be a great leader or something. She drew her bottom lip into her mouth. Hmm . . . maybe it wasn't meant to be positive. Maybe what it really meant was that all the Seths in the world appointed themselves to be cocky and vain, intimidators and manipulators of other people.

Yes, Seth was a self-appointed ego-maniac. That fit much better.

Just to be sure, Grace went back and clicked on the mythology version of his name. She scanned the words quickly, and as she did so, a slow smile stretched across her face. Turned out that Seth was also the name of the Egyptian god of chaos.

Suddenly it all made sense. Not only had Seth brought his self-appointed ego to the auction, but he'd wrought total chaos. No wonder Grace had run. Anyone in their right mind would have run from a god of chaos.

At least she'd done so with her head held high.

Armed with her newly acquired knowledge, Grace closed the laptop with a satisfied snap, feeling much better. If she ever came up against another Seth again, she'd be ready.

Five

♡ ♡ ♡

$\mathcal{G}$race shifted the bag of groceries she carried to the opposite hip as she paused in front of her brother's first-story apartment. She breathed in the damp air and looked longingly at a jogger coming toward her down the street. If only she could be at the park right now, running her favorite route, and not standing outside this apartment. While lovely on the outside, with a colonial townhouse feel, the inside was a different matter. Grace could almost feel the dreariness seeping through the door.

Ever since Grace had moved to Seattle to be near Alec, she'd promised herself to show up at least two or three times a week, regardless of whether he wanted her there or not. So here she was, keeping her promise. She glanced at the front window, covered by dark wooden blinds, and took one last breath of fresh air. However dark or stale it was on the other side, Grace wasn't about to admit defeat no matter how difficult her brother could be.

Squaring her shoulders, Grace rang the bell, knowing he wouldn't answer but wanting to alert him of her arrival. Then she pulled out the spare key he'd given her and slid it into the lock, pushing the door open with her free hip. The smell of stale and musty air invaded her senses, making her want to stay on the outside. But she forced her feet forward and closed the door quickly behind her, shutting out the temptation to leave.

"Hey bro, it's me," Grace called as she walked to the kitchen, feeling like she'd entered a place that shut out all light and happiness. The tap-tapping of the keyboard sounded from down the hall, letting her know that Alec was busy working in his home office. He gave no greeting or indication that he'd heard her come inside.

She sighed and opened the blinds and windows in both the kitchen and family room, wishing Alec had a box fan that would draw the fresh air inside faster. No matter how many times she hinted to her brother that he could open his windows occasionally, he never seemed to do it. A light coat of dust covered the coffee table and entertainment center, and Grace made a mental note to wipe them clean before she left.

She put most of the groceries away, started a pan of rice on the stove, and pulled out a cutting board so she could chop vegetables for a stir fry. She often cooked for her brother and brought him fresh groceries. It was the only way she could guarantee he ate a home-cooked meal since he didn't like to venture out. Alec used to get after Grace for coming, telling her to stop treating him like a special-needs case, but when she continued to come, week after week, he finally gave up the fight.

Their parents continually told Grace to stop enabling Alec, but Grace knew if she didn't, he'd eat cereal, order takeout, or find some other form of easy cuisine. Alec needed fresh produce and a good meal every once in a while.

So every Tuesday and Thursday night, and typically Sunday, he got one. Grace also made sure to leave enough leftovers for at least one meal the following day.

As the sunlight brightened the room and the fresh air began to make its way inside, Grace felt her spirits lift. She turned on some upbeat music and felt them lift even higher. Someday, things would change. Someday, her brother would find something to live for again. And someday, the heavy weight of guilt that settled against her chest every time she thought of Alec would lessen.

Once dinner was ready, Grace wiped her hands on a dishcloth and went to find her brother. With his profile facing her, he tapped away at his computer, and Grace allowed her heart to constrict for a few moments as she studied him. His sandy-blond hair was in need of a haircut, his face in need of a shave, and his complexion in need of some sun.

The physical therapist in her also noticed that his biceps and triceps weren't nearly as toned as they used to be, and his once-lean stomach now carried extra weight. Then there were his legs—so weak and fragile looking. Grace swallowed. For someone whose name meant "the protector of mankind" this wasn't him. Alec should be strong and erect—a force to be reckoned with.

Grace swallowed the lump in her throat, moved forward, and put her hand on his shoulder. "Dinner's ready."

Alec jerked back and shot her a look of surprise. "When did you get here?"

"A little while ago. Didn't you hear me?" Grace could still hear the radio from where she stood, albeit faintly.

He rubbed at the scruff on his chin as he blinked at the monitor. "Sorry. I've been working on a new code, and you know how I get."

"Yeah, I know." Her brother was always working on some code. If Grace never came over, he'd probably come up for air only when he needed to use the bathroom, got hungry, or slept. She had no idea how many hours he spent working, but it was way too much.

There was a time when Grace thought they'd put the worst behind them, but ever since he started working from home, things had gone downhill.

Why had she ever asked Alec to skip a day of high school and go skiing with her that horrible winter day nearly ten years ago? How many times had she wished she could rewind time and take it all back? Why didn't she just go to school like Alec had planned to do? Why couldn't she have been more responsible, like he was? Instead, she'd convinced him to be irresponsible for a day, and it had cost him the use of his legs.

The guilt bore down on her the same way it did every time she saw her brother. She cleared her throat and averted her eyes. "So, you coming? The food's getting cold."

Alec's hands moved from the keyboard to his lap, and he nodded. "Coming."

Without thinking, Grace moved behind him to wheel him out of the room, but one cold look from Alec had her snapping her hands to her side and leading the way to the kitchen. There was nothing Alec hated more than being treated like an invalid. Grace should have known better.

"So," Grace said as they sat down to eat. "What sort of code are you working on now?"

"Just a program for an internet site. They have a lengthy and complex questionnaire they need programmed. It needs to jump to new pages or skip certain questions based on the user's answers then map out and analyze the results." He shrugged. "Pretty boring stuff, but it pays the bills."

"Whatever," Grace said. "You love that kind of stuff. It's like a never-ending puzzle to you."

He nodded. "Good thing, too, because there's not much else that—" He cut himself off and shoved a forkful of stir fry into his mouth.

Grace didn't know what to say. She lowered her eyes to her plate so Alec wouldn't see the pity that filled them. He hated that almost as much as he hated help.

"You really don't need to keep cooking and shopping for me," Alec said. "I'm a big boy and can do it myself."

They'd had this conversation before. Several times, in fact. And every time, Grace's answer was the same. "I like to do it," she said. "I get lonely and enjoy hanging out with my brother. Is that such a bad thing?"

"Not it if were true." His light-green eyes took on a teasing quality, but Grace knew he wasn't really joking. No matter how hard she tried to hide how difficult it was for her to see him like this, Alec could probably see right through her.

Grace swallowed her food and pasted on a smile. "I was thinking that maybe you could come visit me sometime—you know, at work. See what I do. We have all this equipment there that you're welcome to use if you ever want to work out." She bit her tongue after that last part. She shouldn't have said it, but the words had slipped out before she could check them.

"Are you saying I'm looking out of shape?" he said dryly.

Grace sneaked a glance at him, trying to gauge what was going through his mind—if he was in a mood that could take some positive criticism. Maybe it was time to stop all the dancing around the subject and tell him what she really thought. "No, I'm saying that it would be good for you to get out a little more. You can still workout, you know. In fact, you need to. Otherwise you're at risk for things like blood clots, muscle atrophy, or osteoporosis."

Silence.

"Would that really be so bad?" Alec spoke the words quietly, as if he hadn't meant them to be heard by anyone. As if he would actually welcome an early death.

Grace set down her fork with a sharp clack on the table and glared at her brother. She hated—*hated*—when he said stuff like that. "Yes, Alec, that would be bad. How could you even think—" She broke off, fighting back emotion. Not even the sun shining through the open windows could ebb the pain that had suddenly slammed into her chest.

"I was only joking, Grace. Lighten up," Alec said. Only he hadn't been joking, and they both knew it. Still, he looked sorry for having caused her pain, and if he felt sorry enough, maybe Grace could use that to her advantage.

She leaned across the table and covered his hand with hers. "Just come. Please? I have an opening tomorrow. You can get out of the house, and we can work through a few exercises. You used to love to work out."

"I used to love a lot of things." His eyes drifted toward the open window and took on a pained quality, almost as if the glimpse into the outside world reminded him of something that had been taken away.

Grace returned her attention to her food, feeling defeated. Maybe her parents were right. Maybe she was enabling her brother. Maybe it was time to stop coming around, time to stop trying to convince him to be someone he obviously didn't want to be anymore. Maybe—

"Okay. I'll be there tomorrow," said Alec.

Grace's eyes snapped to his as hope flared inside her. She felt as though she'd just leapt over a massive hurdle. If Alec came once, maybe he'd want to keep coming. Maybe he'd even start to smile again—really smile. And maybe, just maybe, he'd finally start to realize that his life wasn't over, just different.

Six

♡ ♡ ♡

The chopper thundered away, leaving Seth, his two best friends, and their guide at the top of one of the many mountain ranges in Haines, Alaska. Snow whipped in Seth's face, stinging the exposed part of his face like tiny glass shards. But he didn't care. This was day one of a fourteen-day trip that had been planned nearly a year earlier, right after their last heli-skiing trip. It marked the beginning of what would be an epic two weeks.

Seth adjusted his helmet and goggles as he waited for the noise of the chopper to subside. He looked around, getting a 360-degree view that featured one snow-covered mountain after another. The sky was blue, the sun shining, and the early February chill biting. With over 5,000 vertical feet of skiable terrain below him, Seth couldn't wait to strap on his skis and take the plunge. In his mind, nothing compared to skiing down the fresh, deep powder of an untouched run. This was what life was all about—tossing fear aside and jumping in with both feet.

Mike had taught him that.

Garrett thrust his snowboard vertically into the snow and draped his arms over the top of it as he glanced at Seth. "You ready for this?"

"More than ready." Seth pulled the drawstrings of his gloves, tightening them around his wrists to keep the snow out.

A grin appeared on Garrett's face as he shook his head. "I've gotta admit, I'm a little nervous. That's a pretty steep run through some pretty deep snow. I hope our guide knows what he's doing. I don't want to trigger an avalanche or something."

"You worry too much."

"And you don't worry enough sometimes."

Owen dropped his skis in the snow and shoved his boots in the bindings one at a time, clicking them into place. "Today is going down in history as the most epic day ever. And I'm going to get it all on camera." He pointed toward his head, where a borrowed helmet cam stuck up from the top like a pudgy antennae.

Seth chuckled as he shoved his own boots into his skis. This was Owen's first experience heli-skiing, and he was like a six-year-old kid on a sugar high—something Seth would be sure to tease him about later when they watched whatever kind of video feed came from Owen's helmet cam. "Just don't biff it too much, or we'll all get motion sickness when we watch it."

"Whatever. You know I can ski circles around both of you."

"If you can catch us," Seth joked. Born and raised near a ski resort in Canada, Owen was the better skier—not that Garrett had ever really learned, since he preferred to snowboard. But over the past couple of years, Seth's time spent on the slopes had brought his skill level nearer to Owen's—the perk of having a lot of money and a flexible schedule.

"You guys about ready?" The guide's deep voice called out.

Seth glanced at Garrett, who was strapping on his board, then at Owen. Side-by-side, his two friends looked ridiculous. Garrett sported neon orange from his helmet to his ski pants so he'd be easier to find if he got lost or caught in an avalanche, while Owen looked as though he'd raided various people's closets for his ski apparel—which he had. He wore a red and white striped jacket, a royal-blue helmet, and some brown plaid snow pants. Not that Owen cared. He'd been saving for this trip for over two years and couldn't afford new ski gear to go with it. Seth, knowing how chilly it was in the high mountains, refused to let him bring his old, worn-out ski jacket and holey pants. He'd insisted that Owen borrow one of his jackets. The plaid pants came from another friend.

Seth gripped his poles and pushed his skis forward. "I'm ready."

"Remember what we talked about," the guide said. "Stay behind me and don't veer too far off course, or you may find yourself taking flight over the edge of a cliff. I know this mountain well so follow my lead."

"Is there any avalanche danger?" Garrett asked.

The guide shook his head. "We tested up here yesterday. The snow is solid."

"Let's get it on then!" Owen called out. "Time's a-wasting!"

The guide nodded and pushed himself forward, taking the slope head-on with large, smooth curves. Garrett headed out next, followed by Seth. A loud *whoopee* followed as Owen took up the rear.

Seth grinned as he carved his way down the mountain, feeling the familiar rush of adrenaline that came with the wind rushing at him as he created fresh tracks through the powder. A ski resort could never compete with the freedom, the beauty, and the isolation of backcountry skiing—as Owen would soon realize.

Seth let out a yelp of his own, allowing the thrill of it all to seep into his bones. He'd needed this trip.

Ever since the auction two weeks earlier, Lanna had avoided his calls and texts, refusing to return his messages. She'd taken stubbornness to a whole new level, and if Seth hadn't cared so much about her or their friendship, he would have washed his hands of her. But Lanna was the closest thing he had to a sister, and he didn't want to lose that.

Since he couldn't force her to talk to him, Seth had packed his bags and jumped on the plane, more than ready to take a break from all things Lanna Carver. The next fourteen days would be all about release and the thrill of adventure. No worries, no cares—just him, his friends, and the majestic mountains of Alaska.

The guide let out a whoop as he took a jump and executed an impressive forward flip, landing solidly on both skis. Garrett followed the guide, bringing his knees up to his chest in a high jump. Seth grinned and headed for the ramp, increasing his speed and launching himself in the air. Without much thought, he twisted his body into a familiar stunt, executing a perfect 360.

Exhilaration rushed though him as his skies connected with the snow then sank deeply into the powder. Too late, Seth realized his mistake. While his skies stopped rotating, his knees didn't. A dull pop sounded, and a searing pain blasted through one of his knees, traveling up and down his leg. Seth gasped and doubled over, grabbing his leg above the knee to try to dull the pain as waves of nausea washed over him.

Seth had heard about a pain like this. Read about it. Worked out every day to keep his legs strong so he could avoid it. But here it was, on the first day of his fourteen-day heli-skiing trip.

"Dude, you okay?" Owen said, skidding to a stop next to him.

Seth glanced at Owen then down the hill at Garrett, who still snowboarded on, unaware. The remaining skiable terrain stretched out below Seth, taunting him with something he could no longer have. He bit back a curse.

"I'm pretty sure I just tore my ACL."

Seven
♡ ♡ ♡

$\mathcal{V}$oices, the shuffling of feet, and other noises invaded Seth's sleep. He tried to force his eyes open, but it felt as if someone had glued them shut.

"Shouldn't he be awake by now?" Garrett's voice sounded.

"Anytime now," said an unfamiliar female voice.

Seth probed through his foggy mind, finally recalling where he was and why. Funny that his knee didn't hurt at all. The anesthesiologist must have given him a local. He tried to pry his eyes open once again, this time succeeding. A brief glimpse of a blurry hospital room appeared before his eyes closed again.

"About time," Garrett's voice came again. "You're mom hasn't stopped calling or texting for updates since before they took you in for surgery. She wants you to call as soon as you can talk."

A hand patted his arm. "Good, you're awake," said the voice Seth now assumed was a nurse. "As soon as you're feeling up to it, I need you to drink something for me."

Seth knew he should try to open his eyes again and fully wake up, but all he really wanted to do was go back to sleep. He wasn't remotely thirsty. Nor was he in the mood to talk to his mother, especially since he'd have to reiterate once again that she didn't need to come. His parents owned a bookstore in another state, and Seth knew how difficult it was for either of them to get away.

"You doing okay?" the nurse asked, patting his arm once again.

"I'm tired, but fine. Thanks," said Seth.

A ringing sounded, and Garrett sighed. "Hey, you ready to talk yet? She's calling again."

Seth lifted his hand, still keeping his eyes closed. Garrett answered the phone then pressed it into Seth's palm.

"Hey, Mom," Seth murmured, still feeling a little out of it.

"I should have come," she said without preamble. "I should be there right now to take you home from the hospital and make sure you do as you're told. I'm not sure Garrett can handle you. Does he know what a horrible patient you can be?"

Seth smiled. That was his mother's way of saying she was worried, which he appreciated. "If I promise to follow all the doctor's orders, will you please stop stressing? I'm fine. Garrett's going to crash at my house tonight, and the doctor said I'll be feeling good in no time."

"Your dad can manage for a few days without me," said his mother, as if she hadn't heard a word Seth said. "Just say the word, and I can be on a flight tonight. I'm sure Lanna can pick me up from the airport."

"You've talked to Lanna?" Seth said with a frown. He wasn't ready for Lanna to find out what had happened to him. He wanted her to forgive him on her own terms, not out of pity.

"No, but I'm sure she wouldn't mind. Is she there right now?"

Seth forced his eyes open to look around the room. The nurse typed something into a computer, while Garrett sat next to the bed, looking bored. "No," Seth answered. "She's not exactly talking to me at the moment." The words were out before Seth realized he shouldn't have said them. He blamed the anesthesia.

"Why?"

He sighed. "Because she's Lanna, that's why. Do you mind if we don't talk about this right now?"

"But who's going to see that you eat something decent? Garrett can't cook, and Owen's even worse."

Seth grinned. Good thing Garrett hadn't heard that. He prided himself on the three dishes he knew how to make. "I promise you, I'm going to be just fine."

A nurse with short blonde hair held out a large Styrofoam cup with a drinking straw. "I need you to drink this for me," she whispered.

"Mom, I've got to go. Nurse's orders. I'll call you once I get home, okay?"

She hesitated. "You sure you're okay without me?"

"Thanks for the offer, but yeah, I'm sure. I'll call you later."

Seth handed the phone back to Garrett and took the drink from the nurse, forcing the cold liquid down his throat.

"How are you feeling?" the nurse asked.

"Like I've been drugged."

She laughed. "Don't worry, that's normal."

"My knee doesn't hurt at all. Is that normal too?"

She gave him a rueful smile and rubbed his arm in a motherly way. "Give it time. The local's only going to last so long. Enjoy it while you can."

Seth nodded, feeling antsy. He couldn't wait to get back to the comfortable surroundings of his house. The large, flat-screen TV. The couch. His bed. "When can I head home?"

"Just as soon as the doctor goes over a few things and signs the release papers. I paged him when you woke up, so he should be here any second."

As if on cue, the doctor breezed through the door with a chart in hand. With his gray hair and wise eyes, he looked confident and capable. When they'd first met, Seth had liked him right away.

"Looks like our patient's awake," said the doctor. "How are you, Seth?"

"Ready to go home."

"I'll bet." The doctor chuckled, flipped through Seth's chart, and set it aside. "The surgery went well, as should the recovery. Whenever you're not doing that list of exercises I gave you, keep your leg in the immobilizer, elevated, iced, and use that compression dressing. We want to minimize the swelling as much as possible. I also took the liberty of having one of my staff set up your first appointment with the best PT in the area. Her name is Grace Warren."

"Her?" Seth wasn't so sure about working with a woman. He wanted someone to push him hard, not coddle him.

"Trust me on this. She knows her stuff."

Seth shrugged, still a little skeptical. But if the best orthopedic surgeon in Seattle said Grace Warren was the best PT in Seattle, who was he to argue? "I just want my knee back, Doc. The sooner the better."

"Which is why I had my scheduler make the appointment. Grace is always booked, but we've worked together for a while now, so she squeezes in my patients as a favor to me. Your appointment's tomorrow morning at ten. Don't be late."

"Yes, sir." Seth almost did a mock salute, but kept himself in check.

"I'll make sure he's there on time," said Garrett.

Seth snickered. "Only if we leave ten minutes earlier than necessary."

Garrett raised an eyebrow. "Hey, you're more than welcome to drive yourself. Oh, wait—*you can't.*"

The doctor's lips twitched as he patted the rail on Seth's bed. "Looks like I'm leaving you in good hands."

Seth relaxed against the pillow, looking up at the ceiling. "If by 'good' you mean a therapist who knows her stuff and the world's safest chauffer, then yeah, I guess I am. I'm sure I'll be better in no time," Seth said dryly.

The doctor offered a look of sympathy. "Well, I wouldn't say 'no time,' but you'll get there eventually."

Suddenly, the estimated six to nine month recovery seemed like forever to Seth. He hoped this PT knew what she was doing so it would be closer to six.

Eight

♡ ♡ ♡

"Grace, your next appointment's here," said the receptionist as she handed Grace a file. She dropped her voice. "And he's a hottie."

Grace bit back a smile. If a patient happened to be a male between the ages of 25 and 35, Kelli thought he was hot. "Thanks. Tell him I'll be with him in a second." Grace finished the sentence she was writing then opened the file of her newest patient. She scanned through the paperwork.

Name: Seth Tuttle
Reason for visit: Post ACL reconstruction rehabilitation.

The moment Grace read the name, she frowned. Although it had been weeks since her last encounter with someone named Seth, the name still acted as a trigger. She hadn't even met her newest patient, but already he made a nervous pit form in her stomach. How would a self-appointed, ego-driven, chaos-wreaking patient do with ACL rehab? She tapped the pen against her lower lip. If this guy was anything like the last Seth she'd met, the next several months might prove to be difficult.

With a sigh, she stood and pasted a smile on her face. But when she rounded the corner and pulled open the door to her waiting room, her smile disappeared.

Oh no. Not *that* Seth. It couldn't be.

From his profile, Seth looked exactly the same as he had the night of the auction. Exactly. Same two days' worth of growth on his face, same sweatpants, same navy hoodie—only this time it lay on the chair next to him, giving Grace a view of his sizable biceps that stretched the sleeves of his t-shirt. She didn't know what upset her composure more, the fact that he was even better looking than she remembered, or the fact that she wasn't nearly as prepared to see him as she wanted to be.

Seth flipped through a magazine, completely oblivious to the fact that he was about to get reacquainted with the woman he'd outbid and kissed.

Grace suddenly wanted to duck back through the door and tell her receptionist that Seth Tuttle would have to reschedule with a different therapist in a different office, and—if possible—a different state. Grace didn't want to be anywhere near the aftermath of the chaos he was bound to cause.

As if sensing her presence, Seth lifted his head and met her gaze with striking blue eyes. She stiffened, waiting for the recognition to come.

"Are you Grace?" he said, all innocence, as though he'd never seen her before.

Grace blinked as realization struck. He didn't recognize her. She should be thrilled by that knowledge—elated, even. Not only did it give her the opportunity for a fresh start, but it gave her the upper hand, in a way. Yet her annoyance won out. All this time, she'd stewed about that night, relived it over and over in her mind, trying to figure out where she went wrong and how she could have handled things differently. While Seth, on the other hand, had apparently forgotten all about her the moment she'd walked away.

She forced her feet forward and lifted her chin. "I take it you're Seth Tuttle?"

"I am." He grabbed the crutches at his side and hoisted himself up easily. Shooting the receptionist a look, he said, "Hey, my friend's parking the car right now. When he comes in, would you mind telling him I've already gone in?"

"Of course. I can send him back if you'd like."

"No, I'm sure he'd rather wait here." Seth turned his attention to Grace and smiled. "So, you're Grace Warren. Dr. Ross tells me you're the best PT in the Seattle area, which I'm hoping is true. I want my knee back as soon as possible and need a PT who can bring it."

Whether it was because he didn't recognize her, or because he questioned her professional skills, Grace bristled. "Dr. Ross is wrong."

Seth raised his eyebrows in question.

"I'm the best physical therapist *anywhere*, including Seattle." With that, she turned on her heel and walked back through the self-closing door, not bothering to hold it open for him like she usually did for patients with crutches or wheelchairs. When the sounds of Seth struggling to get through the door reached her ears, a smile tugged at the corner of Grace's mouth. He did say to bring it.

She strode past Cameron, who was working with another patient, and stopped next to a table, where she waited for Seth.

As he made his way toward Grace, Seth nodded briefly at Cameron then did a double-take and stopped. "Hey, aren't you that guy from the auction?"

Oh sure, he recognizes Cameron, Grace thought dryly.

Cameron glanced up. His face reddened as his eyes darted from Seth to Grace and back to Seth again. "What are you doing here? I mean, Lanna said we were square—that I didn't have to . . . you know."

Grace rolled her eyes as Seth chuckled. "Yeah, we're square. No worries. I only bid to get Lanna to take the money."

"Oh." Cameron visibly relaxed. "Next time do me a favor and clue me in beforehand, will you?"

"Let's hope there won't be a next time." Seth shifted his weight, easing off his left leg. "Otherwise I'll be on Lanna's blacklist permanently."

Cameron chuckled. "Personally, I'd be more worried about Grace if I were you. I seriously doubt you're ever going to get off *her* blacklist."

Seth's forehead crinkled in confusion. "What do you mean? Apologize for what?" Seth's gaze moved to Grace.

She fought the urge to direct a scathing glare at Cameron. So much for a fresh start or having the upper hand.

"Do we know each other?" Seth asked her. "Now that I think about it, you do sort of look familiar."

Grace returned his gaze. "Depends on what you mean by 'know.' If you're the type of guy who goes around kissing girls at random then forgets about them, I guess we don't."

"Wait, he kissed you?" Cameron's voice rang out. "You didn't tell me that."

Grace nearly groaned. Only minutes into their appointment, and Seth was already at it again. A self-appointed god of chaos suddenly seemed like an understatement. He was more like the god of havoc and misery and embarrassment all rolled into one. There wasn't a name for what he was.

A slow smile spread across Seth's face as recognition finally dawned. "You're that girl from the auction, aren't you? Wow. Talk about a small world."

"I can't believe you kissed her, man," Cameron said, still laughing. "You've got some serious guts."

Ignoring Cameron, Seth kept his gaze trained on Grace. "I'm actually glad I ran into you again. I wanted to apologize. You know, for outbidding you."

For outbidding her? That was it? What about the kiss? "Really? That's all you're sorry about?" she asked.

A flirtatious twinkle appeared in his eyes. "Should I be sorry about something else?"

Grace rolled her eyes. She should have expected that.

"Oh, wait." Seth's brow furrowed as he gestured from Grace to Cameron. "Are you two . . .? I mean, I did outbid you for him, right?" He left the question hanging as if it was an actual possibility that Grace would ever date someone like Cameron.

Ugh.

"No," said Grace. "We're not."

"My girlfriend couldn't make it," Cameron explained. "So I asked Grace to come bid on me instead."

Understanding dawned in Seth's eyes. "I knew you two had something underhanded going on."

Grace turned and walked away, hoping Seth would follow and end this ridiculous conversation. She stood next to a table and waited impatiently for Seth to join her. Maybe if she kept things strictly professional from here on out, she would be able to get through this session.

As he approached, she patted the table with her palm. "Take a seat and lie down on your back."

Seth did as she asked, but his lips twitched as though he had to fight back additional laughter. Ignoring it, Grace removed the brace from around his knee and set it aside, trying not to wince when she saw his leg. No matter how many times she worked with patients post surgery, she never got used to seeing the damage surgery caused. Seth's leg was swollen and covered in varying hues of bruises—everything from sickly yellows to murky blues. Clear tape covered the dark red incision sites, making it look even worse.

Still, Grace couldn't help but notice that the unaffected muscles in his leg were toned and strong, bulging at the calves. Apparently he worked out a lot and probably spent some serious time on a bike as well. Grace tried to convince herself she only cared because it meant a quicker recovery time, but really, it made her curious about her newest patient.

She moved to his foot and lifted it. "Okay, so let's see how much mobility you've got." She pushed his knee forward slowly until she met with resistance then made a mental note of the approximate angle and slowly lowered it back down.

Seth brought his hands under his head, lifting it so he could study her. "I still can't believe you're the same girl from the auction. I honestly didn't recognize you."

"I believe you." Grace placed her palm on his patella, out of the way of the incision sites, and pushed his knee down to straighten his leg.

"I mean your hair was curly and in that bun thing, and you were wearing that amazing dress, and now you're . . . well—"

"I'd stop right there if I were you."

Seth's forehead crinkled into a wince. "Yeah, figured that out on my own, thanks," he said through clenched teeth.

Oops. Grace quickly eased off on his knee, realizing she'd pushed down a little harder than normal. But in her defense, it was provoked. And it wasn't as if increased pressure would hurt his ACL—it would just be a little more painful for him.

Grace lifted his leg once again, pushing it slowly toward Seth, making sure to not push too hard this time. "You need to do this every half hour while you're awake for the next few days," Grace said. "Bend and straighten, bend and straighten. If you lie on your stomach on your bed, the added force of gravity will help straighten your leg down as well."

"Got it," he said. "And listen, I'm sorry for not recognizing you, and for being such a—" He stopped as though unsure of which word to use.

"Such a what?" Grace said. "Egotistical jerk?"

"I wouldn't go that far."

Of course he wouldn't, because a self-appointed god of chaos would never think of himself as egotistical. It wasn't in his chemical makeup. "What would you call it then? You told me to outbid you then went ahead and outbid *me,* only to add insult to injury by forcing a kiss on me. Personally, I thought *egotistical jerk* was putting it nicely."

"You didn't exactly pull away," Seth said. "At least not at first."

"Because I was in shock." Grace couldn't believe she had to explain this. "Seriously, who kisses a complete stranger?"

"You said I needed to prove that I wasn't gay."

Unbelievable. He wasn't even remotely sorry. "You couldn't think of another way to do that?"

A cheeky smile appeared. "Another way wouldn't have been nearly as fun."

Grace's jaw clenched, and Seth's hands flew from behind his head to his knee. He groaned. "Okay, okay, I'm sorry. Just stop with the torture already."

Woops, she'd done it again. Grace backed off and cleared her throat. "It's called therapy."

"Yeah, well something tells me that you're being a little harder on me than normal."

Grace thought it best not to respond. Instead, she lowered his leg again, pressing down on his knee with a little less pressure. "There. Better?"

"Much, thanks." His hands went back to lifting his head, and he studied her. "For what it's worth, I really am sorry."

He had a disarming smile, the kind that could make a girl forgive and forget way too easily. Grace forced herself to look away. *Don't be charmed by this guy. Chaos. Ego. Kisses complete strangers without remorse. Remember?*

After several more bending and straightening repetitions, Grace lathered up her hands with some oil then began to massage the muscles and tissue around his knee. Normally, she didn't think twice about massaging a patient's leg, shoulder, or arm. But with Seth, the way her fingers tingled at the touch, it felt personal—almost intimate. What was wrong with her? "This will help break up the scar tissue and reduce the swelling."

"Aren't massages supposed to feel good?" Seth said with another grimace.

"No pain, no gain."

"Says the woman inflicting the pain."

Grace bit back a smile. At least Seth wasn't squirming like some of her other ACL patients did. He was actually pretty tough. "Tell me how you tore your ACL," she said, more than ready to be done with all topics of conversation involving bachelor auctions and kissing.

He let out a breath and relaxed his head against the cushioned table top. "I went heli-skiing, took a jump, and pulled a 360—which was pretty sweet, by the way—only to land in some deep powder and torque my knee."

"Ouch."

"You can say that again, although it was more painful to realize that I was out of commission on day one of a fourteen-day trip."

Grace's eyes widened. First Seth plunked down twenty grand like it was pocket change, and now a two-week heli-skiing trip? Who was this guy? "What, exactly, do you do for a living?"

"I'm a consultant."

Oh, well that explained it. Not. "For who? Donald Trump and Bill Gates?"

Seth chuckled. "No, just your average start-up internet companies. Basically, people hire me to help them set up their websites and market whatever products or services they're selling."

Grace searched his face, not buying it. Web consultants—especially for startup companies—didn't make *that* kind of money. Maybe he was one of those trust-fund kids who'd had everything handed to him on a golden platter his entire life, and marketing was something he did for fun. "I had no idea there was that kind of money in web marketing."

Seth shrugged. "Sometimes there is, sometimes there isn't. I work on commission. If they make money, so do I. If they don't, I get nada. My clients prefer it that way, because most of them don't have a lot of ready cash to invest."

"I see." But really, she didn't see at all, especially considering most start-up companies went under within the first year. Maybe he had a ton of clients or something—ones who didn't mind if he took two weeks off to go heli-skiing.

A knowing smile stretched across Seth's face. "You're wondering how I could drop twenty grand at an auction then turn around and go skiing for two weeks, aren't you?"

Awesome, now he was a mind reader, too. The list kept adding up. But did Grace really want to know more about this guy? With him, the whole "curiosity killed the cat" thing could easily hold true.

"No," Grace said.

"Liar."

The fact that he'd seen right through her only made her that much more determined not to know. She shot him a stop-acting-like-you-know-me-because-you-don't look. "Believe it or not, I'd rather not know. I make it a point not to get too personal with my patients."

Seth's eyes took on a teasing quality. "Too late for that, isn't it? I mean, we've already kissed."

Grace wanted nothing more than to tell him he was right and should start shopping around for a new therapist. But she kept her mouth shut and focused on massaging his knee with a bit more gusto.

"You weren't my patient at the time," she finally said. "But now that you are, I'm only interested in knowing the information that's pertinent to your recovery."

"You mean like what I do for a living?" he said, calling her bluff.

Ugh. There was no stopping him, was there? She cleared her throat and changed the subject. "Was this your first time heli-skiing?"

He raised an eyebrow. "I don't know. Is that pertinent to my recovery?"

"Yes, especially if you're planning to go again next season. I need to know what kind of activities you want to resume so we can get your knee strong enough for them."

Seth's gaze moved to the ceiling with his hands still cradling his head. "In that case, no, it wasn't my first time and definitely won't be my last. I started six years ago with a friend of mine and liked it so much that I figured why not make it an annual thing?"

"Because it's dangerous." The words came out like an automated response. Grace clamped her mouth shut and bit down on her lower lip.

Seth gave her a half smile. "Ah, but I laugh in the face of danger. It's the only way to live."

The statement registered in Grace's mind like a horrible memory. Alec used to say pretty much the same thing, and there was a time when Grace adhered to the notion as well. But now things were different, and she didn't appreciate the reminder or the slew of bad memories that came with them—especially not from someone like Seth, who seemed to have no worries or cares at all.

The wince on Seth's face forced Grace back to the present. Realizing she'd increased the pressure of the massage a little too much, she quickly let go. Why was she letting him get to her so easily? This was ridiculous. She was a professional.

"Sorry," she said.

"No pain no gain, right?" he mustered.

"Right." From that point on, Grace purposefully kept the conversation to neutral, impersonal topics as she worked him through the rest of his session. By the time she'd finished, it felt like hours had passed.

With swift movements, she strapped his brace back on and handed him his crutches. "Keep at those exercises, and we'll see you back here on Thursday." She paused. "Unless, of course, you'd rather work with a different therapist?" The question hung there, and Grace hoped against hope that he'd take her up on the suggestion. She wasn't sure she could endure another session like this one.

But Seth only chuckled, not looking at all embarrassed or uncomfortable. "No, I like your 'no pain, no gain' philosophy. It works for me. See you Thursday."

With that, he turned and hobbled away, leaving Grace not looking forward to Thursday at all.

Nine

♡ ♡ ♡

Seth flopped against the back of his black leather couch and stared at his 80-inch flat-screen TV. He and his friends had just spent the last hour playing some Xbox Kinect game, and Seth had never been so bored. "That was nothing like actual kayaking. It didn't even come close."

Garrett lifted his feet to the coffee table and dropped his head to the back of the couch. "What else is there to do? You can't play basketball, ski, rock climb, or mountain bike. You can't even do something lame like bowl."

"We can go to a movie," Owen said with zero enthusiasm. Unless a new action flick had come out, movies landed at the bottom of their Fun Things To Do list. Owen raised his arms over his head and yawned. "I can't believe I turned down a date for this."

"You turned down a date?" Seth shot him a look of surprise. Owen never turned down an opportunity to hang out with a woman. "Why?"

Owen shrugged. "She wears high heels with jeans, can't leave her house without an umbrella just in case it might rain, and thinks paintballing is dipping balls in paint."

Seth sniggered, wondering what type of girl Owen would eventually end up with. Over the years, he'd dated all types and found issues with every single one of them. For a guy who didn't bother doing his hair most days, he was incredibly picky.

Not that Seth was much different. He'd dated his fair share of girls and still hadn't found one he cared to settle down with either, which was fine with him. He wasn't ready to be tied down when there was still so much to experience. Now, if there was a woman out there with a sense of adventure—someone who preferred experiencing sports to watching them on TV—well, maybe he'd reconsider.

An image of Grace came to mind, and Seth found himself wondering what type of person she was. Would she care if he went paintballing and mountain biking with his friends? Would she be the type to want to come along or hold him back? Did she even like to mountain bike?

"Maybe we should give online dating a try," Garrett suggested. "Having a few cute girls around might make video games and movies more interesting."

Owen shook his head. "They'd probably make us play Just Dance and make us watch chick flicks. Who wants that?"

Garrett grunted in agreement. Seth, on the other hand, wouldn't mind watching Grace play Just Dance. With her slim build and natural grace, she'd probably dance circles around everyone else.

Seth shook his head, trying to clear his mind of all thoughts of Grace. Why was he going there anyway? He frowned at the TV. "There's got to be something fun I can still do. C'mon, guys, think."

"We could still go paintballing," Owen said. "You'd just be an easier target."

Garrett laughed.

Seth rolled his eyes—although paintballing sounded much more appealing than video games at the moment.

"I say we just follow Brandon and Ethan's lead and ditch Seth until he gets his knee back," joked Garrett. "He's going to be zero fun for the next several months anyway."

"Gee thanks," said Seth. But they were right. Seth *was* zero fun to hang out with right now. He was actually incredibly grateful that Owen and Garrett were the type of friends to stick around.

"Nah, we just need to rethink our way of doing things a little," said Owen, tapping his index finger against his lips. "Hey, my sister's the forward for her high-school basketball team. Maybe we could go to a game sometime."

Seth and Garrett groaned in unison. Okay, so maybe movies weren't last on the list anymore. Seth would take a movie over a girls' high-school basketball game any day.

"Give me a few days," Seth said. "And I'll come up with something better than that."

"Like *that's* going to be hard to do," muttered Garrett.

"Shut up. " Owen chucked a pillow at Garrett, who snatched it up and threw it right back. Within seconds, a pillow fight ensued, making Seth roll his eyes once again. His friends were great and all, but Seth suddenly wanted more than this. He wanted something deeper. Something with soft curves, warm lips, and deep, sea green eyes.

Seth shook his head to clear it. What was he thinking? Grace reminded him of Lanna—the girl who wouldn't speak to him because he'd given her twenty grand. The last thing Seth should want was to get into a relationship with another woman like that, no matter how beautiful or interesting she was. It was just the medicine and boredom talking.

From here on out, the only thing Seth wanted from Grace was for her to get his leg back in shape.

Ten minutes into his appointment, Seth had all but forgotten about his promise. From the moment he'd struggled to get through the self-closing door, Grace had welcomed him with rigid professionalism. Like before, her dark hair was pulled back into a ponytail. She wore black yoga pants, along with a fitted white polo that had been appliquéd with the name of the practice. Even in bland clothing, she looked good—a dressed-down version of the beautiful woman in blue from the night of the auction. Seth still couldn't believe he hadn't recognized her right away. She had the same piercing green eyes, high cheekbones, toned body, and impassive expression.

Was she happy to see him again? Annoyed? Seth couldn't tell.

"Looks like you've made some progress," Grace said as she checked how far he could bend and straighten his knee. Even though the movement pained him, her cool fingers on his leg felt good. Really good.

"I take my physical therapist's orders very seriously." Seth grinned, hoping for an answering smile that didn't come.

"Good," she said. "That means we can start working on strength. How's your pain level?"

"Fine right now. But then again, I haven't ticked you off yet," Seth teased, attempting to coerce a smile from her. But all he got was a raised eyebrow.

"Are you planning to tick me off?" she said, releasing his knee.

"Not on purpose."

"Oh. It just comes naturally then."

"Something like that."

Grace seemed more on guard and careful today, as though a simple smile would somehow breach that professional/personal line she didn't like to cross. Come to think of it, Seth had never seen what her smile looked like.

That would have to change.

Grace studied the paper on her clipboard, tapping it lightly with a pencil. "Since your mobility is improving, I'd like you to start with some leg lifts—both on your back and stomach. Then we'll do some heel pushes, calf raises, and end with the bike. Sound okay?"

"Bike?" Seth perked up. "So soon?" He loved to bike. In fact, the sooner he could strap his mountain bike to his SUV and hit the trails, the better. Maybe this recovery wouldn't be as bad as he thought.

"The revolutions on the bike will get your legs bending and straightening, which is the best thing for your knee," Grace explained.

"So mountain biking's okay?"

She shot him a confused look, as though she didn't know if he was joking or not. "Are you serious?"

"Yes." Seth's knee was feeling much better, and if riding a stationary bike wouldn't hurt it, why would a mountain bike?

She shook her head. "No, you can't go mountain biking. It will jar your knee and very possibly torque it as well, which would land you right back in the operating room. For now, stationary bikes only. *Please.*"

Seth frowned, his gaze moving to the crutches that rested against the bench. "Can I at least lose the crutches?" He didn't mention that he rarely used them anymore. They made things awkward and uncomfortable—especially when it came to things like getting through that stupid self-closing door. What kind of PT office had a self-closing door anyway?

Grace returned her attention to the clipboard. "I'd like you to keep using them for a few more days—at least until you can walk without much pain. Otherwise you'll create a limp pattern, which we don't want."

It was on the tip of Seth's tongue to say something about how limps were cool or something like that. But he swallowed the words, mostly because being cheeky wasn't getting him anywhere with Grace. Instead, he let his head flop down and obediently raised his leg like she'd asked—or *attempted* to raise it anyway. So crazy how something Seth could have done easily only a week before now felt like he had twenty pounds strapped to his foot.

Grace looked down at him, her lips pulling up into an almost smile. "Wow, I'm impressed," she said.

"About what?" The few inches he'd been able to raise his leg didn't look at all impressive to him.

She shrugged. "I expected a sarcastic remark about how limps are cool or that women find them sexy or something like that."

As immature as it made Seth sound, he liked that she knew him so well already. It felt like an accomplishment, as though he'd finally made some headway with Grace. He cocked his head to return her gaze. "Do *you* think limps are sexy?"

The hint of a smile disappeared. "No."

"Then I'll keep using the crutches."

At her look of annoyed surprise, Seth returned his attention to the ceiling, holding back a self-satisfied grin. Let her stew on that for a while.

Twenty minutes later, Seth gratefully tucked the crutches under his arms, resting his weight on them in an attempt to ease the throbbing in his leg. It felt as though someone had taken a mallet to his knee then kicked it for good measure.

Maybe Seth shouldn't have attempted to flirt quite so much.

Ten
♡ ♡ ♡

Seth scribbled his name on the patient check-in form and nodded a hello at the receptionist. According to Garrett, he no longer walked with a limp, so Seth had happily donated his crutches to Goodwill the day before. As he'd dropped them in the box, he considered taking a picture to send to Lanna. It had been nearly a month since the night of the auction—since she'd last spoken to him—and Seth was sick of it. Maybe if she saw that he gave to other charities as well, she'd finally find it in her heart to forgive him.

"Grace is expecting you, so feel free to go on back," the receptionist said.

"Thanks." Seth had purposely scheduled the last appointment of the day with the hope of getting some extra time with Grace.

No longer hindered by crutches, Seth pulled the self-closing door open and walked easily through. He headed toward the workout area then paused when he spotted Grace near the back of the room, working with a blond guy in a wheelchair. They were the only two people in the room, which meant Seth's plan had paid off. As soon as the blond guy left, he'd get Grace all to himself. Seth smiled, admiring the way her yoga pants clung to her toned legs and the way her shirt followed her curves. What would her hair look like out of that ponytail? Would it feel as soft and silky as it appeared?

Seth watched her work, admiring the way her muscles contracted as she assisted the guy with some exercise bands. Beautiful and confident, Grace patiently coaxed and encouraged. She exuded a casual elegance not many girls could pull off. No wonder she'd kicked off her heels the night of the auction. They weren't her. She was more the type to wear a pair of comfortable shoes beneath her dress or go barefoot.

Seth smiled, remembering the night of the auction and how her high heels dangled from her fingertips as her bare feet stalked away. At the time, he hadn't thought much of it. But now he wished he'd gone after her, apologized, and found a way to get her to go out with him. Things were trickier now that Seth was a patient. Grace had made it very clear that she didn't date patients—not even ones who'd already kissed her.

"Give me three more," Grace said to the guy in the wheelchair.

He strained to pull on the bands one more time, finally dropping his arms to his side. Beads of sweat glistened across his forehead. "I think I'm done for the day."

Grace pulled up a chair and sat down. Her elbows rested on her knees and her palms came together as she looked at the guy. "Don't hate me for saying this, but I feel like you're holding back. I wanted to start you in the pool next week because you need cardio as much as strength, but we're not making as much progress as I'd hoped. *Are* you holding back?"

The guy leaned forward and held out a staying hand. "Listen, Grace, I appreciate what you're trying to do, I really do, but you're right, I'm not giving it my all, because I don't *want* to give it my all. This isn't me anymore, and the sooner you realize that, the better." He paused. "It was a mistake for me to start coming here."

Surprise and concern reflected in Grace's wide eyes. "Hey, if you think I'm pushing you too hard, I'll back off, okay? Just please don't give up. Not yet."

The guy shook his head. "I'm sorry."

He started to wheel himself away, but Grace placed her hand on a wheel, stopping him. "I don't understand. What do you have against working out? There are thousands of paraplegics who live wonderful, active lifestyles. You can do this."

"How nice that you know so much about people like me."

She let out a sigh, still keeping her hand on the wheel. "C'mon, Alec, you know that's not what I meant. I just hate to see you hide away all the time. There's so much more to life than staring at a computer screen."

Alec's jaw stiffened. He sat up straight, looking Grace in the eye. "You're one to talk. When was the last time you went out? When was the last time you did something for the joy of it? You sit here and accuse me of not living my life, when you're doing the exact same thing. You come here then spend your evenings researching new therapy techniques or trying to coerce me out of my apartment. At least I have a reason for the way I live my life. What's yours?"

Grace visibly flinched, but said nothing. Only sat there in her chair with her lips clamped shut.

Seth's protective instincts kicked in, and he found himself taking a step closer.

Alec began rubbing his temples, as though trying to ward off a headache. "I thought if I came and did this a few times, you'd stop pressuring me. But I was wrong. You're worse now than ever before." He shook his head and let out a breath. "We both know you moved here because of me—because you don't think I can take care of myself. But I'm a big boy, Grace, and I can. I need you to stop bringing me groceries, stop making me dinner, and stop pressuring me to come here. I need you to back off." He paused. "Please."

Grace's hand fell from the wheel, and Alec pushed himself forward, wheeling himself directly past Seth without a second glance. He paused to hit a small button in a recessed opening on the side of the wall then waited as the door opened wide and stayed open long enough for him to wheel himself through. Seth frowned, thinking about how many times he'd struggled to get through that same door while Grace stood by and watched, probably laughing on the inside.

Seth shook his head and took a step forward, ready to give her a hard time about it. But when he saw the worry lines creasing her forehead and the pain in her eyes, the words died in his throat. That guy in the wheelchair had really done a number on her.

Who was he anyway? An old boyfriend? Or worse—a current one? Did Grace really move here for him? Seth felt a prick of something that felt like jealousy. Apparently, she didn't keep a professional distance from all her patients. How had Alec managed to sneak past her walls? Or had they been involved before he became her patient? Seth checked the impulse to follow the guy and find out. He forced himself to stay put, waiting for Grace to notice him.

She sat in her chair, leaning forward with her chin resting on her hands as she gazed out the window. Although Seth could only see her profile, something in her expression wrenched his heart. He'd seen that look before. On Lanna, right after the auction and before she'd walked away from him. It was the same broken expression.

Seth suddenly wanted to pull Grace into a hug and fix whatever was broken inside her. But that was crazy. He hardly knew her, and the last thing Seth should want to do was get personal with another girl like Lanna.

He cleared his throat and moved forward.

As if coming out of a trance, Grace's head snapped up. Her eyes widened in surprise, and she quickly stood. "I'm sorry, have you been standing there long?"

"Long enough to know I'm not being treated nearly as well as that guy." Seth hooked a thumb over his shoulder where Alec had just left. "You forgot to mention that the door opened automatically."

She let out a half sigh, half strangled chuckle. "Sorry. I, uh . . . forgot."

"I bet." Seth leaned casually against the bench and folded his arms, glad to see that some of the sadness had disappeared from her eyes. Maybe some mild goading would make it go away altogether. "Know what else you forgot to mention?"

"What?"

"That you make dinner for your patients as well. When can I expect you to drop by my place? Or do you only do that for guys in wheelchairs?"

Lips no longer twitching, Grace shot him a that's-none-of-your-business look. Then she pointed to the exercise bike and said tersely, "Why don't you warm up on the bike for ten minutes? After that we can go over some more strengthening exercises and see how your leg is coming along."

Seth wanted to kick himself, possibly even duct tape his mouth closed. When it came to Grace, he didn't seem to know when to stop. Maybe he needed therapy on more than just his knee. "I'm sorry. I didn't mean to pry."

"Why do I find that hard to believe?" Grace said. She let out a breath of frustration then sighed. "For the sake of your knee, I'll let it slide for today."

Seth nodded, still curious about the guy in the wheelchair, but not enough to risk ticking Grace off again. He swallowed his many questions and climbed on the bike, starting slowly until his knee got the hang of it, then building up speed. He'd totally bombed in the personal department, but at least he could show Grace that he was still a good patient. Seth had worked hard—both here and at home—and was pleased to notice that his leg muscles were getting stronger already.

While he rode, Grace tinkered around the room, writing something down or fiddling with a machine. Seth even caught her staring out the window at one point with the same sad, broken look in her eyes.

When his ten-minute warm-up finally ended, Seth climbed off the bike with an incredibly sore knee and wiped the perspiration from his forehead with a hand towel. "I can't wait for that not to hurt anymore," he said.

Grace's eyes flickered to his, looking almost haunted. "At least you'll recover."

It took Seth a moment to realize that she was still thinking of Alec—whoever he was. He studied her for a moment, wanting to know why Grace seemed to care so much about him and where her sadness came from.

"What happened to him?" The question was out before Seth could rethink it.

Grace's gaze moved to the window again. She looked uncharacteristically vulnerable. "A skiing accident, same as you," she said, surprising Seth with an answer. "Only instead of his ACL, he injured the T-11 segment of his spinal cord, resulting in permanent paralysis from his waist on down."

"Oh." Seth had no idea what else to say. Sorry? That totally bites? Of all the rotten luck? Everything that came to mind lacked any sort of substance, so he kept quiet, feeling like a jerk for teasing her earlier.

"He's my brother," she added, almost like an afterthought.

Seth felt a wave of relief pass over him. So Alec wasn't an ex-boyfriend or a wannabe boyfriend. Seth almost smiled, but quickly checked the impulse by reminding himself that it wouldn't be appropriate.

Outside, Alec was just now getting into his car. Not sure what had taken him so long, Seth watched as he opened the door, awkwardly scooted himself inside, then snapped a wheel off his chair and moved it into the car. The second wheel came next, followed by the rest of his chair. Impressed by the efficient process, Seth wondered what it would be like to drive with only hand controls.

"Looking at him, you'd think he had it all figured out, wouldn't you?" Grace said.

"What do you mean?"

"That he's accepted his injury and has learned to deal with it."

Seth shot her a sideways look. "He hasn't?"

She shrugged. "In some ways, yes. He's learned how to get around, how to drive a car, how to make the transition from his wheelchair to his bed or shower or wherever else. But he never goes anywhere. He stays in his stuffy apartment most of the time with his blinds closed and the world shut out."

Seth studied Grace's profile. He had so many questions—about her brother, about her, about everything. But he didn't dare ask any of them for fear she'd close up again.

Grace nodded toward the parking lot. "It took me three years to convince him to come work out with me. And now, after only a few tries, he's giving up and fleeing back into his protective shell. Why?" She said the words quietly, as though talking to herself.

Again, Seth felt the urge to pull her into a hug and offer what comfort he could. But did she even realize she'd lowered her protective barriers and shared all that with him? Probably not. If he hadn't lucked out by coming right after Alec left, Seth probably never would have known about her paraplegic brother or the real reason Grace had ended up in Seattle.

As Alec's car finally disappeared from sight, Grace seemed to snap out of it. Her eyes met Seth's in an almost startled realization that she'd just crossed a line she hadn't meant to cross. "I can't believe I just told you all that. You're practically a stranger."

Seth nudged her with his arm. "Oh, c'mon. We've already kissed, remember? That's got to at least get me into the acquaintance category."

Grace let out a small snicker and glanced around, as if suddenly remembering where they were and what she should be doing. "I think you're just trying to get out of the rest of your workout."

"Who, me? Never."

Her lips twitched. "Well, I hope you can stay a little late. You're my last patient today, and we need to get through your entire workout."

Seth couldn't help the silly grin that came to his face. Who knew his plan to schedule the last appointment of the day would turn out so well? "I'll gladly stay as late as you want. And just so you know, if you're ever interested in moving me out of that acquaintance category and into something more along the lines of kissing friends, my lips could use a workout as well."

She rolled her eyes. "And here I was beginning to think you could act your age."

Seth laughed. "Where's the fun in that?"

Shaking her head, Grace looked away, but not before Seth saw the corners of her mouth twitch once again.

Someday he would get her to full-on smile, or better yet—laugh. Wouldn't that be something.

"Up you go." Grace patted the table.

As Seth allowed Grace to check on his progress, his mind started churning. He thought of Grace's brother and how quickly Alec had gotten into his car—about what life would be like for Seth if he'd done more damage than tear his ACL. Would Seth be the type to shut out the world, or would he embrace his new life and seek out the possibilities? He wanted to believe the latter, but who knew for sure? Hadn't he moped around his apartment just the other day because all he could do was play video games?

Just then, an idea struck. A brilliant idea. Seth could rent a bunch of wheelchairs, take them to the gym where he and his friends met to play basketball, and get his friends to play wheelchair ball. It was the perfect solution. Why hadn't Seth thought of it before? Maybe Alec would want to join in as well.

Grace had Seth stand to do some calf raises, and as he lifted his body up and down, he said, "Hey, you think your brother might be interested in playing wheelchair basketball with me and some of my friends?"

Grace's eyebrow raised. "Are you serious?"

Seth shrugged. "Why not? It's a Paralympic sport, isn't it?"

"But you're not a paraplegic."

"No, but according to you, I'm not allowed to play regular basketball yet, so why not wheelchair ball? Unless, of course, you won't let me do that, either."

Grace's expression turned thoughtful. She raised her arm and rested it on the exercise bike next to him. "So what, you're just going to rent a bunch of wheelchairs?"

"That's the plan, yes."

"And your friends are on board with this?"

"Yeah. They think it's going to be a riot." At least they would once Seth told them about it.

Grace drew her lower lip into her mouth and worked it back and forth before releasing it. "You sure you have room for one more?"

"There's always room for one more."

Grace smiled—actually smiled. It lightened her eyes the way Seth knew it would and made her that much more beautiful. Seth wanted to fist pump the air. Evidently today was a day for miracles.

"I'll see if I can get Alec to come," she said. "When are you meeting and where?"

Oh, um . . . Hopefully the gym at the junior high where they usually met, but he'd have to call a friend to make sure. Then there were the wheelchairs to procure. "If you give me your cell number, I'll text you the details once I get them nailed down."

She hesitated a moment, then scribbled something on a pad of paper and held it just out of reach from him. "I only want one text from you, okay?"

"But what if plans change?" Seth asked innocently. "How will you know if I'm not allowed to text you again?"

She rolled her eyes. "Okay, fine. I only want to be texted about basketball, and that's it. No saying things like your lips need a workout or anything like that. Got it?"

Seth suppressed a smile, or at least tried to. "Fine. Basketball talk and that's it. Promise."

She hesitated a moment longer before handing over her number. Seth examined her tiny scrawl, thinking that he might have to frame it and put it on display as a sort of hard-earned trophy. Then he stuffed it into the pocket of his hoodie and grinned. "Do you typically give your number out to patients, or am I just special?"

Her eyes narrowed, and her gaze dropped to where his hand was clamped over the pocket.

Seth laughed. "Don't worry. I always keep my promises. Basketball talk only." Little did she know that basketball could be applied to pretty much everything.

"Somehow, I'm not feeling very reassured."

Seth laughed again. How well she knew him already.

Eleven
♡ ♡ ♡

$\mathcal{G}$race waltzed into her brother's home office and set a takeout box containing his favorite fast-food hamburger and fries beside him. She was on a mission, and she refused to leave before that mission was accomplished.

Alec eyed the food warily. "Listen, Grace, I was serious when I said—"

"Eat," she said. "Then we're going out."

He let out a frustrated sigh and opened his mouth to say something—probably a protest—but Grace planted her hand on the table with a sharp rap. "After being such a royal pain all these years, you can do one more thing for me. C'mon. One night. That's all I ask."

Alec rolled his eyes, but at least he didn't protest. He took the takeout box and pried the lid open. "What do you have in mind?"

"It's a surprise." One he might disown her for, but hopefully he would come around in the end. If not, Grace would finally take her parents advice and leave him be—not that she'd have any choice, because Alec would likely never speak to her again.

"I don't like surprises," Alec said as he shoved a fry into his mouth. "For all I know, you'll take me to a cliff and shove me off."

Grace smiled, happy he was cracking jokes instead of resisting. "Tempting, but no. It'll be much more painful than that."

Alec groaned. "You're taking me back to your clinic, aren't you?"

"No. And that's all you're getting out of me, so finish eating and c'mon." With that, Grace left him alone and retreated to the kitchen, where she unloaded a few groceries—mostly produce—then loaded a few dishes into the dishwasher, washed off the counters, and waited, fingers tapping, for Alec to finish his dinner.

When he finally emerged from his office, Grace insisted on driving. She waited as he scooted into her passenger seat, and then she quickly pulled the wheels off his wheelchair and shoved everything into her trunk. There. Alec was now at her mercy and couldn't leave even if he wanted to.

Grace tried to appear calm as she headed down the road, but a sliver of doubt crept in, making her wonder if she was doing the right thing by giving Seth carte blanche to wreak chaos on her brother's life as well. But if she didn't, would things ever change? Probably not.

A flurry of butterflies raged in her stomach as she drove. It felt like a Hail Mary—her last desperate attempt to get Alec to see that there really was life outside his dreary apartment and wheelchair. By the time Grace pulled to a stop in the parking lot of the junior high, her palms were sweaty from gripping the wheel so hard.

Alec stared at the building in front of them, making no move to open the car door. "What are we doing here?"

"I told you, it's a surprise," said Grace, her voice a little shaky. What would happen when they went inside and Alec heard the sound of a basketball hitting the gym floor? Would he balk? Yell? Clamp his hands around his wheels and refuse to let her push him into the gym? Would she be forced to take Alec home before Seth and his friends even saw that they were there? She hadn't really thought beyond getting him here.

Grace drew in a breath and climbed from the car then pulled Alec's wheelchair from the trunk and quickly assembled it. With a wary look, he swung himself onto the chair and brushed off Grace's efforts to push him. "I can do it on my own, thanks."

"You're acting like a two-year-old."

"And you're acting like a helicopter mom, so it works."

He had a point. Why was Grace here anyway? Was she really doing this for Alec? Or was it for her—a last-ditch effort to appease the guilt she still carried? Maybe a little of both. She didn't know anymore.

Grace walked ahead silently, toward the door at the far side of the building that Seth had texted her about. He'd actually texted her about a lot of things during the past few days, and as promised, they always related to basketball in one way or the other.

> *Don't forget to keep your eye on the ball at work today.*
>
> *Just nailed a 3-pointer. (That's code for landed a new client.)*

And her personal favorite, though she'd never admit it: *My Gatorade just dribbled down my chin—I mean "double-dribbled," because it happened twice. How embarrassing.*

Biting back a smile at the memory, Grace pulled the door open and waited for Alec to wheel himself through.

Sure enough, the moment they entered the building, voices and laughter echoed down the hall, followed by a ball bouncing off a backboard.

Alec immediately froze. "What are we doing here, Grace?" he said, making it clear that "It's a surprise" wouldn't cut it anymore.

Grace hesitated, not sure what to do. Should she tell him the truth and insist he go in and give it a try? Should she send an "SOS" text to Seth? Or should she duct tape his hands together and his mouth shut then wheel him in like a prisoner?

"Grace." It sounded like a warning.

The last option suddenly seemed like a really good idea. If only she'd brought duct tape. "I, uh—"

The door opened down the hall, magnifying the sounds of the basketball game. Something clanked a few times against the door, followed by muttering, and a guy in a wheelchair appeared. Grace hated how her heart raced at the sight of Seth, as though he were some handsome hero coming to her rescue, but she'd never been happier to see him.

"Hey, you made it. Good." Seth wheeled himself toward them. "I was getting worried you weren't going to show, which would be a bad thing since we're one player short."

Grace didn't dare look at Alec. She could only imagine the thoughts going through his mind. "Sorry we're late," she said. "It took a little longer to get here than I thought."

Alec remained silent, probably working through various scenarios involving the best way to murder his sister.

Seth stopped in front of them and extended his hand to Grace's brother. "You must be Alec."

Alec hesitated then took his hand, giving it a quick shake. "Sorry, but I have no idea who you are. Grace . . . surprised me."

Seth's grin widened. "She didn't tell you where she was taking you?"

"No."

"And you actually trusted her?" Seth chuckled. "You're braver than I would have been."

"Or just stupid."

Seth laughed. "Well, there is that."

Alec's lips twitched, and Grace felt the first stirrings of hope. If Seth could break through Alec's defenses after only a few sentences, maybe there was hope that he could convince her brother to stay.

"This is Seth," said Grace, introducing him. "He's one of my patients."

"Her best and favorite patient."

Grace wasn't about to argue, not when she so obviously needed Seth's help. "Let's just say he knows how to leave a lasting impression."

"Lasting . . . I like that." Even in the dim light of the hallway Seth's eyes twinkled, making Grace roll hers.

Alec continued to stare at Seth, taking in his wheelchair. "You're a paraplegic?"

"No, just an idiot who tore his ACL. Hence the reason for this." Seth tapped the wheels on his chair. "It's the only way your sister will let me play ball."

Alec nodded, his jaw working back and forth. His hands found the wheels, as if ready to push himself away. "Well, good to meet you. Maybe I'll see you around."

Seth cocked his head to the side. "Oh c'mon, you're not really taking off, are you? We need you. It might sound like we know what we're doing, but we're all clueless, even after watching a YouTube video of a Paralympic game. It's not nearly as easy to maneuver these things as it looks."

"It would probably be easier if you had the right kind of chairs," Alec said dryly.

"Yeah, probably." Seth chuckled. "But beggars can't be choosers, and considering I had to go to three different places just to get these, I had to take what I could get." Seth paused, jerking his head toward the gym. "So, you in?"

Grace held her breath as Alec hesitated. Was he actually considering it, or trying to figure out the best way to let Seth down and get out of there? *Please let it be option one.*

Alec finally shrugged. "Sure, why not? I used to love basketball."

"Awesome." Seth grinned. "Let's go introduce you to everyone. You can give us all a few tips before someone breaks one of these chairs."

Grace's heart pounded as she followed them down the hall. Did what just happened really happen? Had Seth really convinced her brother to stay? She suddenly felt like pulling him out of his chair and giving him a giant hug. Once again, her eyes followed his movements as Seth continued to wheel himself forward. What would it feel like to put her arms around him? Probably good—too good—which is exactly why she should never do it, no matter how much he deserved it or how tempted she might be.

The sound of the gym door clanking against Seth's wheelchair brought Grace back to her senses. She grabbed it and held it open for them.

Seth flashed her a meaningful look as he passed. "What? You're not going to make me get through it on my own?"

"Maybe next time," she said, making him chuckle.

Inside the gym, Seth introduced everyone then quickly formed two teams. With Alec, there were six altogether, and Grace suddenly felt like a misfit. Should she stay on the sidelines like Alec's babysitter or wait in the foyer?

Seth glanced at Grace and nodded toward the corner of the room. "There's an extra chair over there if you'd like to join in on the fun."

Sure enough, another wheelchair leaned against the wall. But the last thing Grace wanted to do was get in the way. She'd rather be a spectator. "I'll pass, but thanks anyway."

"Oh c'mon, Grace," Alec taunted. "You can be on our team. Now that they have me, we could really use a handicap to even things out."

Grace's eyes narrowed. She opened her mouth to retort when one of Seth's friends—a guy named Owen—started chortling and slapping his knee. "Did the handicapped guy just say he needed a handicap? Because that's just funny." Owen must have realized how his comment might have sounded, because the laughter died as quickly as it came. He shot Alec an apologetic look. "No offense, man."

Alec laughed, rich and deep. "None taken."

Grace's heart nearly stopped at the sound. How long had it been since she'd heard Alec laugh? It sounded almost foreign to her, like a distant memory—one she didn't realize how much she missed until now.

A lump lodged in her throat, and her eyes met Seth's in wonder. *How did you do that?* she silently asked. *How?* In only a matter of minutes, he and his friends had accomplished what she'd been trying to do for years. She felt both grateful and jealous at the same time.

Who was Seth, exactly? What had prompted him to invite Alec tonight? What had made him show up at that auction weeks before? Why were all these guys willing to show up and play basketball in wheelchairs for him? While Grace wanted to keep believing that he was an ego-driven wreaker of havoc, evidently there was more to him than that—a deeper, more complicated side that Grace wasn't sure she wanted to know.

Shoving her thoughts aside, Grace walked a few steps to the side of the court and retrieved the ball from the floor. "How about making me the ball girl? Something tells me you're going to need one."

All of the guys chuckled, even Alec. A cozy warmth ribboned around Grace's heart, filling her soul with something that went beyond joy. For the first time in years, Alec had laughed at something she said. It felt like Grace had been given a tiny miracle—a glimpse of the old Alec she used to love and idolize.

And she had Seth to thank for it.

Twelve

♡ ♡ ♡

"Only twenty more seconds," Grace said.

Twenty seconds had never felt so long. Seth's face practically exploded from the exertion it took to do a simple wall sit. His injured leg screamed at him to let up, but he wasn't about to do that—not with Grace standing next to him and counting down the seconds. His pride wouldn't let him.

"Five, four, three, two, one."

Seth's knee buckled as he slumped to the ground, extending his injured knee forward while his elbow rested on his uninjured bent knee. He shook his head as he caught his breath. "This is crazy. A month ago, that would have been no big deal."

Grace sank to the floor beside him and rested her head against the wall. Five minutes before, Cameron had waved a goodbye, saying, "Grace, you work too hard," then walked out the door, leaving them alone in the room.

Once again, Seth had scheduled the last appointment on purpose, hoping for some more alone-time with her. Since Grace's appointment times seemed to start earlier and go later than all the other therapists', he figured it was a possibility. No wonder Dr. Ross had to pull a few strings to get Seth an appointment with her. She really was a popular therapist, and now that Seth had gotten to know her better, he understood why.

Cameron was right, though. She did work too hard. Seth could see it in her eyes—the exhaustion, stress, and worry. Or maybe she just didn't allow herself any stress relief. Did she even know how to have fun? To set work aside and enjoy life? Somehow, Seth didn't think so, and it was something he wanted to change.

Grace offered him a look of sympathy. "Don't worry, your strength will come back. I know progress seems slow right now, but you've come so far already. Just promise me you won't slack off. This is about the time when a lot of patients start cutting back on their workouts, partly because they're sick of it and partly because their knee starts to feel stronger and they think they don't need it anymore. Those are the patients who end up re-injuring themselves or who never fully recover." She twisted her head and met his gaze. "Don't be one of those patients."

"Would you really care if I was?" Seth probably shouldn't have voiced the question, but every minute spent with Grace made him like her even more. Seth wanted to know if she thought of him as just another patient, or if she might care just a little bit more.

"Yes, I would."

Seth's mouth pulled into a smile. He liked that answer. "Why?"

"Because I care about all my patients."

Seth's smile melted away. He should have expected that, but it didn't keep him from hoping that he'd made more of an impression than that.

Grace patted his knee and stood, offering her hand to help him up. "And it's because I care that I'm going to make you ride the bike now."

Seth groaned. He wanted to throw the stationary bike out the window, strap his top-of-the-line mountain bike to the roof of his car, drive it to his favorite trail, and go for a real ride. He wanted to see trees and bushes fly past, feel the wind on his face, and breathe in the intoxicating, earthy smell that made mountain biking so addicting.

Seth was sick of pedaling for all he was worth and going nowhere.

"Isn't there anything else I can do instead?" Seth said. "I'm begging you. Please don't make me ride that bike today."

Grace drew her lower lip into her mouth the same way she did every time she mulled something over. Seth found it adorable.

"How about the rower?" she suggested. "I was planning to wait until next time, but I think you're ready."

Seth wasn't sure what he expected, but a rowing machine didn't hold much appeal either. Still, it wasn't the bike, so he nodded in agreement and finally accepted her hand. Although he didn't need the help up, Seth never missed an opportunity to touch Grace. Her hands always felt soft and cool, making him want to hold on for longer than necessary.

"Speaking of progress," Grace said, relinquishing his hand, "how do you feel about swimming?"

"If it gets me off that bike, I'll take it."

She smiled—something she'd started to do more often around him. "Sorry, but it's more for recovery, which means you'll still have to work out on the bike."

"I had a feeling you were going to say that."

Grace gestured for him to sit on the rower and made some slight adjustments then nodded for him to start. Seth

Working It Out

did, trying to picture himself on Lake Union in a kayak, cutting smoothly through the water. But there was no breeze, no fresh air, and no smell of lake water. Unfortunately the rowing machine just wasn't the same, and before long he started to feel the stirrings of boredom.

Grace looked up from making notes on her clipboard. "Hey, I, uh, want to thank you again for what you did for Alec. I'm still not sure how you convinced him to keep playing, but he's looking forward to tomorrow. So really— thank you. You have no idea how much it means to me."

Seth nodded, glad he could be of help. "No problem. Alec's a cool guy." Seth actually found it hard to reconcile the guy Grace had described with the one who'd played ball the other night. Alec was funny, knew his way around a wheelchair, and could throw a great shot. He was the kind of guy Seth would choose to hang out with.

Grace tapped the pen against her lower lip, watching Seth closely. "Mind if I ask you a question?"

"Shoot." Anything to get his mind off the mundane movements of rowing.

Grace sat in a chair next to him and clasped her fingers together. "The night of the auction, why did you show up and cause a scene? I mean, why not just donate the money instead?"

Seth's eyebrow shot up in surprise. Although Grace was beginning to lower her guard more often around him, she'd never actually started a personal conversation. It both thrilled and made Seth nervous at the same time. In a way, Grace reminded him of one of those roly poly bugs he used to play with as a kid. If Seth held perfectly still, the bug would feel comfortable enough to uncurl and come out of its ball, but the slightest jarring would send it tucking itself right back into its protective shell.

Ever since Seth had met Grace, he had a way of saying things that made her tuck into a tight ball. But now that she

83

was finally opening up to him, he was leery of saying the wrong thing. Would she react like Lanna and refuse to see his side? Or would she understand?

"Uh . . ." Where did Seth begin?

"You don't have to answer if you don't want," she said quickly. "I didn't mean to pry or get personal."

But that was exactly what Seth wanted—*to get personal.* "No, that's okay. You just caught me off guard, that's all."

Grace laughed—actually laughed. It sounded rich, bubbly, and melodious, nearly taking Seth's breath away. All this time, he'd tried jokes, teasing comments, anything to hear that sound, but nothing had worked until now.

What had he said again?

"Sorry," Grace said, letting her laughter die off. "It's just nice catching you off guard for once. You know—payback and all that."

Seth made a mental note to let her get some payback more often. "Just so you know," he said, "If you ever let me go for a ride on a real bike outside, that would totally catch me off guard."

Grace laughed again, making the smelly and stagnant room suddenly feel a little less like a gym and more like a cozy retreat. Seth could watch her and listen to that sound all day long.

"You'll be able to ride a real bike soon, I promise," she said.

"Will you come with me when I do?" It was the closest that Seth had ever come to asking her out. He held his breath in anticipation of her answer. But when her brows furrowed, and he could practically see her rolling back into her secure little ball, Seth regretted the words.

"I meant during one of our sessions," he quickly amended. "I could bring my bike here and we could take it to the park down the street."

Her expression cleared, and she nodded. "Yeah, sure— when you're ready."

An awkward silence settled around them, making Seth want to curse. He felt like they'd taken two steps forward and two back. So much for progress.

Be patient, he reminded himself. Maybe if he opened up a little, she would too. Seth continued to row, bending and straightening his aching leg as he searched for a way to get back to the conversation about Lanna and the auction without making it obvious he was grasping at straws.

When he couldn't come up with a decent segue, he finally said, "Sorry, I wasn't trying to avoid answering your question before. I just didn't know how to explain without making you think worse of me than you already do."

"Why would I think worse of you?"

Seth sighed, focusing on the movements of the rowing machine. "Well, it goes like this: Right before Lanna's brother died, he asked me to look after her. But Lanna—who is practically a charity case herself—doesn't think she needs any help, especially not from me. She sees it as a personal handout and would rather exhaust herself planning one fundraiser after another than accept anything from me."

Seth paused, not wanting to go into the details of a night he'd rather forget. But he'd already started and couldn't exactly stop now. "When I found out she was planning an auction, I saw it as my chance to finally donate a lot of money and force her to take it whether she wanted to or not. I thought I was doing the right thing—you know, the greater good and all that—but all I succeeded in doing was to tick her off. She hasn't spoken to me since."

The corners of Grace's mouth tugged into a smile. "You seem to like ticking people off, don't you?" It was more of a statement than a question.

"Believe it or not, I really don't. Especially not someone as stubborn as Lanna." Or Grace, for that matter. Seth stopped rowing and grabbed a hand towel, wiping it across his forehead.

"I take it you two are close?" Grace asked casually, glancing at her clipboard as though she didn't really care about his answer.

"She's like a sister." Seth's only sister.

Grace lifted her head and studied him, tapping her pen against her lower lip. "I'm surprised she didn't ask you to be one of the bachelors."

"Oh, she did. I passed."

"Oh," said Grace, setting down her clipboard. "Then she didn't refuse *all* your help."

Seth leveled her a look, the same look he'd given Lanna when she'd initially made the suggestion. "She refused the help I was willing to offer."

"I see." The way Grace said it made it sound as though she understood something Seth didn't. He didn't like feeling like he was missing something, but did he really want to understand?

"What do you see?" Seth asked, still not sure he wanted to know.

Grace nodded toward the machine. "Keep rowing."

Seth started back up, wincing when his knee protested the movement. Only a minute or two was all it took to freeze it back up again. What a pain.

"All I'm saying," said Grace, "is that Lanna would probably gladly accept your help as long as it's not in the form of money."

Of course she thought that because Grace was just as stubborn as Lanna. "And all I'm saying is that I would never, *ever* consider auctioning myself off to who-knows-what-kind of person just so Lanna could raise a little more money for her charity."

"I'm not saying you should."

Seth flicked a surprised glance her way. "Then what are you saying?"

Grace leaned back in her chair and folded her arms. "Have you ever thought of offering to help her raise the money? Or, now that they're probably doing okay thanks to your donation, what about offering to help tutor some of those kids in her after-school program?"

"You want me to volunteer?" Was she serious? The idea held zero appeal for Seth. He wasn't the tutor type, nor was he particularly good with kids. There was a reason he was a business consultant and not an elementary school teacher.

No, giving money was more his thing.

"Sure, why not?" said Grace. "Or do you have something against giving up a few hours of your time to help the less fortunate?"

Yes, Seth did actually. He liked spending his time the way he wanted to spend it. But something told him he shouldn't admit that to Grace. He'd have to plead the fifth on that one.

"Because from where I'm sitting," she continued. "Other than wheelchair basketball, working out, and playing video games or watching movies, you really can't do much right now."

"I work, too." Occasionally.

Her lips twitched. "And how many hours does that 'consultant' job of yours take?"

"It depends on the week."

"On average."

Seth sighed and stopped rowing again. He wasn't crazy about the direction this conversation was headed or how it made him feel—as though he only cared about himself, which wasn't true. Seth gave money to the homeless, donated to charities, and opened doors for the elderly. He'd hired a mechanic to fix Lanna's car without her knowing, organized basketball games for his friends, and had even convinced Grace's brother to keep playing with them. He wasn't totally self-centered. But the way Grace looked at him right now made him feel like he was pretty close.

Seth frowned, feeling the need to put himself in a more positive light. "How about this?" he finally said. "I'll agree to volunteer if *you* agree to go with me."

It was a brilliant suggestion, actually. If Grace declined, Seth wouldn't feel obligated to volunteer. And if she said yes, she would have to spend time with him outside of work. Either way, he won.

"Oh . . . I, uh, don't think that's a good idea."

"Why not?" Seth said with mock innocence. "Don't tell me you're against giving up a few hours of your time to help the less fortunate."

Grace leveled him a warning look. "No, but you're my patient. It wouldn't be appropriate to do something with you outside of work."

"But you came to the basketball game," Seth pointed out.

"That was different."

"How so?" Seth asked. "It's not like I'm asking you on a date or anything."

"I know, it's just—" She fidgeted, looking flustered.

Seth cocked his head to the side, molding his expression into one of sympathy. "Think of the children, Grace. Think of the children."

She rolled her eyes and threw up her hands in a gesture of defeat. "I walked right into that one, didn't I? Okay fine, you win. I'll go." She gestured toward the machine. "Now row."

Seth grinned and resumed rowing, suddenly feeling as though he really were in a kayak, cutting through the waters on Lake Union. The sun warmed his skin, a breeze whipped at his face, and the smell of lake water lingered in the air. Or was that the smell of triumph?

Thirteen

♡ ♡ ♡

Grace looked through Seth's windshield, noting that the brown cinderblock building looked old and tired, as though it had lived its life and now wanted to move on. Artistic graffiti covered one side of the wall, almost like a mural, and a sign that read *Magnificent Minds* was affixed to the wall next to a red painted steel door. A teenage boy rode his bike down the sidewalk and stopped outside the door, where he chained his bike to a stand. He had to pull twice on the door to get it to open then disappeared inside.

From her comfy seat in Seth's Land Rover, with its new-car smell, Grace felt out of place. They should have taken her more understated Nissan. At least the silver of her car would have blended in a little better than the deep orange of Seth's.

"If you think the outside looks bad, wait until you see the inside," Seth said from the driver's seat.

Grace glanced his way, noticing the way his brown Quicksilver baseball hat made his eyes appear darker than usual. His face was clean shaven today, tempting Grace to run her fingers across his jaw line. "You've been here before?"

Seth nodded, studying the building. "A few times."

When he didn't make a move to open his door, Grace unfastened her seat belt. "Ready?"

Seth continued to stare at the door. "Lanna hasn't spoken to me since the night of the auction and doesn't know I'm here."

Grace's hand remained on her seatbelt. "You didn't tell her we were coming?" What was Seth thinking? Didn't he know that showing up with no warning wasn't the best way to apologize? Would Lanna even have anything for them to do?

Seth met Grace's eyes. "Lanna isn't the type to get mad, but after the stunt I pulled, she . . ." He shook his head, his voice drifting off as he bit his lower lip and glanced back at the building.

He looked vulnerable, nervous even, something that Grace had never seen on him before. It caught her off guard. He'd always been so confident, so sure of himself. He had it all. Looks, money, talent, a natural charisma. And yet here he was, sitting in his expensive automobile, completely intimidated by the nondescript building in front of them—or rather, by a particular girl inside the building.

An unwanted prick of jealousy struck Grace in the heart, which was ridiculous, since she wasn't in the running for Seth's affections. Still, she couldn't help but wonder what it would feel like to have Seth care about her that way.

Shoving the feeling aside, Grace laid a hand on his arm. "I met Lanna at the auction, and she seemed like the forgiving type. I bet it will mean a lot to her that you're here."

Seth shook his head as though he didn't believe her. "She's as stubborn as—well, you." Under the rim of his cap, his eyes met hers again, only this time he wore a lopsided smile.

"Me?" What was that supposed to mean? Grace was strong-willed and determined, maybe, but stubborn?

Seth continued to hold her gaze. "Ever since I first met you, you've reminded me of the girl on the other side of that door." He gestured toward the building. "Something tells me that you and Lanna are going to get along really well. If nothing else, you both have a common enemy from the auction."

Grace smiled. For some reason, being compared to Lanna felt good, as if she'd somehow earned some of Seth's esteem.

"You should do that more often," Seth said, watching her with a look she couldn't quite decipher.

"Do what?"

His finger reached out to touch the corner of her mouth, sending chills up her spine. "Smile. It looks good on you."

Grace's heart sped up as she stared back, wondering what he was thinking. Was he feeling this crazy, almost electric feeling that seemed to zing through the car around them?

His hand dropped back to his lap, and his eyes left hers. He drew in a breath and reached for the handle. "Let's get this over with."

They left the car behind, and Seth yanked open the steel door, making a face as it screeched in protest. "I offered to pay for a new door, but would she let me? No."

Grace smiled. Any woman who could stand up to Seth deserved to be applauded. "I like her already."

"I figured you would."

Grace moved forward into a small reception-type room with an empty desk off to the side. It had that musty, old-house smell mixed with a hint of vanilla—a plug in air freshener next to the desk. Muted and muffled voices echoed from a back room at the end of the hall.

The door screeched open again, and a young African-American girl walked in with long, tightly curled hair. She flashed Grace and Seth a curious look before heading down the hall. With a quick glance at each other, they followed.

As the girl entered the room ahead of them, a female voice called out, "Hey, Rayna, how are you, girl? We missed you yesterday."

"Hey, Miss Lanna. Sorry. I couldn't come. I had to babysit."

"Well, we're glad you're here today. Your favorite chair's open, right over there by the window. Take a seat, and I'll be with you in a—" She stopped when Seth entered the room, her eyes widening. She shot a glance at the half-dozen kids already in the room and stood, moving closer. "What are you doing here?"

"We're here to volunteer," Seth said.

Grace waited for him to continue, but he didn't. She shot him a look. Really? After all this time, that's all he had to say? Ignoring her silent plea, Seth simply stood there, waiting for Lanna to fill in the awkward silence that was getting worse by the second.

Grace shook her head. *Men.*

"Ok-ay," Lanna finally said. Her eyes flickered to Grace's, crinkling slightly in confusion. "I'm sorry," she said, extending her hand. "I didn't mean to be rude. I'm Lanna. Are you here with Seth? You look familiar."

Grace nodded and shook Lanna's hand. "I'm Grace," she said. "I'm his therapist." She left the "physical" part out on purpose.

"Therapist?" Lanna's eyes widened. "Are you serious?"

Grace molded her expression into one of sympathy and nodded. "After a lot—and I mean *a lot*—of therapy, Seth realizes he has some unresolved issues, so he invited me along to make sure that you understood how sorry he is for how things went down at the auction. Since he can't bring himself to say that out loud"—Grace shot Seth a meaningful look—"he's here to volunteer for however many hours it takes to earn your forgiveness."

Lanna still looked confused, but a tentative smile played on her lips. "Wow, you must be a really good therapist to finally get him to see that."

Seth rolled his eyes. "Grace is my *physical* therapist, not my psychologist. But she's right about two things: I *am* sorry, and I'm here to volunteer. But only for *today*," he said, emphasizing the last word.

Lanna nodded. "Understood. And for what it's worth, I'm sorry too." She opened her arms. "Truce?"

Seth accepted her hug with a small smile and an expression of relief mixed with happiness—one that tugged on Grace's heartstrings. "Truce," he said.

A young boy, probably about ten, tapped Lanna on the shoulder, breaking them apart. "Miss Lanna, I can't figure this out." He held up what appeared to be his math homework.

Lanna bent to his level. "Hey, Chad. See this guy right here?" She pointed to Seth. "He's going to help you with your homework today. Will that be okay?"

The boy shot a tentative look at Seth then nodded solemnly. Taking his cue, Seth reached for the homework page. "I happen to be a pro at math, so you're in good hands. Let's go have a seat and see if we can figure these out." He winked at Grace before following the boy back to his seat.

Lanna watched him walk away, smiling, then turned back to Grace. "Are you really his physical therapist?"

Grace nodded.

"Is there a reason he's seeing you?" She paused, then rushed on to say, "I mean not *seeing*, seeing, but seeing like—" She winced, and her brow crinkled. "Oh geez, I'm making a mess of this, aren't I?"

Grace laughed and shook her head. "About a month ago, Seth tore his ACL during a heli-skiing trip. I just happened to be the therapist his doctor referred him to."

"He did *what*?" Lanna's voice rose to attract the attention of a few kids nearby. She looked so distressed that Grace reached out to touch her arm in a comforting gesture. "Nothing to worry about. As you can see, he's going to be fine."

Lanna blinked, shaking her head. "I can't believe I didn't know that. I feel like the worst kind of friend right now."

Grace smiled. "Well, considering Seth feels like the worst kind of friend for what happened at the auction, I'd say you're about even. Really, though, he's fine."

Lanna cocked her head to the side, studying Grace with a quizzical expression. "I'm surprised Seth told you about that. He's not normally that open with people."

For whatever reason, Grace liked thinking that Seth had opened up to her—something he wouldn't do with just anyone. It made her feel better about everything that had happened with Alec.

"I think I may bring out the worst in him," Grace said, not knowing how else to respond.

Lanna's snicker had Seth glancing their way, as well as some of the kids. As soon as Lanna noticed, she dropped her voice. "Forgive my curiosity, but are you two . . . you know, dating?"

Grace couldn't pretend to be surprised by the question because of course Lanna would think that. After all, what kind of normal therapist/patient relationship extended to stuff like this? None that Grace knew of. Still, Lanna needed to be set straight. "No, we're not dating—not even thinking about dating. To be honest, I'm not even sure what I'm doing here. He just—" Grace shrugged, not quite sure how to explain.

Lanna nodded in understanding. "He can be very persuasive when he sets his mind to something." She raised an eyebrow suggestively. "I'm just wondering if he has his mind set on you."

An unwanted thrill shot through Grace, followed by alarm at the possibility. That wouldn't be good. She didn't want to be attracted to Seth, charmed by him, or even indebted to him. She simply wanted to make it through the rest of his recovery with her heart intact—something that would never happen if he continued to drag her into his personal life and insert himself into hers.

Lanna nudged her shoulder. "Relax. He's actually a really great guy."

"I know, I just—" She just what? Didn't want her name appearing on his undoubtedly extensive conquest list? Didn't want to be *that* therapist who couldn't keep the professional barriers intact?

Grace frowned. What *was* she doing here? Was this really about trying to help Seth and Lanna mend fences? Or did Grace agree because deep down she *wanted* to spend more time with Seth?

An uncomfortable pit settled in her stomach.

She quickly pushed it away and squared her shoulders. Grace was strong. And a professional. She'd gone with her brother to the basketball game to get him on the right track, and she'd come here to help Seth. That was it. After today there would be no reason to cross over the professional line into personal.

More than ready to change the subject, Grace said, "Seth wasn't the only one who came here to work. What can I do?"

Lanna gave her a knowing smile before pointing to two young girls nearby—both of whom were giggling and talking. "See those two girls over there? My friend Milly usually keeps them on track. But something came up and she couldn't be here today. Would you mind? They're both sweethearts who also happen to be best friends and would rather gab than get their homework done."

"I'm on it." Grace grabbed a chair and pulled it near the girls. She introduced herself and asked if she could see what they were working on. In no time at all, she had them a little more focused on their homework.

As she worked with the girls, every now and then her gaze would drift across the room toward Seth. Sometimes she'd catch him looking at her and would quickly look away; sometimes she'd watch as he tried to explain something to the boy, and sometimes she found him leaning back in his chair, twirling a pencil and eyeing the window with longing.

Seth hadn't been joking when he'd said there was a reason he didn't go into elementary education. But at least he'd come. At least he was trying. And at least Lanna had finally spoken to him. That counted for something.

But what would happen after today? Would Seth ever return? Would he find a way to get a little more involved as Grace suggested, or would he take a step back until Lanna's funds ran dry then try to pull out his wallet yet again? Would Lanna start accepting his help—at least where this program was concerned?

Why did Grace even care?

By the time all the kids had finished up and left, Grace was ready for a brisk walk through the park—anything to get her body moving. How did Lanna come every day to this musty-smelling room and sit here for hours, trying to be both a parent and teacher to these kids? What motivated her? What kept her going? She seemed to have an endless supply of patience and kindness.

Seth yawned and stretched as he walked over to Grace. "That was the longest two hours of my life."

Grace and Lanna both laughed.

"Yeah." Lanna nodded. "I figured this would be a 'been there, done that' sort of thing for you. But thank you for coming just the same. And for the money, though it kills me to admit it. Because of you, we'll be able to stop worrying about how to keep paying the rent on this place for a long while." She paused and looked away, but not before Grace saw her get a little teary-eyed. "I just hope that one day you can come to see the value of this place."

Seth stepped forward and drew Lanna into a brotherly hug. Wanting to give them a little privacy, Grace wandered the room, pushing in chairs and picking up pencils.

"Just because this isn't my type of scene doesn't mean I don't value what you do," said Seth. "Believe it or not, I admire the heck out of you and think that what you're doing for these kids is incredible. Yes, I hate to see you exhaust yourself with all the fundraising you've had to do—which was the main reason I wanted to help. But please understand I didn't do it just for you." He paused. "I did it for the tax break as well."

Grace had to muffle her laughter as Lanna groaned and pushed him away, playfully punching his arm. "You're so impossible sometimes. I honestly have no idea how Mike put up with you for so many years." She cast a glance at Grace. "Quick, get away while you still can."

Grace's thoughts exactly.

Seth chuckled. "Whatever. You know Mike was way worse than me."

"Maybe." Lanna's expression turned melancholy as she looked around the room. "I wish he were here right now."

"He is. In spirit. I guarantee it."

The corners of Lanna's mouth lifted. "It's really annoying how I can never stay mad at you for very long."

"You call over a month not long?"

"Yeah, well, I actually got over it awhile ago. I just didn't want you to know what a weakling I am when it comes to you. Your ego's big enough already."

"Not nearly as big as your pride."

"Oh shut up."

Seth laughed, and Grace clasped her fingers behind her back, looking around for something more to do than eavesdrop. But there were no more tables to realign and no more garbage to throw away. She should probably make an excuse and wait for Seth in the front room, but she couldn't bring herself to say the words. She was enjoying the exchange too much.

"You know," Seth said, "you really should use some of that money and get a few game tables in here or something. This all-work-and-no-play thing really drags. I'm willing to bet the kids would be a lot more inclined to come if you made it fun for them."

Lanna looked around the room as if considering it. "We do struggle getting kids to come, but the tutoring program is top priority. They're already behind in school, and if they don't catch up now, it's only going to get harder for them."

"I get that, but all kids need breaks. I mean, take Chad, for example. After spending all day sitting in a chair at school, I'm sure the last thing he wants to do is to come here and do the same. The only reason he even comes is because his mom works, so she makes him ride his bike here after school instead of staying home alone." Seth sat on a table and folded his arms. "All I'm saying is that if you made this place a little more fun, it would be even more successful than it already is. You could use games as incentives. You know— finish this page or report or whatever and earn a game of air hockey or fifteen minutes on Xbox Kinect or whatever."

Grace had to admit that Seth made a good point. A really good point, actually.

"But those kind of things would be distracting to the other kids," said Lanna.

"This room is huge." Seth gestured to the center of the room. "Build a wall right there and add a door. One side can be the fun side, the other the boring side." His eyes flickered to Grace. "Even Grace agrees with me on this one, don't you?"

Grace shrugged, remaining diplomatically silent. But the air felt suddenly charged with excitement, and she found herself getting caught up in Seth's vision for this place. How fun would it be to take a paintbrush to that wall over there and organize board games and puzzles? To see the kids' faces light up once they saw the transformation?

As quickly as her spirits rose, Grace doused them. What was she thinking? She couldn't get involved even if she wanted to. It would put her around Seth way too much.

Lanna pursed her lips in thought. "I suppose we could splurge a little for something like that. That is, if you wouldn't mind doing a little manual labor," she hinted at Seth.

He rolled his eyes. "Yes, I can help you build your wall—as long as the owner of the building okays it."

Lanna smiled. "He's pretty easy going. I'm sure he won't mind."

"And what about sports programs?" Seth added. "There's an elementary school around the corner, isn't there? If you had enough interested kids, you could form your own team and ask the school to borrow its gym or fields to practice."

"Whoa, slow down." Lanna rested her hands on her hips. "I mean, that all sounds well and good, but who's going to coach a team like that? You?"

Seth shrugged. "Sure, why not? Spring soccer is coming up, isn't it? I'd have to check the schedule, but I think I know enough about the game to coach a city-league team—

assuming I have a great assistant, of course." He shot Grace a meaningful look. "A trainer or sports medicine sort of person would come in really handy."

Grace immediately tensed. When would Seth get it through his thick head that she was his therapist and only his therapist? End of discussion. She waved the question away. "Oh, you don't want my help. I'd make a terrible assistant. But Alec used to play soccer for our high school team. You should ask him."

Seth raised an eyebrow. "Do you think he'd do it?"

"If anyone can convince him, you can." Which was true. Ever since that first basketball game, Alec had been hanging out with Seth and his friends more and more. In her brother's eyes, Seth could do no wrong.

"That's not a bad idea. I'll ask him," Seth said to Grace. "But only if you promise to come to some of the games and cheer us on. Or better yet, you could head up a girls' team."

Sometimes Seth reminded Grace of a door-to-door sales person who wouldn't take "no" for an answer. How did Lanna get away with avoiding him for over a month? He was relentless. Grace swallowed, feeling the sudden urge to get out of there. "I'll think about it," she said noncommittally.

"I hate to burst your bubble, Seth," Lanna interjected. "But the kids involved in this program aren't all the same age. We have kids as young as third graders on up to junior-high school kids. We even have a couple of high-schoolers who come occasionally. It wouldn't just be one team you'd have to worry about coaching—more like four or five."

"Oh." Surprise and worry reflected in Seth's eyes, making Grace want to laugh. Would he rescind his offer? Backpedal? Or would he find a way to make it work? "I suppose I could recruit a few other guys to help out," he said finally.

"And then there's the money to consider," Lanna added. "The kids' parents could never afford it, not even something as inexpensive as city league."

Seth caught Lanna's eye. "That doesn't have to be a problem—so long as you'll let me cover it." He let the suggestion hang out there.

Grace felt like dropping her head to her hands and groaning. What was Seth thinking to suggest that? Would he never learn? Did he really want to undo all the progress he'd made with Lanna today? Honestly, he could be so—

"I'd be okay with that," Lanna said, surprising both Grace and Seth—based on the way his eyes widened.

He blinked in confusion. "Are you seriously telling me that after ignoring me for over a month, you're now suddenly willing to accept my money?"

Lanna waved his question away as if she couldn't believe she had to explain. "You're doing this for the kids, not me. That changes everything."

Seth had never looked more confused. He lifted his hands in a gesture of defeat. "I'll never understand you, Lanna, but whatever. Let me make some calls, and I'll get back to you."

Lanna grinned and threw her arms around Seth, hugging him tight. "Thank you, thank you, thank you!" She pulled back and looked up at him. "Where was this Seth when we first opened this place?"

"Being smart and staying out of it."

Grace smiled at the exchange even as her heart constricted. In that moment, she felt like she was getting another glimpse of the real Seth—the one who was kind and good and loyal. Yes, the chaos wreaking guy was still a part of him, but underneath all of that was a heart of pure gold.

The discovery made Grace squirm, mostly because she felt her defenses weaken. She didn't want the god of chaos to have a heart. It made things too confusing.

Lanna pulled back to pat Seth on the chest before smiling at Grace. "I hope you come back, Grace. Something tells me that you had a lot to do with this."

Grace blinked in surprise. "What? Me? No. I had nothing to do with this, trust me." She didn't want any credit for this turn of events, nor did she want to feel any pressure to come back and get in deeper than she already was.

Grace looked to Seth for help, but instead of setting Lanna straight, he watched her with an expression she couldn't read. The usual teasing glint in his eyes was gone, replaced by something more serious and intense. Her heart pounded.

A small smile appeared before Seth looked away and tweaked Lanna's nose. "We're going to head. But assuming you'll now answer my calls, I'll be in touch."

"Looking forward to it." Lanna said. "And thanks again, Seth, this really means a lot to me."

"No problem." Seth met Grace's gaze once again and held out his hand for her to take. "Ready to go?"

She felt her resolve slipping, but couldn't let it go completely. She stared at his hand, wanting to touch it, hold it, to interlace her small fingers with his strong ones. But she was his therapist, not his girlfriend.

Therapist.

His fingers wiggled. "My keys, please? I saw you pick them up when you were cleaning earlier."

Huh? Grace glanced down. Sure enough, his keys were clutched in her hand. There was even an imprint on her palm from squeezing them too hard. Her face flamed, and she quickly handed them over.

"It was great to meet you, Lanna," Grace said. Without another word, she turned and headed for the front of the building, wanting to crawl into the trunk of Seth's car and hide. When she reached the outside air, she drew in a deep, steadying breath then grabbed the passenger door handle, ready to yank it open and dive inside. But it wouldn't budge. The car was locked.

Duh.

Forced to stand there, clasping and unclasping her hands, Grace waited for Seth to catch up and unlock it. But instead of clicking the button on his keyless remote, he walked toward her, stopping directly in front of her.

Grace stood frozen as he reached around and manually unlocked the car. His chest bumped against her shoulder, sending tingles up and down her arms. In and out she breathed, telling her racing heart to slow down and her body to stop responding. It was only a touch. A simple touch. Nothing to get all worked up about.

But then Seth looked at her in that intense way again, his face only inches from hers. Grace trembled, feeling like all of her defenses and inhibitions were falling in a garbled up heap around her. Nothing made sense anymore. Not Seth. Not her feelings. Nothing. Grace didn't know what she wanted or didn't want anymore.

"If you'll step aside, I'll open your door for you," Seth said.

Once again, Grace's face flamed, and she quickly stepped aside. That was twice in only a matter of minutes. How could she be so dense? What was wrong with her? A normal person would have stepped aside the moment he'd reached for the lock. A normal person would have realized he'd asked for his keys earlier, not her hand. She might as well post a sign across her forehead that read, "Yes, I'm attracted to you and apparently don't have a brain when you're around." Not that she needed a sign. Her reaction was obvious enough.

A knowing smile appeared on Seth's face as he held the door open for her. Grace slid into the car, wishing, more than ever, that she'd never climbed inside in the first place.

Once Seth was seated next to her, Grace stared out the passenger window, away from his smile and away from him.

"What about grabbing some dinner on the way home?" Seth suggested as he reversed his car. "I'm beyond starving, and you probably are, too."

Grace's stomach growled in response. She placed her hand over it, willing it to shut up. It was like her body was on a mission to betray and embarrass her, and she was sick of feeling so out of control.

"I really don't think that's a good idea," Grace said.

"Really? Eating's not a good idea? Are you sure? Because you, of all people, should know that food's a necessary fuel for the body."

Grace kept her gaze trained on the passing scenery, feeling drained. "You know what I meant."

"How about a rain-check then?"

Grace let out a breath and turned to face him. She couldn't play this game anymore. As nice and charming as Seth could be, he wasn't the committing type. He was the fly-by-the-seat-of-his-pants and get-the-girl-who-presents-a-challenge-to-go-out-with-him type. Once Grace finally gave in, the game would be over, and she would be left—well, not okay.

"Listen, Seth, I think you're a great guy, but you've got to stop doing this."

"Doing what?" He gave her a look of innocence, as though he really didn't know.

Grace resisted the urge to roll her eyes. Fine. If he wanted her to spell it out, she'd spell it out. "Asking me out, flirting, messing with me—you name it, you've got to stop. I. Don't. Date. Patients. Okay?"

"What about when I'm not your patient?"

Grace felt like beating her head against the dashboard. If only he really were a door-to-door salesman so she could shut the door in his face and walk away. Couldn't he see that this wasn't a joke for her? That they were talking about her heart?

Grace rested her head against the headrest and let out a frustrated sigh. "Why do I get the impression that you're the type of guy who always gets what he wants?"

"I wouldn't say *always*," Seth said. "But when I really want something"—He shot her a meaningful look—"I don't give up easily."

Exactly what Grace was afraid of.

Fourteen

♡ ♡ ♡

Seth leaned back in his rented wheelchair as Alec gave high fives to Garrett and Brandon. They'd just played a three-on-three game of basketball, and Alec, Garrett, and Brandon had pretty much slaughtered Seth, Owen, and their other friend, Ethan. Alec was good. Not only could he outmaneuver everyone, but ninety percent of his shots found their way into the net. For a guy who'd only played basketball for fun in high school, he definitely knew how to shoot—even after a ten-year hiatus. It was the reason everyone wanted him on their team.

"Great game, guys," Alec said to Garrett and Brandon. "You're really getting the hang of those chairs." Sweat dotted his forehead and soaked parts of his shirt, but he looked happy. If only Grace were here to see it. Much to Seth's disappointment, she hadn't shown up since that first game.

Garrett stretched his legs out in front of him and rubbed his quads. He glanced at Alec. "I don't know how you do it, sitting in that chair day after day. My abs are screaming and my legs are cramping."

"He doesn't have a choice, idiot." With his foot, Owen gave Garrett's chair a playful push, twisting it to the side.

Garrett shoved Owen's foot away and twisted back around, glaring at his friend. "He knows I didn't mean it like that. Right, Alec?" He suddenly didn't look so sure of himself.

"Yeah." Alec leaned forward and rested his elbows on his knees. "But Owen's right, I don't have a choice. Day after day, this is my life. I go out of my way to find wheelchair ramps, take up too much aisle space, and feel like a dwarf. Just leaving the house is a major production." The feeling in the room thickened with discomfort. "But," Alec added with a shrug. "I can kick everyone's trash in a game of wheelchair ball, so it's not without its perks."

The guys all chuckled, Seth included. In many ways, Alec reminded him of Grace. They had that same calm, almost stiff exterior that masked a dry sense of humor. When playing ball, Alec really let his guard down, and when he did, he fit right into the group. Seth couldn't help but wonder what Grace would be like if she did the same. Something told him there would be no turning back for him if she did.

Ethan stood to his full height of 6'6" and stretched his arms over his head. "I've got to get going. Thanks for putting this together, Seth. Want me to take the chair home again?"

"If you're planning to come Wednesday, then yeah, that'd be great."

Ethan made quick work of folding his chair before waving goodbye. The rest of the guys followed suit—with the exception of Alec, who wheeled himself to the opposite end of the gym and began shooting one ball after another, missing more than normal. Since Seth couldn't lock up until Alec decided to leave, he folded his chair and left it by the door then walked across the gym to where Alec sat. The basketball hit the rim with a clang before slamming to the floor and bouncing toward Seth.

He grabbed it and tossed it Alec's way, standing near the basket to retrieve more balls.

"It's okay, I got them," Alec said when Seth reached for another wayward ball.

Seth tossed it back. "It's no problem."

"Just like it's not a problem for me to get it," Alec said a little stiffly, as if offended. "It just takes me a little longer."

Seth stifled a smile. Yes, Alec was definitely Grace's brother.

When the next ball hit the rim and bounced to the far left, Seth jogged to grab it before chucking it toward Alec. "It would be a lot easier if you'd just make a shot."

"Says the person who just got his tail kicked."

Seth grinned as he retrieved another ball. Only this time, instead of returning it to Alec, he tucked it under his arm. "Hey, I've been meaning to ask you something."

"What's up?"

Seth walked toward Alec and dropped down beside him, tossing the ball back and forth between his palms before throwing it to Alec once again. "So a friend of mine runs this afterschool program for kids, and somehow I got roped into organizing a couple of soccer teams. The city-league program officially starts in two more weeks, which gives me just enough time to put a few teams together and hopefully get some practices in before the first scheduled game." He paused, wondering how Alec would react. "So how about it? You interested in coaching?"

Alec's eyes widened in a you-did-not-just-ask-me-that sort of way. "Me—coach soccer? Are you serious?"

"Yeah. Grace said you were one of the star players for your high school team, so why not?"

Alec shot Seth a look of annoyance. "Because you need legs for soccer, Seth. How am I supposed to teach a bunch of kids how to play when I can't move mine?" Without really aiming, Alec hurled the ball at the basket. It bounced off the backboard and careened the opposite way, filling the silence with a reverberating sound every time it hit the ground. Alec watched it go with a frustrated look on his face.

Seth didn't move to retrieve the ball this time. Instead, he studied Alec, wondering how they'd gone from joking around to this. For the first time since he'd met Alec, he felt like he was seeing the guy who'd walked out on Grace that day in her clinic.

"What's really eating at you?" Seth said.

Alec threw up his hands as though Seth should already know. "I just hate being reminded of what I can't do. I used to ski, play basketball, rock climb, run triathlons, and"—He shot Seth a look—"play soccer." He shook his head in a gesture of frustration. "Now I can't even coach a youth soccer league."

Wow, talk about pent-up frustration. Seth studied Alec for a moment, resting his elbow on his bent knee. "You know what amazes me?" he finally said.

"What?"

"That there really are no insurmountable challenges."

Alec rolled his eyes and groaned. "Please don't tell me you're going to give me a pep talk right now, because I get enough of that from Grace."

"Take Beethoven, for example," Seth continued as if Alec hadn't said anything. "He lost his hearing but ended up composing some of the most brilliant music in history. Claude Monet went blind in his old age but continued to paint. Then there's Stevie Wonder, Michael J. Fox, Stephen Hawking—"

"Don't you dare say Christopher Reeve."

"And Christopher Reeve." Seth grinned. "Not to mention all those athletes who compete in the Paralympics year after year or people who go on to live regular lives, filled with a good job and a family they love."

"Your point?" Alec said, probably ready for Seth to be done.

Seth shrugged. "All I'm saying is that a whole lot of people have taken away your excuses to wallow. So stop it already."

"Excuse me?" The scathing look Alec directed at Seth had him worried he'd gone too far. But what Alec needed was a good kick in the butt, and Seth wasn't about to back down.

"C'mon, man, there's no reason why you can't do anything you want to do, including coaching a youth soccer league or getting back into skiing or whatever it is you want to do with your life. You just have to be more creative. Thousands of people have done it."

For what seemed like forever, silence descended, making the enclosed gym feel claustrophobic. Alec sat in his chair with a half glare, half sullen look on his face. "Grace put you up to this, didn't she?"

"No, but I see the way she worries and stresses about you. I saw tears in her eyes the day you charged out of your workout with her, and I've seen how happy it's made her that you started playing ball with us regularly." Seth glanced at the ball resting on the floor at the other end of the gym and sighed. "It's not all about you, you know. The way you choose to live your life affects those close to you as well."

Alec let out a breath and slouched against the back of his chair. When his eyes met Seth's again, he looked resigned. "You're right. Grace deserves better from me."

"And you deserve better from yourself." Feeling like he'd said all that needed to be said on the subject, Seth hopped to his feet and jogged to retrieve the ball, tossing it once more toward Alec. "So how about a compromise? If you agree to coach from your wheelchair, I'll do the same. We'll make it a competition and see whose team has the most wins at the end of the season."

The corners of Alec's mouth tugged into a slow smile, and something sparked in his eyes. "Haven't you learned anything from playing basketball with me? You'd never win. So do your team a favor and even the playing field by standing on your own two feet. I'll figure out a way to teach those kids soccer." With that, Alec swished the basketball into the net.

Seth grinned, feeling like the shot was a turning point—a good turning point. Maybe now Alec would stop looking at his disability as something that made him unequal to the rest of the world and start seeing it for what it really was: a chance to prove that he could still do everything he wanted to do.

"You're on," Seth said. "And may the best coach win."

"Oh, I will."

Fifteen

♡ ♡ ♡

*M*usic blared from an open window in Alec's apartment, making Grace stop short. She glanced up in awe. All of the blinds and windows were wide open, letting in the fresh, damp air. It had been two weeks since she'd dropped by, and she suddenly wondered if she was at the right place. A quick glance at the numbers on the door assured her she was.

The overcast sky suddenly seemed sunny and bright.

With a smile, Grace balanced the bag of groceries on her hip as she shoved her spare key into the lock, knowing Alec would never hear her knock over the music. Besides, she'd sent him a text earlier letting him know she was coming. Ever since Alec had agreed to keep playing ball with Seth, Grace had taken a step back, hoping that Seth could work even more magic.

Evidently he had.

Inside, a wonderful smell filled the apartment, reminding Grace of the Sunday dinners her mom used to make. She walked across freshly vacuumed carpet to the kitchen where everything seemed to sparkle and shine, like a Mr. Clean commercial.

Wow.

"Hey, sis," Alec said, wheeling himself down the hall toward her. His hair was freshly cut, his face shaved, and his clothes ironed. Actually, based off the tag hanging from his sleeve, they were new.

"Who are you and what have you done with my brother?" Grace tugged the tag free and glanced at it. A fifty dollar shirt from Nordstrom. Her eyes widened.

"You can put those groceries away because I made dinner," Alec said as he wheeled past her. "Baked ziti with extra cheese—your favorite."

Grace trailed behind, blinking as he pulled a small casserole dish from the oven, followed by a loaf of French bread wrapped in foil. Her heart constricted. "You went grocery shopping?"

"I didn't have much of a choice," he answered, his tone teasing. "You let my cupboard get bare, and I was hungry."

"And your clothes." She pointed. "They're new. Did you order them online or . . ." She let the question die off, not daring to hope that he'd actually left his house to purchase clothes.

"The salesperson I met at Nordstrom was really helpful. Do you like what she picked out?" He glanced down at his clothes. "Oh, and my socks are new too. I'd wiggle my toes to show them off if I could."

Sure enough, his socks looked new as well—and completely ridiculous with green and yellow stripes. Grace withheld the laughter bubbling up inside her. "Was the salesperson colorblind?"

He frowned and looked at his feet. "Actually, I picked these out. You don't like them?"

"They're just, uh . . . very colorful," she finished lamely.

113

Alec grinned. "They also smell way better than my other ones." He slid his hands under one leg and lifted his foot. "Want to take a whiff?"

Graced eyed him with a raised eyebrow. "You seriously want me to smell your socks?"

"Sure, why not?" He grinned.

"You're mental."

Alec chuckled, and a wonderful happiness weaved its way into Grace's heart, warming and swelling it. Grace suddenly felt like she'd been transported back in time—back to the day when Alec constantly smiled and teased and made everyone laugh. When he'd fill her locker with water balloons, laugh hysterically when they burst on the ground around her, and help her clean up the mess afterwards. When he'd pull out his guitar and change the lyrics of popular songs to something ridiculous. When he was—well, Alec.

Grace didn't realize how much she'd missed him until now.

She wanted to throw her arms around her brother and shout, "Welcome back!" She wanted to call her parents to share the good news. And she wanted to call Seth to tell him thank you, thank you, thank you.

Looking back, Grace couldn't believe how much she'd misjudged Seth. He was like a tree feller, crashing through the forest with a machete and slicing down trees. At first she'd considered it a massive disturbance and catastrophe, but not anymore. Now it felt like he'd had a purpose all along. Like he'd been clearing dead wood to make a path to a beautiful new place—a place she never wanted to leave.

Grace turned away and blinked tears from her eyes as she took her time emptying the bag of groceries. By the time she'd finished, she had her emotions in check and could sit across the table from Alec without letting him know how affected she really was.

"So I've been thinking about giving skiing another try," Alec said as they ate.

All happy thoughts left Grace's mind as her eyes flew to her brother. "What did you say?"

Even though it had been ten years, the image was still there, clear and crisp as ever. Alec's broken and bruised body bent in a way a body shouldn't bend. Two strangers lifting him onto an ugly orange sled so a snow machine could carry him down the mountain to a waiting ambulance. A doctor who didn't know Alec or understand how much he needed his legs pronouncing him a paraplegic.

And now Alec wanted to give skiing another try.

"Seth was telling me about his heli-skiing trip and how they've taken up paraplegics with sit skis. I guess they had a bunch of pictures of one guy doing it. Anyway, it got me thinking, you know? Seth even did some research and found a company not far away that could fit me to one." Alec looked so excited, so animated. His face was practically glowing. "I know the season's pretty much over, but I was hoping you wouldn't mind giving me another try at working out so I could be ready for next season. I could really use your help getting my lazy butt back in shape."

The warm bite of French bread turned to pasty sawdust in Grace's mouth. She swallowed, forcing it down then quickly chasing it down with some large gulps of water. How long had she ached to hear her brother say he wanted to get his body back in shape? But not so he could go skiing again—especially not *heli*-skiing. What had Seth been thinking to suggest that? He'd just torn his ACL, for crying out loud, and now he wanted her brother to give it a try?

This was all so wrong. So completely wrong. Evidently Seth wasn't content to leave her beautiful, new, and happy place alone. He had to take his machete to it once more and ruin everything.

Once a wreaker of chaos, always a wreaker of chaos.

"Seth was also telling me about these wheelchair mountain bikes they make," Alec continued as if Grace's world wasn't caving in around her. "They have four wheels so you have to find wide trails to take them on, but they're made specifically for paraplegics."

Enough! she wanted to scream. *I don't want to hear anymore.* What was Alec saying? Why would he want to risk becoming a quadriplegic—or worse, die? Wasn't paraplegia bad enough?

Grace suddenly felt sick to her stomach.

"So," Alec prompted. "If I promise to be a better patient, will you work out with me?"

Grace glanced at him, wanting to tell him that yes, she would, but not so he could further injure himself. How could he expect her to agree to that? But it had been too long since she'd seen the excitement in his eyes, the happiness, the will to do something with his life. She refused to be the one to crush it.

No, she'd leave that honor to the machete-carting Seth.

"Of course," she said.

Cold and wet, Grace fisted her hand and pounded on the door, wanting to knock it down, as well as the man on the inside of the beautiful Craftsman style home. Darkness had fallen, and the pouring rain had not only made it difficult to find his house, but had given her anger more time to grow. Over and over, she banged, letting all of her frustration and fear unload on the pristine, white wooden door.

The door flew open, revealing Seth's surprised face. He wore a snug-fitting t-shirt and jeans with bare feet sticking out beneath the hems.

"Grace? What are you doing here?" he said. "Not that I'm not happy to see you or anything—just totally surprised."

Both of her hands clenched at her sides. "How could you!" she said. "How could you bring my brother back from the dead only to send him to an earlier burial! How could you!"

Seth's hands rose slowly, as if to ward off her anger. "Whoa, calm down, Grace. What are you talking about?"

"Heli-skiing? Really? You just tore your ACL, and you're telling my brother he should try heli-skiing? What were you thinking? Do you have any idea how lucky you were to come away from that trip with only an ACL tear? Do you have any idea how close Alec came to being a quadriplegic? Do you? Because that could still happen, you know. Sit-skiing is still dangerous—probably even more so than regular skiing. What were you thinking?"

"You said that already." Seth let out a breath and leaned against the doorjamb. He looked so unaffected and unrepentant that her fingers itched to slap that look off his face.

She glared at him, hating him for not taking life more seriously, for not valuing her brother's life, and for wriggling his way into her heart. Something inside her cracked, and tears started to sting the backs of her eyes, making her hate him all the more.

"Finished?" he asked.

Grace looked away from him, feeling miserable. Yelling at him was supposed to make her feel better. It was supposed to coerce a heartfelt apology from him, accompanied by a promise to somehow stop her brother from looking into sit skiing and mountain biking. What was wrong with wheelchair basketball and coaching? What was wrong with going out to dinner and to the movies like normal people?

Grace should have known Seth would be incapable of stopping there. He couldn't resist trying to bring everyone into his high-risk world of extreme play—even her paraplegic brother. It had been useless to come here, thinking she could convince him otherwise.

Before the tears gave way, Grace spun on her heel, intending to run to her car. But a strong hand caught her arm. "Where do you think you're going? We haven't even begun to talk about this."

Grace pulled her arm away and frowned. "So talk already. I'm done."

"I seriously doubt that," Seth said under his breath. Then he jerked his thumb over his shoulder. "Would you like to come inside first? You're wet, and it's more comfort—"

"No."

"Okay, but I just got done with a workout, and my knee's aching, so I hope you don't mind if I take a seat." He plopped down on the step right outside his door and straightened his injured leg. His hands clasped around his bent leg as he looked up at her.

Grace folded her arms and took a step back. "Why did you tell my brother he should try heli-skiing?"

"I didn't," Seth said. "He asked about my injury, and I told him how it happened. He wondered whether any paraplegics had ever tried it, and I told him that based on the pictures I'd seen in the company's office, several people had. I didn't put the idea into his mind, he did."

"And wheelchair mountain biking? Was that his idea as well?"

Seth shook his head. "No, that was me. Mountain biking's kind of my thing, and I saw a guy doing the wheelchair version of it a few years back, so I told your brother about it. Not because I wanted him to give it a try or anything, more because I thought it was pretty cool."

"Cool?" Was he joking? "You think careening down a rocky, uneven mountain on four wheels with only hand controls is cool? Are you insane?" Evidently Seth had fallen off his bike one too many times and hit his head hard.

Seth leaned forward and stood slowly, moving closer to Grace. She took a step back, feeling rain on her face and nearly falling when her foot found air instead of concrete. Seth's hand reached out to steady her then he tugged her closer, out of the rain. Her skin sizzled where his fingers gripped her arm.

Seth's eyes searched her face, so close that if he dipped his head, he would be within kissing distance. She felt the warmth of his breath, and her breath caught in her throat. He wouldn't really kiss her, would he? Not when she was feeling the urge to punch that rugged nose of his. Not even Seth was that stupid. Her body stiffened, ready to shove him back if he moved any closer.

"It *is* cool, Grace," he finally said. "And so are all the paraplegics I see pushing their way to the end of a marathon, competing in the Paralympics, swimming, playing basketball, skiing, or not letting their body keep them from doing whatever it is they happen to love. It's incredibly cool."

Fresh tears pricked at Grace's eyes, but she refused to let them fall. If they were talking about anyone else, this wouldn't be an argument. She'd be in full agreement. But when it came to Alec, the worst-case scenario overshadowed the coolness factor big-time.

"Didn't you see the look in Alec's eye when he told you about it?" Seth said. "The excitement? The spark?"

Grace nodded as a traitorous tear escaped, running down her cheek. That was the worst part about it all. Before Alec's accident, she'd seen that spark many times—whenever he came up with some new adventure or harebrained idea for them to try. Which was also how Grace knew it wasn't just talk. Alec would follow through with everything—even the mountain biking.

"What if he gets hurt again?" Grace said. "What if his diagnosis changes from paraplegia to quadriplegia? Or worse? What then?"

"That's his choice to make—his risk to take."

"You don't get it." Grace turned away from Seth and dropped down on the top stair of his porch, too exhausted to stand any longer. Rain dotted her jeans, but she didn't care. "He wants me to start working out with him so he can get in shape for this summer and next year's ski season. But I can't do it. I can't. I'll blame myself if anything bad happens, and it will be like high school all over again. I just don't have it in me to do a repeat of the last ten years. I don't."

Seth sat beside her and leaned forward enough to see her face. "Are you telling me you blame yourself for his paraplegia?"

"Of course I do. It was my fault." She stared out into the dark and rainy night, focusing on the rippling reflections of the moon in scattered puddles. Her surroundings should have felt soothing and peaceful, but they weren't. It felt more like an eerie and haunted forest.

"We grew up in Colorado and both loved to ski," Grace said. "But on the morning of March twenty-sixth, we woke up to twelve inches of fresh powder in our yard, which meant even more snow in the mountains. My parents agreed to let us go skiing, but Alec had a test coming up and didn't want to miss one of his classes. I was determined to go, though, and since he didn't want me going alone, he skipped school and came anyway." The lump in Grace's throat seemed to grow larger as she relived that horrible day. "There was a terrain park at the resort, and Alec loved trying new tricks off one of the larger ramps. I cheered him on and dared him to do a back flip. When he did, one of his skies caught on some snow. It threw him off balance, and he landed on his back."

Grace stared at the puddles as the plink, plink of raindrops landed in them. *Talk about it, let it out,* a counselor had once encouraged. *It's the only way to move on.* So Grace had talked about it with her counselor, her parents, and Alec. She'd cried and apologized over and over and over again, and Alec had told her that it wasn't her fault. It had been his choice to go, his decision to try the back flip, his ski that had been caught. But no matter how much she talked or how many people told her it was only an accident, that heavy, horrible feeling of guilt would never leave. Even now, ten years later, it felt heavier than ever.

Seth's arm came around her back, and Grace let him pull her close. His hand moved up and down her arm in a soothing gesture, but he said nothing. Which was a relief. How many times had she heard, "It wasn't your fault. It was an accident. Stop blaming yourself." How many times had people tried to comfort her using words that did absolutely no good?

"Do you think your brother still blames you?" Seth finally said.

Grace rested her head against his shoulder, soaking up his warmth and his strength. "No, but I still blame myself."

Seth nodded. "Who wouldn't?"

Grace lifted her head and looked him in the eye. It was one of those rare moments when they didn't twinkle back. Instead, they were filled with understanding and sympathy. "I still feel as horrible as I did that day the doctor told us the news," she said.

Seth's fingers moved to brush some hair from her face then trailed down her cheek, leaving a myriad of goose bumps in its wake. "Which is exactly why you should help him work out and be there when he gives skiing another try."

That was the last thing Grace had expected to hear. The touch that had been so soothing, so wonderful, suddenly felt like a jolt, and she jerked away. "What?"

His arm fell from around her shoulders, making Grace shiver even with her hoodie on. "Why do you feel so guilty, Grace?"

Wasn't it obvious? "Because my brother's a paraplegic."

"Yes, but what you really feel guilty about is that he can't do the things he used to be able to, right? That everyday things are hard for him?"

Where was Seth going with this? "Well, yeah. I basically took his life away."

Seth leaned back on the palm of his hands, and a little of that teasing spark darkened his eyes. "No you didn't, Grace. Learning to do the things he used to do will make him feel alive again. But if you fight this, if you try to take that away . . ." He voice drifted off.

Grace frowned, not liking that perspective at all. "So I'm supposed to put on a positive face and help get his body back into shape, only to watch him risk it again doing crazy stunts?"

"Yes."

That seemed so wrong to her. So opposite of everything she felt. Besides, there was so much more to life than skiing or mountain biking. Why couldn't Seth and Alec see that?

"Life isn't all about having fun, you know," she said. "It's about learning and growing, making a difference and doing something meaningful. Why can't Alec focus on that instead?"

Seth studied her for a moment, his expression thoughtful. "You're right, there's more to life than fun. You're the one who taught me that. But that doesn't mean you shouldn't have fun while doing all those other things, and I think we can both agree that your brother is in some serious need of some fun in his life."

Grace suddenly felt all antsy and out of sorts. It happened every time she felt so sure about something, only to be proven wrong. She hated being wrong, especially if it made Seth right. "I don't like you very much right now."

A chuckle sounded, and Seth's arm came around her once again, pulling her up against him. "Then it's a good thing I like you enough for the both of us," he said, making her feel even more out of sorts, only in a different way. He nodded toward his door. "What do you say we go inside and blow this off with some boxing?"

"What?" Was he serious? Grace leaned to the side so she could see his face.

"You do want to punch me, right?"

He *was* serious—well, as serious as Seth could be when he was teasing her. "Yeah," she said, wondering where this was going.

His arm fell from around her, and he stood, holding out his hand for her to take. "Then come inside and punch away."

Grace couldn't help but smile. How could she resist an invitation like that? But she should resist. She should walk back to her car, climb in, and leave temptation behind. If only he weren't smiling at her in that way and making her feel all warm and bubbly. Grace couldn't bring herself to say no. "Only if you have some kind of chocolate and nut combination to offer." There, that was her out. If Seth didn't have something that fit the description, Grace would leave. She would.

His eyes practically twinkled. "Does Rocky Road count?"

It was like he knew Rocky Road was one of her favorite ice-cream flavors—one she always turned to when life went sour. Like tonight.

Whatever willpower Grace had left slipped through the cracks, and she found herself placing her hand in his and allowing him to pull her up.

He had promised she could punch him.

Sixteen
♡ ♡ ♡

$\mathcal{L}$ight footsteps echoed behind Seth as he led the way to his kitchen. Tonight had definitely taken an unexpected turn for the better, and Seth planned to milk it for all it was worth. The odds of Grace ever showing up on his doorstep were slim to none. The odds of her coming inside, even slimmer. Yet here they were, on a mission to find Rocky Road ice cream in Seth's freezer. Thank goodness he had some.

Owen had brought over a pint one night, right after Seth's surgery. Since Seth didn't have the heart to tell him he hated the stuff, it had sat there, uneaten. Seth kept meaning to throw it out, but hadn't gotten around to doing it, and now he was glad. From here on out, he'd keep his freezer stocked, just in case Grace happened by again. If Seth had beaten the odds once, who knew? Maybe it would happen again.

Seth strode to his freezer and pulled out the ice cream. He slid it across his granite countertop toward Grace and pulled out a spoon, holding it out to her. "It's all yours."

Grace eyed the spoon before meeting his gaze. "You don't want any?"

"I'll let you have the honors tonight."

Grace accepted the spoon with a frown. "But I make it a point to never eat in front of anyone—especially not ice cream. That would be so . . . wrong."

Seth leaned against the counter and folded his arms, still not quite sure how he'd managed to get Grace inside, sitting on one of his barstools. The way she now watched him expectantly made the whole scene feel surreal. "You'll have to get over it, because I hate the stuff. It doesn't even taste like normal chocolate, and then there's the whole soggy nut thing." He screwed up his face. "Not a fan."

Eyebrow arched, Grace asked, "Why is it in your freezer then?"

"On the off chance you stopped by." Seth gave her a lopsided smile. "I had a feeling it was one of your favorites and planned to use it to coerce you inside. It worked."

Grace pried the lid of the ice cream open, only to frown. "How long has it been in your freezer, exactly?"

Seth leaned forward and peered inside. Shiny, chocolately goo covered in ice crystals stared back, looking nastier than normal. He wanted to simultaneously laugh and groan. "From the looks of it, a really long time," he finally said. "You should've come sooner."

Grace's lips started to twitch. A quiet snort sounded, followed by a snicker, then full on laughter. Grace pushed the ice cream away and rested her head on the counter as she laughed and laughed. Seth recognized the sound. It was the kind of uncontrollable laugh that came after someone had officially lost it.

Calm, collected, impenetrable Grace had lost it. In Seth's kitchen. The thought made him smile—as did the

125

image of her with her face buried in her arms, shoulders shaking. Seth wanted to pry her off the counter and let his shoulder muffle her laughter, or better yet, his mouth. Instead, he walked around the island and pulled up a chair next to her. He rested his elbow on the counter and propped his head up with his hand as he watched her, amused.

When she finally raised her head, she had to wipe a few tears from her eyes. "I'm sorry," she said, shaking her head. "I don't know what's wrong with me. It really wasn't that funny."

"No kidding."

Grace wiped at her eyes once again then looked around. "Let me guess, the 'boxing' you referred to involves those large blow-up gloves that don't do any real damage."

"Nope." Seth grinned. "More like the computerized kind called Xbox Kinect. Feel free to punch me to your heart's content."

The giggles started all over again, and Grace reburied her head in her arms. Her soft brown hair fell to the side as her shoulders shook, and Seth couldn't resist reaching out to touch it. As his fingers lightly combed through hair that was softer and smoother than it looked, Grace's shoulders stopped shaking and her head raised slowly. A worried, almost anxious, expression appeared on her face as she returned his gaze.

Normally, Seth would shrug and say something light-hearted—something that would erase the nervous tension, like "Sorry, thought I saw some gray for a second." But he didn't feel like lightening the mood. He felt like closing the gap between them and seeing if her lips were as soft as her hair.

His hand cupped her chin, and his thumb lightly touched her lower lip. She sucked in breath but didn't move. Ever so slowly, Seth's fingers moved along her jaw, brushing away her hair before cupping the back of her neck. Then he leaned closer, watching her face, her eyes, trying to gauge what would happen if he really did try to kiss her. Would she let him? She wasn't moving away, so he leaned even closer, until his mouth was a breath away from hers.

She drew in a shuddering breath, still not moving or saying anything. Seth took it as a positive sign and closed the gap, covering her lips with his. Just like he expected, they were warm and soft and moist and . . . moving against his— responding. Almost immediately, something ignited inside Seth, spreading through his body like an amazing adrenaline rush. Never before had a kiss felt this right, this powerful. Grace intoxicated him.

His fingers threaded through her hair, pulling her closer. When he felt the touch of her hand on his arm and her fingers curling around it, a thrill shot through Seth. As much as Grace tried to fight it or say she didn't want it, she was enjoying this as much as he was. Encouraged, Seth leaned in closer, pressing her against the counter as his mouth moved over hers, searching, seeking, and finding.

A murmur escaped her lips, and Seth left his seat behind as his other arm found its way around her back. She fit against him perfectly, as if her body had been molded as the perfect counterpart to his. Nothing had ever felt so good or right.

The strains of U2's "Pride" sounded, invading the moment like an annoying fly buzzing around. Seth ignored it, hoping Grace would too, but after a few seconds, her body started to stiffen, and her hands moved from his back to his chest, pushing him gently away. Seth wanted to curse and shove the phone down the garbage disposal. This wasn't how he wanted the kiss to end, not with Grace pushing him away.

His mouth left hers, and he suddenly felt bereft. U2 finally went away, and Seth held Grace's gaze, willing the fear and concern he saw in her eyes to dissipate. His hands moved gently up and down her arms as he searched for the right words to say, something that would replace the fear with happiness. Something that would bring back her smile and laughter.

But the strains of U2 filled the silence once again, and Seth felt like cursing.

"You should answer that," Grace finally said.

"Not until you agree that what just happened wasn't a mistake."

Anxiety appeared in her eyes. She looked away, drawing her lower lip into her mouth. A moment later she moved away from him, sliding out of her chair.

"Grace, don't go," Seth said. "Please. We need to talk about this."

She shook her head as the phone started to ring for the third time. "I've got to go. And you really should get that. It's probably important."

Seth walked around the island, grabbed the phone, and shoved it into the refrigerator, shutting the door firmly on a song he would never like again. His palms landed on the cold, granite counter as his eyes pleaded with hers. "Grace, please."

A spark of humor appeared in her eyes. "Is that supposed to make your battery last longer?" She probably meant it to lighten the mood, but Seth wasn't interested in joking around right now, not when so much was on the line.

"No," he said. "It's supposed to make whoever that is go away. We need to talk, Grace."

The humor left Grace's eyes, and she took a step back. "I think it would be best to pretend that never happened."

"No." Seth pushed away from the counter and started toward her, but when she retreated once again, he stopped. "There's no way I could ever forget that kiss, and I doubt you can either."

Wrong thing to say, because she shook her head emphatically then turned and bolted for the door. It took

Seth grabbing hold of the counter to keep himself from running after her. The slamming of his front door echoed through his house, sounding like a buzzer signaling the end of a game or match—one that he'd lost big-time.

Seth grabbed the pint of frost-bitten Rocky Road ice cream and launched it at the fridge door, as if it could somehow fly through it and smash into his cell phone. When the container landed on the floor with an unsatisfying thud, he kicked it away and yanked open the door. Then he grabbed his cell phone, ready to strangle the person whose name appeared last on his caller ID.

Lanna.

Seth glared at the phone, suddenly wishing he was still on her bad side.

Seventeen
♡ ♡ ♡

"Earth to Grace." Cameron's hand waved in front of her face, rudely interrupting her unsettled thoughts.

Annoyed, Grace swatted his hand away. This was her lunch break—*her* time. Why couldn't he see she wasn't in the mood to talk?

Cameron lifted his hands in surrender, giving her a don't-shoot-the-messenger look. "Just wanted to let you know that your favorite patient is here."

Grace's eyes widened as panicked butterflies filled her stomach. Seth's appointment wasn't for a couple of days, which happened to be the amount of time she needed to prepare herself to see him again. There was a reason she hadn't answered any of his calls or texts over the past two days. She wasn't ready to talk. Did he really think that showing up at her work, unannounced, was a good idea? Because it wasn't. It was a horrible idea.

Grace couldn't face him yet, not when the memory of that kiss still burned in her mind like the worst temptation ever. She now understood how some people could become alcoholics after just one drink. One kiss was all it took for her to become addicted to Seth. Maybe there was a support group she could join, consisting of all the girls who had ever experienced one of Seth's kisses.

Grace grabbed Cameron's arm. "Tell him I'm not here."

Cameron stared at his wrist. "Okay, ow," he finally said.

Grace let go of his wrist, but her gaze still bore into him. "I'm not here," she hissed. "Got it?"

"Looks like you're here to me," said a deep voice behind Cameron.

Grace felt an odd mixture of relief and disappointment when she heard Alec's voice. She glanced around Cameron and spotted her brother sitting in his wheelchair, giving her a strange look. "You did say to come today, right?" he said. "Or did I get the day wrong?"

Grace glanced at her watch as though the digital numbers would somehow make everything clear. She vaguely remembered telling Alec he could come during her lunch break, but had she meant today? Grace couldn't remember. She shook her head, trying to clear it. "Sorry. I completely forgot."

Alec raised an eyebrow. "Who did you think I was?"

"My thoughts exactly," Cameron added.

Grace felt her face warm. She pushed her chair back and stood. "No one. Cameron just caught me off guard, that's all."

"Yeah right." Cameron gave his head a shake, forcing his hair away from his eyes as he glanced at Alec. "I told her that her favorite patient was here, and she totally freaked out. So . . . if *you're* not her favorite patient, who is?"

A slow smile spread across Alec's face. "I think I have a pretty good idea."

"Really? Who?" Cameron said.

Grace glared at her brother. "I don't have a favorite patient," she said firmly, turning her glare on Cameron. "Isn't it your lunch break too? What are you still doing here?"

Once again, Cameron's hands went up in surrender, as though worried she might attack. "Just being curious, that's all. C'mon, I've got to know. Who is he?"

Grace brushed past him, glaring once more at Alec. "You're going to be in some serious pain after I get through with you."

"Can't wait." Alec grinned.

"Seriously?" Cameron said, trailing behind. "You're just going to leave me hanging like that?"

"Yes," Grace said, stopping next to the bench press. "Now go to lunch, will you? Isn't Talia waiting for you?"

"Oh, right." Cameron headed toward the door, giving her one last glance over his shoulder. "This isn't over, you know. I will find out."

Grace waited for the door to shut before breathing a sigh of relief. That is, until she caught Alec watching her. She frowned. "Don't ask, because I don't want to talk about it."

"Good, because I don't either," he said. "The last thing I want to do is get caught in the middle of you and Seth."

Grace felt like she was on the verge of going insane. For two days, she'd tossed and turned, fretted, and relived that kiss over and over again. And each time, all it did was churn her insides into something that felt like butterflies mixed with sour butter. If that wasn't bad enough, her distraction was at an all-time high. She'd put milk in her pantry, dirty clothes in her dryer, and mixed up the name and workout of more than one patient over the past couple of days. That kiss had given "god of chaos" a whole new meaning.

Grace sank down on the bench and dropped her head to her hands. "He kissed me," she blurted, unable to keep it inside any longer. "Why did he have to kiss me?"

Alec let out a groan. "I so did not want to hear that."

"He's my patient!" Grace said, sending a pleading look his way. She needed someone to listen to her, to make her see straight once again. "He's always messing with me, always disorganizing my life, making me do things I don't want to do and getting into my head. He's charming and nice one minute and annoying and frustrating the next. I can't live this way anymore!"

Alec's eyes widened slightly before he let out a half snicker, half laugh. "Wow," was all he said.

"'Wow'? Really? That's it?" Surely Alec had something more intelligent to say.

Another snicker, and Alec shook his head. "Sorry, sis, but I've never seen you this way before. I mean, you're so . . ." His palms turned up, indicating he'd come up empty.

Grace, on the other hand, had no problem describing what she was. "I'm a mess!"

He nodded. "That's one way of saying it."

Grace grabbed a hand towel and chucked it at her brother. "You're no help at all."

"What do you want me to do, go challenge Seth to a duel or something?"

"No." Grace rolled her eyes. "I want you to say something to make this crazy anxiety go away. I want Seth to cancel his appointments and find another physical therapist to pester. *I want peace.*"

Alec looked longingly at the bench press, as if he'd rather lift weights than talk about his sister's love life. "If you don't like him, just tell him."

"That's the problem. I *do* like him—too much!"

Alec's gaze shot back to her. He blinked, then blinked some more, as if trying to make sense of something that didn't make any sense at all. "Let me get this straight. You like Seth, he kissed you, which you probably also liked, and now you want him to go away? That makes zero sense."

"He's my patient!"

"So?"

"He's also the egotistical god of chaos!"

"You lost me on that one."

Grace stood and began pacing the room, grateful that everyone else was on their lunch break. It was bad enough that Alec was here, witnessing her mental breakdown. "Seth isn't the committing type. He's into fun and more fun and doesn't understand what it means to be responsible. I mean, look at his career. He's a part-time consultant who flits in and out of people's lives like a mosquito."

"Mosquito?"

"Yes! Like an annoying, pestering mosquito you just want to swat away."

"But you said you like him."

"I do! That's the problem!"

"Then he's not like a mosquito, because nobody likes mosquitoes."

"What?" It was Grace's turn to blink, which she did, over and over again as she stared at her brother. She really had no idea what she'd expected him to say, but definitely not that. Of course the mosquito comparison didn't fit, but the last thing Grace was looking for was a lesson on metaphors. She needed advice. Good advice. Something she apparently wouldn't get from her brother.

Grace wandered over to the window and looked out, placing her hands on her hips. The overcast sky contained a slew of bushy, dark clouds that promised rain—a perfect match to her mood.

"Listen," said Alec, wheeling up beside her. "I'm sorry I haven't been much help, but I honestly don't know what to say. Have you considered talking all this over with Seth? I mean, if you tell him your concerns, maybe he'll prove you wrong. From what I know of him, he seems like a pretty decent guy. Maybe you've misjudged him."

"His name's Seth. I haven't misjudged him."

"Oh, for the love of Pete," said Alec. "Please don't tell me you still judge the guys you date by a name they were given at birth—a name they had no control over. You, of all people."

Grace faced him, her hands still on her hips. "What's that supposed to mean?"

"It means your name's Grace—you know, *merciful* and *forgiving*?"

Grace frowned and turned back to the window. This conversation had totally backfired. Instead of Alec giving her a hug and telling her that everything would be okay, that Seth *was* the committing type who would never break her heart, she was being accused of judging him unfairly. Which maybe she was, but that was beside the point. Where was sibling loyalty? Compassion? Understanding?

"All I'm saying is that if you like Seth that much, you should at least give him a chance. What do you have to lose?"

"A lot, which you should already know." Grace stared down at him. After Alec's accident, his high-school girlfriend walked out of his life, leaving him alone to nurse both a broken body and a broken heart. Grace had always hated her for that.

Alec sighed. "You're right, and I'm sorry. You do have a lot to lose, but not nearly as much as you could lose if you push Seth out of your life. Trust me on that one. After my accident, I was afraid that Allison would decide I wasn't worth the effort, so I broke up with her before she got around to dumping me. I figured it would be easier than sitting around, waiting for that ball to drop. It's probably one of the things I regret the most because I've always wondered 'what if.'"

All this time Grace had thought Allison had been the one to walk away, when really it was her brother. She suddenly felt like a very bad judge of character. "But I thought—"

"I know."

It was amazing how a few sentences—mere words—could completely change Grace's perspective and settle the anxious butterflies in her stomach. Her brother was right. She really didn't know how Seth would handle a relationship or if he was capable of signing up for the long haul. All she knew was that she missed him and wanted more.

Grace hugged her arms close as she studied her brother, allowing a small, sympathetic smile to touch her lips. "Ever thought of looking her up?"

"She's married."

"Oh."

"Yeah." Her brother pushed his wheelchair toward the bench press. "Mind if we work out now? I promised Seth I'd meet him in an hour about that youth soccer league. He's supposed to give us our assignments today."

"Oh." For whatever reason, Grace felt as though she'd found out about a party she hadn't been invited to, which was ridiculous because Seth *had* invited her. She was the one who'd turned him down.

Well, no more. Alec was right. It was time to put her fears aside and give Seth a chance. From here on out, there would be no more turning Seth down or pushing him away.

Eighteen

♡ ♡ ♡

"Macy, wrong way! You're goal is that way, remember?" Seth pointed to the opposite side of the field, ready to pull his hair out. Enough girls had signed up to form two teams, and since Owen, Garrett, and Brandon had insisted on coaching one of the three boys teams, the lot had fallen on Seth and Alec to take the girls—something he regretted now, especially since he wasn't exactly happy with the female gender at the moment.

"Beth, only the goalie can pick up the ball. You have to use your feet."

"But it hurts when I kick."

"What?" Seth jogged over to inspect the little girl's shoes. Although they looked old and worn out, he couldn't see any reason why they'd hurt her. He let out a breath. "What makes them hurt?" he said with as much patience as he could muster.

Beth's large green eyes dropped to her feet, and she clasped her hands behind her back. "They're too tight."

"Are you saying your shoes are too small?"

She nodded. "My mom doesn't have money for new ones, so I have to wait until my cousin gives me her old shoes. But they're always too small."

Something hit Seth hard in the chest, melting away his frustration. He wanted to pry off Beth's shoes, drive her to the nearest shoe store, and get her every shoe she liked in her size. How awful would it be to wear shoes that were too tight? The only time Seth had ever felt that was when he'd tried on the wrong size at the shoe store. He'd complained to his mom, and she immediately took them off and found him the right size.

Seth dropped down on his knee so he could look Beth in the eye. "What size are your feet?" he said gently.

"I don't know."

Seth pursed his lips in thought then stood and blew loudly on his whistle, gesturing for all the girls to come in, including the girls Alec was working with on the next field over. When they'd all surrounded him, Seth gave their shoes a quick perusal. Although some looked newer than others, each pair was worn and not in the best shape.

He raised his voice so all the girls could hear. "It's come to my attention that I completely forgot to get your shoe sizes for your new soccer shoes."

"We get new shoes?" Macy asked in hushed tones, as if Seth had just presented her with a dream trip to Disneyland. Only it wasn't Disneyland. It was a pair of shoes.

He swallowed the lump in his throat. "Of course. If we're going to be the best teams in the city, we're going to need good shoes. Does anyone know what size shoe you wear?"

They stared at him blankly.

"Okay." Seth glanced down at his clipboard that contained the practice schedules and permission slips he was supposed to give out. He tugged the permission slips loose and started distributing them. "I'm going to need everyone to take off one shoe. Then I'll come around with a pencil and trace your foot on the paper so I know what size you're going to need. Okay?"

The girls grinned and nodded then dropped to the grass and started tugging off their shoes. For the remainder of practice, Seth traced each of their feet and made a mental note to ask Lanna for new permission slips. By the time the next practice rolled around, all of the kids would have both soccer shoes and a new pair of sneakers.

"You do know that those permission slips are for the girls to take to their parents, right?" Lanna's voice intruded. "You're not supposed to make footprints out of them."

Alec snickered as Seth glanced up, squinting into the sun at Lanna. "Oh good, you're here. We're going to need some more permission slips."

"Why, so you can make handprints, too?"

Seth shot her a half smile. "Something like that."

"He's getting soccer shoes for the kids and needed to know their size," Alec said.

"Oh." All humor left Lanna's eyes as she searched Seth's face. "Really?"

"It's part of the uniform," Seth explained.

She smiled and nodded her approval. "Well, yeah, of course. I can't believe I forgot about that." She turned her attention to Alec and held out her hand. "Hi, I'm Lanna. I don't think we've met."

"Alec," he said, shaking her hand. "I'm the guy who thinks he can teach these girls how to play soccer by explanation rather than demonstration."

"Whatever," said Seth. "He duct-taped shoes to sticks so he could teach the girls how to kick the right way."

Her smile widened. "I can't wait to see that. Thanks for being here."

"No problem."

Seth finished tracing the last foot then stood and patted the pages of footprints together. "I think that's it for today, girls," he announced. A few parents had shown up to collect their kids, so he wandered over to give them the schedule for the practices and games. The rest he distributed to the girls who planned to ride their bikes home or walk, making them promise to give it to a parent.

He returned to find Lanna laughing at something Alec had said. "What's so funny?" Seth asked.

"Alec was just telling me about your new way of playing basketball," Lanna said. "I should have known you wouldn't let your injury keep you from playing. You're unstoppable that way."

"Yeah, well, I would have quit after the first attempt if it wasn't for Alec. He gave us a bunch of pointers, and now he's only slightly better than the rest of us."

"Whatever," said Alec. "Any advantage I had went away a long time ago, which is fine with me. It makes beating you that much more satisfying."

Seth grinned. "Just wait until these soccer games get started, and we'll see how satisfied you feel when my girls end up as the champions."

"If you can get them to remember which way to kick the ball."

"True." Seth chuckled, feeling exhausted all of a sudden. The past couple of days had taken their toll.

Alec let out a breath, glanced around, then placed his hands on the wheels of his chair. "It's been real, Seth, but I've got to go." He nodded at Lanna. "Good to meet you, Lanna."

"Likewise," she said.

One last nod and Alec turned, pushing himself over the uneven grass to his car.

Lanna stared after him. "Okay, who is that guy, and why haven't I met him before?"

Seth raised an eyebrow. "Don't tell me you're interested in Alec." Lanna said nothing, but the way her eyes continued to follow Alec's movements told Seth otherwise. He laughed and shook his head. He should have known the do-gooder in Lanna would be drawn to someone like Alec. She probably couldn't help it. "He's Grace's brother."

Her eyes snapped to his. "Really?"

"Really." Seth threw the ball her way. She didn't react in time, and it slipped through her fingers, tumbling to the grass behind her. Seth jogged over and kicked it lightly back to her, hoping to start a scrimmage to get his mind off the reminder of Grace, but Lanna scooped it up and tucked it under her arm. Her gaze immediately returned to Alec, who was now getting in his car.

Seth rolled his eyes and grabbed the ball from her, feeling the sudden need to warn her. "I wouldn't go there if I were you. Falling for a member of the Warren family brings nothing but frustration and trouble. Trust me. Walk away while you still can."

Lanna finally looked at him, a teasing smile on her face. "What's the matter? You finally fell for someone who doesn't want to follow you around like a loyal puppy, lap at your heels, and hang on every word you say?"

Seth frowned. "Bark and nip at my heels is more like it."

She laughed. "Sounds like she's perfect for you."

"Yeah, well, try convincing her of that." Seth had thought he'd done exactly that, if her response to their kiss had proved anything, but afterward, when Seth had wanted nothing more than to pull her back into his arms and pick up where they'd left off, Grace had fled. Now his calls went unanswered and his texts unreturned. He'd even asked Alec for her address and went to her apartment last night, but her windows were dark, and no one answered. Now he was stuck waiting for his next appointment.

Lanna's hand rested on his arm, bringing him back to the present. "Don't worry, she'll come around. No girl can resist you for long."

Seth reached up to scratch the back of his head, feeling suddenly twitchy. "I wish I had your confidence, but I might have rushed things."

"You? Rush things? No," Lanna said dryly.

"Hey, I've been a very patient patient. I wanted to ask her out right away, but I held off and gave her time to warm up to me." The kiss at the auction didn't count.

A smile tugged at the corner of Lanna's mouth. "Meaning you flirted and teased and got her to go out with you in roundabout ways, like that day you brought her to the center, right?"

Seth frowned. When she put it like that, he didn't sound patient at all. "How else was she going to warm up to me? Not that it matters now. When I kissed her, she ran away like a scared rabbit." Seth hadn't intended to tell Lanna that—or anyone, for that matter—but the words were out before he could rethink them.

"You kissed her?" Eyes wide, Lanna gaped at him.

Now Seth really wished he'd kept that part to himself. He suddenly felt like the kid who'd grabbed a fistful of chocolate cake because he couldn't wait for someone to serve him a slice on a plate. Not that he'd learned his lesson. If he could rewind time and do it all over again, the only thing he'd do differently was put the phone in the fridge *first*.

Feeling his frustration come back full force, Seth dropped the soccer ball and kicked it across the grassy field.

A hand on his arm had Seth catching Lanna's eye once again. Her smile was filled with sympathy. "You're the type of person who doesn't stick your toe in the water to see if it's warm or cold before going in. Instead, you race to the diving board and launch yourself off, splashing everyone else with one of your cannonballs. It's the way you approach every situation. Which is really great and something I love about you. But sometimes, with certain people, a cannonball is a bit much, you know? A toe in the water would be better. Maybe Grace is that type of person."

Seth's eyebrows drew together. Although he saw Lanna's point, he'd already executed a few cannonballs and didn't understand how he could go back to simply sticking his toe in the water. Or was she saying it was too late for that? "So what do I do now?"

Lanna hesitated. "Maybe you should take a step back and let the waters get calm again, then try approaching her again with a little less oomph, if you know what I mean."

Seth didn't, not completely, anyway. "And how do I go about letting the waters calm? Find a new therapist and stay away from her completely?" He didn't like the sound of that at all.

"No," said Lanna. "I'm saying that you're her patient, so be her patient—a regular, non-flirting, does-what-he's-told, patient."

"Sounds boring," Seth said. Not to mention impossible. He couldn't imagine being in the same room with Grace and not trying to coax a smile or goad her into saying something that would make her blush. Nor could he imagine not touching her when given the chance. But if that's what it took to turn the situation around, he'd give it his best shot.

Lanna gave his arm a pat. "Give her time, and she'll come around. You'll see."

Seth only hoped she was right.

Nineteen
♡ ♡ ♡

$\mathcal{G}$race drummed her fingers against the counter as she attempted to concentrate on one of her patient's files. But it was no use. Seth would walk through the door any minute, and her heart felt as though it might burst from racing way too fast. Almost as soon as she'd made up her mind to give Seth a chance, the phone calls and texts had stopped. He was so unpredictable that she had no idea what to expect from him when he walked through that door. What would he say? Do? How would he act? How should *she* act?

The door handle turned, and Grace tensed. But it was only Cameron, coming back from his lunch break. Whew.

Calm down, it's only Seth. You've had lots of therapy sessions with him before. This is no different. But the jittery feeling refused to subside. Grace should have answered one of his calls or texts. She should have called him and gotten that first awkward conversation over with. At the very least, she should have sent him a text saying sorry for running out on him the other night. Now she was stuck having to face him again in front of Cameron.

Oh joy.

"I'm such an idiot," she muttered.

"What did you say?" Cameron said, making her jump.

She glanced up, meeting his bemused expression. "Huh?"

"Did you just call yourself an idiot?"

Had she said that out loud? Grace swallowed a groan, trying to think of a reason she'd be calling herself names at 1:30 in the afternoon. "Oh, yeah. I, uh, just forgot some notes at home."

Cameron pointed a finger at her as though accusing her of something. "That's what happens when you take your work home with you. You really should take my advice and learn to leave work at work. It's very liberating."

Grace nodded and turned back to the file, grateful he hadn't seen through her lie. The click of the door sounded again, and she stiffened, forcing her eyes to stay on the file as though she hadn't heard anything. Was that Seth? Was he walking toward her with that heart-stopping smile?

Just act like nothing happened. It's just a regular day, and he's just a regular patient. A really hot, amazingly good kisser of a regular patient.

Oh geez.

Grace dropped her forehead to her hand, trying to get her body to relax and her heart to stop racing. She was a professional. She could do this. She would not freak out.

"Hey, Grace."

She jumped and knocked over her pencil holder, spilling the contents all over the counter. As Grace frantically tried to pick them up, she shot Seth a totally fake smile. "Oh, hey. How's it going?" The pencil holder seemed to shrink because the pens and pencils no longer fit. She finally dropped what remained on the counter and stood, smiling way too brightly. "Ready for your workout?"

The heart-stopping smile appeared. "That's why I'm here."

"Right." Her hands fidgeted, finally clasping together in front of her. "I, uh, think you should start with a fifteen-minute swim. Then we'll go from there." Perfect. That would give her fifteen minutes to regain her composure and stop acting like a nervous teenager on her first date.

"But I thought swimming was for recovery—you know, *after* the workout?"

Curse him for listening . And for probably seeing right through her.

"Normally that's the case," she backpedaled. "But today it's going to be your warm up. I thought I'd give you a break from the bike and rower." She held her breath, waiting for the inevitable teasing to begin. Would he accuse her of using *his* swim for *her* recovery? Or would he tell her to jump in the pool and take the recovery swim while *he* warmed up on the bike?

Seth only shrugged. "You're the boss." Then he headed down the hall toward the changing room, saying nothing more. No teasing smile. No sarcastic remark. Nothing.

With a frown, Grace watched him go, mentally kicking herself yet again for not responding to his calls or texts. Of course he would act like nothing had happened. Grace would react the same way if she'd tried to reach out and had been met with a solid brick wall of no response. Technically, the ball was now in her court, and it was all her fault. She didn't like it there. She wanted to volley it back and tell him to keep it. She didn't want it.

But maybe he didn't want it either.

Grace leaned against the counter and folded her arms, ignoring the scattered pens and pencils. Her gaze flickered to the windows surrounding the endless therapy pool where Seth had just entered, wearing only blue and white plaid board shorts. Her breath caught. From his biceps and deltoids to his obliques and abdominals, every muscle in his upper body was beautifully sculpted. The sight of him instantly brought back the memory of those strong arms around her, his solid chest pressed against her, and that kiss—oh that kiss.

Seth glanced her way and gave a little wave when he caught her staring. Heat flew to her cheeks, and Grace forced her attention back to the file on her desk, rereading a sentence she'd probably read a hundred times. But it still didn't stick. If Seth planned to keep acting as though nothing had happened, how would she go about letting him know she'd had a change of heart? Walk up to him and say, "Hey, about that kiss—mind giving it another try?" After reiterating over and over that she didn't date patients, she'd sound like a total hypocrite.

She *was* a total hypocrite.

Her fingers drummed against the counter. Good grief, what was wrong with her? This was ridiculous. Grace was a mature, independent, and confident woman. As soon as Seth returned from his swim, she would face him with her head held high and her mind intact. If he flirted, she would flirt. If he asked her out, she'd calmly reply that she'd love to go. And if he ever kissed her again, she'd definitely kiss him back.

She was Grace Warren, after all—a woman who faced life head on.

"Psst."

Grace jumped, nearly knocking over the pencil holder once again. She looked up to find Seth rubbing his damp hair with a hand towel and looking so good she wanted to kiss him right then and there.

She cleared her throat. "Done already?" Time had never passed so quickly.

"Fifteen minutes, as ordered."

Grace waited for him to do something Seth would do,

like plop down on her desk, grin in that teasing way of his, and say something flirty, something meant to upset her equilibrium. But he didn't. He merely glanced over his shoulder toward the weight area and raised an eyebrow. "So, what next? Bike? Rowing? Bosu ball? Lunges? Or possibly some light jogging? My knee's feeling great."

Grace blinked for a moment before mentally shaking herself. Did he really want to work out and not flirt? Jog, not joke around? Was he finally going to keep things professional now that she didn't want him to? Talk about Murphy's Law kind of timing.

"Earth to Grace."

Snap out of it. This wasn't the time or place for flirting anyway—or any sort of personal conversation, for that matter. What had he said again? Oh, right. Jog. He wanted to jog. Grace stood and shook her head. "Sorry, but not yet. You need to give it another few weeks at least."

"But—"

"Trust me."

He sighed and leaned against the wall, folding his arms. "It's been over nine weeks, Grace. I've done everything you've asked and then some. I work with you and even harder at home. My leg's strong, and jogging will make it even stronger."

She'd had this conversation before. Many times, with many different patients. Sometimes it happened earlier, sometimes later, but eventually, they would all get to this same point of frustration when progress didn't happen fast enough for them. Normally, Grace would give her practiced response—one meant to encourage and inspire patience. But today, with Seth, her heart broke a little at the look of frustration on his face. She knew he wanted to get back on his mountain bike or go for a run, and she hated that she couldn't say yes. But Grace would hate it even more if she gave him the go-ahead and he ended up re-injuring himself.

With a sigh, Grace said, "Follow me." She moved past him and walked to the Bosu ball, where she put one foot on it and executed a deep, single-leg lunge to the side. Then she stepped aside and gestured for him to do the same. "Give me ten of those, and we'll talk about jogging."

Seth smiled in that confident way of his and moved to do as she asked. He placed his foot on the ball and slowly sank into a wobbly, shallow side lunge. His knee shook and his face turned red as he pushed himself back to standing position. His second attempt was even more pathetic.

Grace cocked her head to the side and offered a sympathetic smile. "You're not ready."

"I went jogging yesterday and was fine," he said. "My knee felt great."

Of course he'd jogged. In fact, Grace wouldn't be surprised if he'd done it more than once. Seth wasn't the type of person to be held back when he thought he could do something. But that didn't mean he was ready.

"Of course your knee felt fine," Grace said. "Jogging is a forward and backward motion. You do it every day when you walk or ride a bike. But as you just proved, it's the side-to-side motion that you need to worry about. If you were to step on a crack, get thrown off balance, or tweak your knee in any way, your muscles aren't strong enough to self-correct yet, and you'd probably land yourself right back where you started."

Seth watched her, saying nothing.

"Trust me," Grace said. "I'm speaking from experience when I tell you that you're not ready to jog yet. In another few weeks, possibly. But not yet."

"You're really cramping my style, you know that, right?" He let out a breath and stared at the Bosu ball as though it were to blame. "Fine, you've made your point. No more jogging."

Grace placed her hand on his arm and gave it a squeeze. "You'll get there. I promise."

"Yeah, yeah."

For the remainder of the session, Seth was the type of patient she'd wanted him to be in the beginning—all work and no play. He didn't make her laugh, didn't make her blush, and didn't give her one opportunity to flirt back. She found herself missing the old Seth—the confident, chaos-inducing Seth that she had grown to care so much about.

Why had Grace run away from that kiss? Why hadn't she figured out sooner that she wouldn't be able to stop herself from falling? Why couldn't she just blurt out her feelings now and not care that they had an audience? Why did the ball have to land in her court, and why couldn't she knock it back with a solid thwack? Was it pride or fear holding her back? Or maybe a little of both?

More than ever, she wished for a do-over.

Twenty

♡ ♡ ♡

Grace slowly made her way down the hallway of Magnificent Minds toward the voices coming from the back room. When she walked in, she stopped short. The once cavernous room was now half the size, made smaller by a wall painted black with chalkboard paint. The remaining walls gleamed with a cool mural of kids playing, reading, and talking. The windows were open, and the combined smells of paint and fresh air made the room feel new and alive. Over a dozen kids sat at scattered desks, working and talking quietly, and through a door on Grace's right came muffled sounds of laughter and the ping, ping of an air hockey table.

Grace blinked at the transformation and how different it looked and felt. No longer stale and boring, the room now offered children a place for both learning and fun—exactly what Seth had envisioned. When he committed to something, he followed through and then some.

"Grace? Hey, how are you?" Lanna's voice sounded loud in the quiet of the room, and dozens of eyes glanced her way.

Feeling conspicuous, Grace offered a little wave as she made her way toward Lanna, who worked with a couple of kids at a table. Another woman Grace recognized as Milly from the auction sat with a small group near the windows.

But no Seth.

Grace's heart deflated a little. She hadn't really expected to find him here, since tutoring wasn't his thing and coaching soccer kept him on the field, not inside. But it didn't keep her from hoping that renovations were still underway and there was a chance he could be here. Now that Seth was down to weekly therapy sessions, Grace missed him, especially since their time together wasn't the same as it was before the kiss. He continued to be the ideal patient, and Grace—well, she no longer wanted the ideal. She wanted the god of chaos.

As Grace approached Lanna, she smiled. "I got off work a little early, so I thought I'd drop by to see if you needed any help. This place looks incredible, by the way."

With obvious pride, Lanna glanced around the room. "I know, right? When Seth sets his mind to something, he goes all out."

"I can see that."

Lanna told the children at her table that she'd be right back then stood to give Grace a hug. "It's so great to see you again. Thanks for coming."

"No problem." Normally, Grace didn't feel comfortable hugging just anyone, especially not someone she barely knew, but Lanna had a way of making it feel like they'd known each other for ages. She probably made everyone feel that way. "Feel free to put me to work."

Lanna pulled back and scanned the room, pointing to a table where a few young girls sat reading. "That group over there has fifteen more minutes before they can play in the game room." She lowered her voice. "The girl in pink is new to our group. Her name is Mia, and she's way below the average reading level for her age group. Bella is helping her with the words she doesn't know, but I'm sure she'd love a break so she can get her own reading done. Do you mind?"

"Of course not." Grace walked to the group of girls and pulled up a chair. For the next fifteen minutes, she worked with Mia, who turned out to be a doll. With jet black, wildly curly hair, and dark skin and eyes to match, one look was all it took for Grace's heart to melt. She happily took the little girl under her wing, and in what seemed like minutes, a bell chimed. The girls at the table all squealed and jumped up, running toward the game room. Grace trailed behind, wanting a glimpse of the other side.

As Grace peeked through the door, the sight made her smile. Several IPads were affixed to one wall so the kids could stand in front of them to play various games. A few kids danced to a tune from "Just Dance" in front of a large flat-screen TV. An air hockey table and a ping-pong table took up the space in the middle of the room. Large beanbag chairs were scattered around the room, and a bookcase containing dozens of board games and puzzles stood against the far wall. The final touch was the framed motivational posters resting against freshly painted steel-blue walls.

The room felt homey and fun, yet challenging at the same time. It felt like Seth.

A wonderful sensation nestled its way into Grace's heart as she looked around and saw touches of Seth everywhere. With kids running, laughing, and chatting, the room was the epitome of chaos, but it was a good chaos—like Seth. Why had she been fighting her feelings toward him so much? It made absolutely no sense now that she saw firsthand the product of his kindness and imagination.

"Okay, boys, your time's up," Lanna's voice called out behind her.

"Just one more game!" one kid said.

"Sure," Lanna said. "Just as soon as you finish the rest of your math homework."

Groans sounded as the boys reluctantly left the game room behind and returned to the work room. Lanna smiled indulgently as they passed before turning to Grace. "As much as Seth's ideas have made this a fun place for the kids to be, sometimes I worry it's too fun."

Too fun? No. It was perfect. "From what I can see, you're keeping them out of trouble by giving them a place where they can work and play hard. I think it's wonderful." A lump formed in Grace's throat as she met Lanna's gaze. "Does Seth drop by much?" She tried to keep her tone nonchalant, but there was still an underlying *Any chance he'll be here today?* hopefulness she couldn't do away with completely.

Lanna gave her a look of sympathy, as though she knew exactly what Grace was asking. "Occasionally, but not very often. He's pretty busy with work and soccer practices right now." She paused. "Would you like me to tell him that you dropped by?"

Would Seth even care if she did? Grace finally shrugged. "It really doesn't matter."

Lanna nodded. Then she clasped her hands together and rocked back and forth on her heels in a nervous gesture. "So I met your brother the other day," she blurted. "He's doing a great job coaching some of these kids."

"Yeah, he seems to really like it. I'm glad he agreed to do it."

"He's really nice," Lanna hedged. "And cute."

Grace raised an eyebrow and forced herself not to smile. Lanna was interested in Alec? No way. Although now that Grace thought about it, they might be a really good fit. "He's also incredibly stubborn and way too smart for his own good."

"He's sure been great with the kids on his team. Patient, funny, and kind—the best combination. He even showed up here a time or two to help out."

"Really?"

Lanna nodded.

The news surprised Grace. Actually, a lot of things about Alec surprised her lately. But what really motivated his visits to the center? Was he drawn to the kids—or to their beautiful and petite advocate? Maybe some of both?

From the corner of her eye, Grace watched as Lanna continued to rock back and forth on her heels, looking around at nothing in particular. When she caught Grace studying her, she chewed on her lower lip for a moment before saying, "Do you happen to know if he's seeing anyone?"

Grace laughed, mostly because if Lanna really knew her brother, she'd never have to ask. "Honestly, I don't think he's 'seen' any girl for a really long time."

"Why not?"

Grace shrugged. "Can't say for sure, but reading between the lines, I'd say that he doesn't think he's got much to offer. After his accident, he broke up with his girlfriend because he was afraid she'd dump him eventually, and he really hasn't gotten back on the saddle since. At least not that I know of."

Amidst the chaos of kids running around, talking, and laughing, Lanna's expression turned contemplative, as though she had no problem tuning everything out. Finally, her eyes met Grace's once again. "Well, I'm not usually the type to ask a guy out, but I may have to get over that."

Although Grace hadn't known Lanna long, she liked her. A lot. Lanna was the type of girl who could be really good for her brother. "If you want to date Alec, then yeah, you probably will." Grace paused. "And I hope you do."

Lanna cocked her head to the side. "You wouldn't mind?"

"Not at all," Grace said, thinking about the last girl who'd fallen for her brother. "Just don't take it personally if he turns you down."

A grin spread across Lanna's face, and a glint appeared in her eyes. "Oh, I won't. But if there's one thing I've learned from Seth over the years, it's how to wear someone down until they eventually give in. I'll get Alec to go out with me if it's the last thing I do."

Grace smiled, but at the same time, a worry that had nothing to do with Alec and everything to do with Seth settled like an uncomfortable pit in her stomach. If Seth wasn't the type to give up, why had he stopped calling or flirting? Why was he acting like a regular patient whose only agenda was to get his knee strong enough to run and mountain bike again?

"Hey, you okay?" Lanna asked. "I didn't offend you or anything, did I? I was only joking. I mean, if Alec's not interested in me, I promise not to keep bugging him."

Grace blinked in an effort to clear her thoughts. Then she waved Lanna's concern away. "Oh, I didn't think you were. I was just, uh . . ." She paused, not sure how to explain. Normally, Grace didn't blab about her worries to just anyone, but something about Lanna made it easy—as though Grace was talking to an old and trusted friend.

"To be honest, I was thinking about Seth," Grace finally said.

A question appeared in Lanna's eyes, but she said nothing. Just waited for Grace to continue.

Grace fidgeted, not sure how to explain or if she really wanted to explain. But one look around the room—Seth's room—was enough to convince her that the only thing she had to lose was Seth. Maybe Lanna could help prevent that from happening.

Grace sighed. "When I first met Seth, he didn't come across as the serious type. I sort of felt like an item on his bucket list—something to cross off before moving on to the next item. But now that I've gotten to know him a little better and realize that's probably not the case, he's different around me. He doesn't flirt or try to get me to go out with him anymore. I guess I'm just worried that I've missed my window of opportunity."

"I seriously doubt that," Lanna said. The contemplative look reappeared on her face as she tapped her finger against her lips. "Want to know what I think?"

Coming from someone who wasn't afraid to be blunt, the question made Grace squirm a little. Did she really want to know what Lanna thought? "What?"

Lanna met Grace's gaze and smiled. "I think that maybe it's time that we both got over our pride."

If only that wasn't easier said than done.

Twenty-one
♡ ♡ ♡

The moment Seth showed up for his appointment, Grace presented him with a cupcake covered in dyed green coconut that looked like grass. As a topper, she'd printed off a small picture of a runner and taped it to a toothpick.

"Ta da," she said. "You've officially made it twelve weeks post-surgery today."

Seth glanced at the cupcake but made no move to take it. "Are you trying to rub in the fact that I'm not allowed to go jogging yet? Because that's not funny."

"No." Grace picked up his hand and set the cupcake on his palm. "I'm trying to tell you that today we're going jogging. Outside."

A dark eyebrow lifted. "Jogging . . . as in faster than a walk?"

"You're pretty smart for a guy who tore his ACL attempting a 360 in deep powder."

The corners of Seth's mouth tugged up. "I never would have met you if I hadn't." Almost immediately, his mouth straightened, and he looked away as though he hadn't meant to voice that thought. But the words had already been spoken, and Grace wasn't about to let the moment pass. She'd been waiting for an opportunity like this for weeks.

"So kissing me at the auction didn't count?" she said, attempting to goad him into flirting with her—or at the very least remind him of another, far more memorable kiss.

His eyes met hers, looking hesitant, as if he wasn't sure what to say. Which was a first. "You know what I meant."

Not exactly the flirtatious response Grace had wanted, but if he thought that meeting her was a positive aspect of tearing his ACL, she'd take it.

"Well, I'm glad you did then." Grace bit down hard on her lower lip, immediately wishing the words back. Did she really just say she was glad he'd torn his ACL? What kind of person said that? "I mean," Grace quickly revised. "I'm glad I got to know you better, too—not that you tore your ACL." Oh geez, this wasn't going nearly as well as she'd hoped.

For a moment Seth's mouth formed a smile, and his eyes took on a teasing quality. But then he ducked his head and glanced once again at the cupcake Grace had made for him. He held it up. "We're really going jogging?"

Grace nodded. Maybe she should do as Lanna had suggested and just ask him out. But what if he wasn't interested any longer? The way he'd dodged her awkward flirting attempts and quickly found a way to change the subject made her nervous. Had Seth decided she wasn't worth it?

No. She tossed the worry aside. That kiss they'd shared was much more than a mild flirtation. She could still remember the heat, the power, the jolt of something extra that went beyond mere attraction. Seth had to have felt it, too. Grace just needed to figure out why he was now backing off. There had to be another reason.

She sighed. "Before we go, I need you to lie down on that table so I can apply some Kinesio tape to your leg."

Seth grimaced. "Do you have to? That stuff rips my hair out."

"Baby."

Seth's lips twitched, but he dropped down on the table, obediently lifting his leg for her to apply the tape. Grace did so with slow precision, first cutting the wide tape into thin strips then smoothing it slowly across his leg muscles, deliberately taking her time. She'd grasp any excuse to touch him.

Once she'd finished taping, Grace held out her hand to help him up. He eyed her for a moment before taking it, then pulled himself up to a sitting position.

Grace reluctantly let go and mustered a perky expression. "Ready for your first post-surgery jog?" She smiled. "Well, first approved one, anyway."

"More than ready." He jumped off the table and led the way to the side door.

They walked outside and headed toward the park at the end of the block. When they arrived, Grace had him do a few warm-up exercises before giving him the go ahead to jog. Then she trailed behind, studying his gait to make sure he showed no signs of limping or favoring his injured knee in any way. Once she ascertained that everything looked fine, she increased her speed and caught up.

Normally, with other patients, Grace would fall back and keep an eye on them as they jogged the lengthy trail that circled the park. But with Seth, she had no desire to watch and wait—not when she'd rather jog next to him. After today, her appointments with him would drop to twice monthly. The thought made her feel as though he was slipping away, that it was only a matter of time before he was out of her life completely.

Grace felt antsy all of a sudden, as though she needed to do something to stop that from happening. Without really thinking it through, she blurted, "Hey, want to meet up

Monday morning for a jog?" It was as close as she could come to taking Lanna's advice about asking him out.

Seth shot her a sideways glance before returning his attention to the path ahead. "But my appointment isn't for another week."

"Two, actually," Grace corrected. "You're now at the point where we really only need to meet about twice a month."

Seth adjusted his gait, slowing his speed slightly. "So what's Monday?"

Did she really have to explain? Wasn't it obvious? Or was she just really that bad at this? "Two friends going jogging together."

Another sideways glance. "But I thought you didn't like to mix personal with business."

Grace rolled her eyes. Was he making it difficult on purpose? Grace should have expected this, and would have, if she'd taken the time to think her offer through a little more before blurting it out. "It's just jogging," she said. "Do you want to go or not?"

"I don't know," he said. "Will you treat me like a patient if I do?"

"What's that supposed to mean?"

"Are you going to tell me to slow down if I go too fast? Make me warm up? Or are you going to leave the therapist title at home and just jog with me?"

Grace rounded a corner and continued to move smoothly along beside him. Not too fast and not too slow, the pace he set was right on. "If you stay about the speed we're going now and do a warm up on your own, then no, I won't say anything."

He chuckled. "And if I don't?"

"I'm a therapist—it's who I am. I can't turn it on and off like a light switch."

"Fair enough."

After another long pause, Grace shot him a sideways glance. *So?* she wanted to ask. *Are we on for Monday or not?* But she held her tongue, not wanting to sound too desperate. She'd already asked him twice anyway. The offer would stay as-is on the table, and if he wanted to pick it up, great. If not, it would stay there untouched.

"What time?" he said after a moment.

Grace bit back a smile of triumph. "Is 6:00 too early?"

"No." Seth continued to look ahead with an impassive expression, giving Grace no indication about what he thought or if the prospect of spending time with her outside of the physical therapy arena excited him. "Where?" he asked.

"Here?"

He nodded. "6:00 on Monday it is."

The spare key turned easily in Alec's lock, and Grace pushed the door open with her hip while carrying several grocery sacks. She kicked the door shut and stumbled toward the kitchen. "Alec? You here? I brought stuff for dinner."

Alec appeared from his bedroom at the end of the hall, wearing a green- and blue-striped button-down shirt and dark slacks. He looked good, really good—too good for a casual evening in.

Grace arched an eyebrow. "Going somewhere?"

"Didn't you get my text?"

Grace shook her head. "I accidentally left my phone at the clinic today. Why?"

He chewed on his lower lip for a moment, as if weighing his words. "Sorry to bail on you, but I've got other plans tonight."

Trying not to show her surprise, Grace walked into the kitchen and set the bags on the counter. "What kind of plans?"

"I'm just . . . going out with a friend is all."

Apparently whatever plans Alec had weren't ones he wanted to share with Grace, which made her all the more curious. She began unloading the groceries. "*A friend*—as in just one?"

"Just one," was all he said.

"Do I know this friend?"

Alec leveled her a look. "You're nosy."

Grace shrugged. "Someone has to answer all of Mom's questions the next time she calls, and we both know it won't be you."

"Which is exactly why I'm not going to tell you." Alec's hands landed on the wheels of his chair as he maneuvered his way toward his room once again.

Grace folded her arms and leaned against the counter, raising her voice so he could hear her. "Maybe I'll just hang around until you leave then follow you the way I used to back in high-school."

Alec glanced over his shoulder and rolled his eyes. "You're such a pain sometimes, you know that?"

"Look who's talking." Grace pushed away from the counter and moved toward him. "Is it Lanna?" After their conversation the other day, it was the only thing that made sense.

A look of surprise registered on Alec's face. "How did you know?"

Grace ignored the question. "Did you ask her out, or did she ask you?"

"She did. Why?"

Grace smiled. Good for Lanna. But at the same time, Grace experienced a pang of jealousy that Lanna had been able to do what she couldn't. Sure, Grace had asked Seth to go jogging—as *friends*. How pathetic was that? For weeks, Seth had flirted, asked her out, and found ways to get her to meet him outside the clinic. And every time, Grace had shot him down. But now that the tables had turned, Grace couldn't bring herself to do the same.

If she had any guts, she'd walk over to Seth's place right now and kiss him the way he'd kissed her.

With a frown, Grace resumed unpacking the groceries. When Alec made no move to go back to his room, Grace looked up and caught him watching her with an expectant look on his face, as though waiting for her to say something. What had he asked her again? She couldn't remember.

Alec leveled her a look. "Are you going to tell me how you knew it was Lanna?"

Oh, right—*that* question.

"No," Grace said, not wanting to betray Lanna's confidence—not that Alec couldn't piece it together on his own if he gave it much thought.

She put the last of the groceries away, stuffed the plastic bags into a drawer, and picked up her keys. "I hope you have a great time tonight."

"Will do."

As Grace walked out into the fading afternoon light, she raised her face to the sun. Maybe it was time to follow Lanna's lead and let Seth know that she wanted more than just a jogging friend. That she wanted to spend time with him, go out with him, coach with him, hold his hand, snuggle, and definitely experience more of his kisses.

If Seth felt differently, Grace would deal with it then. But come Monday morning, she would leave no question in his mind that she wanted to be more than jogging friends.

Twenty-two
♡ ♡ ♡

The early morning air felt chilly and humid—the perfect temperature for a jog. Seth breathed in the raw, earthy smell and took in the beautiful surroundings before his gaze settled on Grace, who stood about 100 feet away with her back facing him. Her arms swung forward and back as she warmed up her body with fluid, graceful motions. In tight spandex pants and a matching jacket, with the sunlight casting a halo around her trim and toned body, she looked beautiful. The fact that Seth was here because she'd invited him made it even better.

Ever since he'd taken Lanna's advice and tried to be just like any other patient, Seth's progress with Grace had improved drastically. She'd flirted, looked at him differently, smiled and teased more, and now they were about to jog together outside of work—something he'd never expected to happen.

But at what point could Seth start being himself again and not worry that he'd drive Grace away? Or was acting disinterested the only way to pique her interest? Seth had no idea. But he found himself really hating this game.

Seth slowed his steps, wanting to admire Grace while she was still unaware of his presence. Every part of his body longed to wrap his arms around her and experience the thrill of kissing her again, but it was too soon. Even Seth knew that. Grace had invited him here as a friend, and that was that.

When Grace turned and spotted him, Seth gave her a head nod, keeping his expression impassive. "Hey."

"Hey," she returned. "You came."

"I told you I would." Seth frowned. Since when had he not followed through with a promise? If Grace invited him to go shopping for shoes and he said he'd be there, he would. Seth was a man of his word.

Grace shook her head in a flustered manner. "Yeah, I know. I didn't mean to sound surprised. I'm just . . . glad you're here."

Seth studied her, trying to read her expression. Most of the time, Grace was always so calm and collected—the type to never let anything ruffle her. But every now and then, she acted as though she felt out of her element, as though Seth made her nervous. Like now.

"I'm glad I'm here too." Seth eyed the extensive path around the park that circled a pond and wove through a forest of pines. "How many laps do you usually do?"

"How's your knee feeling today?" she asked, as if that would determine the number of laps they'd jog.

Seth raised an eyebrow. "Don't forget I'm here as your friend, not your patient."

"I'm asking as a friend."

Yeah right. A smile tugged at the corners of Seth's mouth. "My knee's fine, thanks." He gestured to the trail. "Ready?"

She hesitated and bit down on her lower lip. After a moment of awkward silence, she blurted, "Aren't you going to warm up?"

"No." Normally, Seth would take the time to warm up, but after all of the times she'd played the therapist/patient card, Seth felt the need to put Grace firmly in her position as *not* his therapist. Not today, anyway.

Her jaw clenched, working back and forth as she studied him. Finally she looked away and shrugged. "Fine, whatever." But her stiff body language said something completely different.

Seth held back a smile and started forward. "Coming?" he called over his shoulder.

"You really aren't going to warm up?" she yelled back.

"Nope," he said again.

She caught up to him. "You really should warm up."

"That's what I'm doing now."

"Seth, c'mon."

He shot her a sideways look. "Get over it, Grace. You're going to have to stop being my therapist at some point. Think of this as practice."

"Fine," she huffed. "If you want to risk re-injuring your knee, that's your call."

"My point exactly."

She huffed again, making Seth bite back another smile. He didn't know why he found it so fun to tease her, but he did. The way she always rose to the bait made it so easy and, well, funny. It was just one more thing he found endearing about her.

Thinking it best to change the subject, Seth said, "I hear you've been helping out Lanna at the after-school program."

"Yeah," Grace said. "Whenever I can sneak out of work early, I try to go over. I really like working with those kids, and I love what you've done with that space. It's got a great vibe now, and I like being a part of it, you know?"

Seth nodded. He knew exactly what she meant—something he owed to Grace for pushing him to go that first time. "It's actually been really fun for me as well. The fact that Lanna's letting me do more without putting up a fight makes it even better."

"How's the coaching coming along?"

"Great. The girls are really starting to catch on, and we've even won a couple of games."

"I'll have to come sometime," said Grace. "To, you know, see you in action."

First jogging outside of work and now she wanted to come to one of his soccer games? Yes, this was definite progress. Seth shot her a sideways smile. "Sure, you can be the water girl."

"Oh, I see. First I'm the ball girl at your basketball game and now the water girl? What's next? Laundry duty?"

Seth chuckled. "Hey, I offered you a job as assistant coach, and you turned me down flat. It's your own fault."

"Can I take it back?" she asked.

He shot her a sideways look and smiled. "Sure, you can be in charge of warm-ups since you like doing them so much."

"Very funny."

They rounded a bend in the trail, and Grace moved smoothly beside him with seemingly little effort. Seth, on the other hand, was beginning to feel a little winded. He blamed it on not being able to jog for three months.

"Alec said you outfitted all the girls with new cleats and new pairs of tennis shoes," Grace said. "That was really great of you."

She made it sound as though Seth had done something praiseworthy, but Seth didn't feel comfortable being praised for something that needed to be done—especially when he could easily afford to do it. He only wished he would have gotten involved sooner.

He shrugged. "They needed it, and I could afford it. No big deal," he said.

They rounded the far end of the lake, and Grace placed a hand on Seth's arm, slowing him down to a walk. "But it is a big deal—to those kids and to me." She pulled him to a stop and turned to face him. "You're a good man, Seth Tuttle."

Seth's arm burned where she touched him, and the way she looked up at him made him want to lean down and kiss her right then. Would she let him? Would she respond? Or would that only set him back again?

Seth muttered a quick thanks then started forward once again, needing some time to sort through his feelings. He didn't understand Grace. From the beginning, she'd made a point to keep her distance—to be his therapist and only his therapist. But now things were changing, and Seth didn't know what to make of them. Had she changed her mind? Was she finally coming around? Or was this simply a game of tag, and she was currently it?

A sort of nervous tension latched on to Seth, making him feel anxious. As nice as it was to be chased rather than do the chasing, he was sick of both roles. Did Grace care about him as more than a patient or not?

Up ahead, a few steps led to a bridge that crossed over a small stream. As soon as Seth hit the first step, he purposefully let his knee buckle and fell to the ground, wincing and hugging a knee that felt perfectly fine. Seth wasn't sure what prompted him to pull such a stunt— possibly the need to find out how much Grace really cared— but here he was, on the ground, faking an injury.

"What happened? Are you okay?" Grace dropped beside him. Her hands deftly pushed his aside as she straightened his leg and moved her fingers over his skin. "Did you tear something? This is all my fault. I should have made you warm up. Why didn't you warm up? You should have listened to me!"

169

Her touch felt so good that Seth couldn't resist laying back in the grass and closing his eyes. He even went so far as to grimace.

"It's not swelling anywhere that I can tell," Grace said. "If you lean on me, can you walk? There's an ER not far from here. We can get it x-rayed."

The worry in her voice had Seth grimacing for real this time. What had he been thinking? It was as if he were ten again, tugging on the pigtail of the cute girl in class in an attempt to get her attention. That had never ended well, and neither would this.

"Maybe you should try kissing it better," Seth said.

"What?" Her fingers stilled on his leg. She sounded half worried, half confused, as if she had no idea whether he was talking rationally.

Seth squinted up at her and issued a smile, praying she'd respond with one in return. "My knee's fine, Grace. I was just messing with you."

The way her expression changed from worried confusion to something not nearly as positive made Seth mentally kick himself yet again.

"How could you?" She gave his arm a shove. "I really thought you were hurt. Why would you do that to me?"

Seth blamed his insecurity and immaturity, with a little bit of mischief thrown in. "You're not laughing," he said lamely.

She glared at him as though she couldn't believe he'd just said that. Which was completely understandable, because he shouldn't have said it—or faked a stupid injury either. He should have apologized, or at the very least, asked for a do-over.

Grace opened her mouth as though she wanted to say something then snapped it shut and looked away. Various emotions crossed her face as she shifted positions and sat back on the grass. When her eyes met his again, she didn't look happy. "Do you have any idea what it feels like to see someone you care about get hurt and not be able to do anything to stop it or fix it? It's the worst feeling in the world."

Seth felt like a complete heel, mostly because he knew exactly what that felt like and should have known better. He'd watched Mike's life slowly get sucked away and couldn't do a thing about it.

Idiot.

Seth scooted closer and reached for her hand. "I'm sorry. I really am. I only meant it as a joke and didn't think how stupid it would be."

She peeked at him from the corner of her eyes. "It was pretty stupid."

"Dumbest joke ever," Seth agreed.

"You can say that again."

"Dumbest joke ever."

She nodded, saying nothing. After a moment, her lips twitched and a snicker sounded. She immediately covered her mouth with the back of her hand in a failed attempt to muffle another snicker. Or was that a snort?

Seth leaned closer to make sure it really was laughter and not the pre-curser to tears. Sometimes he couldn't tell the difference. "Are you laughing?" he asked.

She nodded, her eyes bright with mirth.

Seth rubbed the back of his neck then scratched his head, not understanding how they'd gotten from A to B— not that he was complaining—but she didn't make sense.

"I'm sorry." Grace bit her lips together, trying to keep a straight face. "You must think I'm bipolar or something."

"The thought did cross my mind."

She laughed. "So if I just fell for the dumbest joke ever, what does that make me exactly?"

An answering smile tugged on Seth's mouth as he watched her continue to fight her laughter. "I'm going to plead the fifth on that one."

Grace reached over and slugged him. "That's for making me fall for the dumbest joke ever." Then her arms came around him in a quick hug. "And that's for not being hurt."

Before Seth had time to react or return the hug, she hopped to her feet and started jogging away. He suddenly felt cheated out of a moment that might have turned into something more.

"Wait up!" Seth leapt to his feet, realizing that he was once again doing the chasing.

Grace drove away from the park and away from Seth feeling unsettled and frustrated. Other than the quick hug and telling him that he was a good guy, she'd done nothing. She hadn't apologized for never returning his calls or asked him out. She hadn't even set up another time to jog.

By the time Grace pulled to a stop in front of her apartment, she felt like a complete failure. She frowned at her building. Dating and flirting used to come so much easier, didn't it? It had been so long that she really couldn't remember.

Maybe she should just send him a text. In three short sentences, she could apologize and ask him out. All she'd have to do is hit send and wait. Done.

But Grace couldn't bring herself to do that, either. She would not resort to a text. She would not. Grace would grow up, act her age, and do it in person.

Tomorrow.

But as the day wore on, the unsettled feeling worsened to the point where Grace felt sick to her stomach. She couldn't eat or focus and even had to ask Cameron for help remembering a certain exercise.

That was the final straw.

As soon as her last patient before lunch left, Grace headed for her office and closed the door firmly behind her. Before she could second guess or talk herself out of it, she called Seth's number. Her hand shook as she waited for the call to go through.

"Hey, Grace," he answered almost immediately. "This is a nice surprise."

"Hey," she said.

A short pause.

"What's up?" he asked.

It's now or never. Now or never. Out with it! "Do-you-still-want-to-go-out-with-me?" Grace cringed at how fast the words came out.

"What?"

Her cringe deepened. Of course she'd have to repeat it. Of course. It was like her penance for being a wimp. "Do. You. Still. Want. To go out with me?"

He chuckled and lowered his voice, as though he didn't want to be overheard. "Of course I still want to go out with you. But I thought you weren't interested."

"I wasn't."

"Wasn't? As in past tense?"

"As in past tense." Weeks ago, in fact.

"That's good to know." His voice sounded like a smile— the gleeful kind that appeared when things went exactly the way Seth wanted them to.

Silence.

More silence.

Grace bit her lower lip, wondering what she should say next. She hadn't exactly thought this conversation through very well. Was he waiting for her to ask him out or at least make a suggestion? She frantically tried to come up with something, but her mind drew one blank after another.

The silence became almost painful.

Finally, Seth said, "Let me get this straight. You called to tell me that you're now willing to go out with me, right?"

Grace felt lamer than ever. "Something like that."

"And you figured I'd have the perfect idea for a date off the top of my head?"

Yes. No. Maybe. Argh. Grace didn't know. "You never seemed to have a problem with ideas before."

Seth laughed. "You could always ask *me* out, you know."

She could. She should. That's what she'd intended to do, but—oh, why was this so hard? "In case you couldn't tell, I'm a little rusty at this."

Another chuckle sounded. "Let me put you out of your misery then. How about Friday night at 6:00? I'll pick you up, and we'll do dinner and something else. That work?"

"Yes."

"You sure?"

"I'm sure."

"Okay then. See you Friday." His voice still sounded like a smile—an I'm-laughing-at-you sort of smile. Grace suddenly wanted to crawl into a dark hole and hide.

"Oh, and Grace?" Seth said.

"Yeah?"

"Looking forward to it."

"Me too." Grace slowly lowered the phone from her ear, not sure what to think. The conversation had gone nothing like she'd imagined it would, but it was over. And now she had a date with Seth on Friday at six.

Anticipation began to replace the unsettled feeling in the form of giddiness.

Twenty-three

♡ ♡ ♡

Grace opened her door to find Seth standing on her front porch. Butterflies flapped in her stomach as she looked him over. Dressed in faded jeans and a sweatshirt that had seen better days, he looked casual—too casual—especially compared to Grace.

Seth eyed her up and down, his mouth splitting into a lopsided smile. "You look gorgeous, as usual, but you're probably going to want to wear something else."

Grace glanced down at her black skinny pants and new red shirt—the one she'd purchased a few days before in anticipation of this date. Other than the dress she'd worn at the auction, Seth had only ever seen her in workout clothes, and Grace wanted tonight to be different. Special. Not an old sweatshirt-and-faded-jeans type of a date.

Evidently Seth didn't read minds.

One by one, the butterflies in Grace's stomach stopped flapping.

She leaned against the doorjamb and folded her arms. "You seriously want me to change out of this fabulous shirt—which I bought specifically for this date, I might add, and into"—Grace gestured to Seth's ensemble—"something like that?"

His grin widened as he took a step closer, resting his hand on the doorjamb next to her head. He leaned in close enough to make the butterflies take flight once more. "It *is* fabulous—especially on you. Which is why I'd hate to see it splattered in paint."

Grace frowned. Paint? What did he plan to do, put her to work on another room at Magnificent Minds? No, wait. Seth's style ran more toward—her eyes narrowed. "You're taking me paintballing, aren't you?" The last time she agreed to go paintballing—way back in high school—her body had come away not only covered in paint but in bruises as well. Those paint-filled bullets weren't exactly soft and gentle.

"My 'splattered in paint' comment gave it away, didn't it? Shoot. I wanted to surprise you."

Grace should have expected something like this. Planned for it, even. This was Seth, after all—someone incapable of doing the predictable thing. "We're really going paintballing?"

"Yes, and you're going to have a blast."

"But what about your knee?" Grace said, grasping at any excuse to cry off. It didn't matter that he already thought her overprotective.

Seth pushed away from the door and leveled her with a look. "You're not allowed to worry about that, because this is a date, not a therapy session."

Grace nodded, unable to think of another reason why Seth should be the one to change and not her. What was so wrong with a nice romantic dinner followed by a casual walk someplace equally romantic, like the Graham Arboretum?

She'd pictured Seth holding her hand, putting his arm around her, and stealing a kiss or two or three.

Not turning each other into works of abstract art.

That's what she got for making Seth plan the date. Come to think of it, he probably picked paintballing on purpose as revenge.

Grace sighed and stepped back, opening her door wider. "Feel free to wait in here. I'll be a few minutes."

She returned to her room and changed into some old jeans with a hole in one knee, as well as a thick sweatshirt she'd received for running a half-marathon a year before. Although Grace hated the thought of ruining her favorite sweatshirt, she hated the thought of welts on her skin even more. This was the thickest sweatshirt she had and would protect her better than anything else.

With a heavy heart, Grace pulled back her hair, which she'd painstakingly curled into a ponytail, and removed her favorite dangling earrings—the ones she saved for special occasions. With one final glance in the mirror, she went to find Seth.

Grace pasted on a smile and spun in a slow circle, showing off her latest, much less fabulous outfit. "This work?"

"Cool sweatshirt," Seth said. "You sure you don't mind getting paint all over it?"

Grace waved the comment away. "What, this old thing?"

Seth pulled the door open. "Don't worry, I have an extra one in my car that you can borrow. It's been through a few paintball wars and is pretty thick."

Grateful for his consideration, Grace smiled. "Thanks, I'll probably take you up on that." Even if this wasn't the dream date she'd imagined, Grace would take it if it meant spending time with Seth.

He drove out of the city toward Tacoma, finally stopping at an adventure park, touting the best paintballing experience ever. In the lobby, they ran into a group of people. Two of them Grace remembered as Garrett and Owen from the wheelchair basketball game and several she didn't recognize. Seth made quick introductions, but Grace didn't commit them to memory. She was too worried about being the only one who couldn't remember how to load or shoot a paintball gun. Everyone looked so much more prepared and excited.

Grace hugged Seth's oversized sweatshirt to her, breathing in the smell and reminding herself why she was here.

The door opened, and Alec wheeled himself inside with Lanna close behind. She wore military camo and a bright smile, as though she went paintballing every weekend. Was Grace the only newbie?

"Grace!" Lanna pulled her in for a hug like they were best friends who hadn't seen each other in a while.

It made Grace feel marginally better. She shot Alec a look of surprise. "You're paintballing, too?"

"Lanna made me," Alec said. "I tried to tell her I'd be an easy target, but she promised to find us a good hiding place."

Lanna's hands came to rest on Alec's shoulders, and she gave them a squeeze. "He's my secret weapon. He's going to be like one of those snipers who picks people off from a distance."

Grace's heart swelled—not only at seeing them together, but the fact that her brother was here, ready to participate in a game designed for someone with two good legs. She couldn't believe how far he'd come in such a short time. Grace owed so much to both Lanna and Seth. Did they have any idea how wonderful they were? How big of an impact they'd made on the lives of both of the Warren siblings?

Grace's eyes moved to Seth, who was at the counter, filling out forms. His shoulders looked so strong and capable. Even in his old sweatshirt, Grace had never felt more attracted to him. It hit her that Seth was all she'd ever wanted—all she never knew she wanted.

When Seth turned and caught her staring, he waved her over and held out a pen. "They need your signature," he said.

Grace signed her name with a flourish, suddenly excited to see what awaited them in the fields behind the store. If her wheelchair-bound brother and petite little Lanna weren't intimidated to play, she refused to be either. A surge of energy shot through her, and Grace suddenly felt like grabbing a gun and saying, "Bring it."

Outside, when the shrill alarm sounded, and as the initial shots rang out, Grace smiled. If she ever wanted to get Seth back for choosing the most un-romantic date ever, this was her chance. Seth was going down.

Twenty-four

♡ ♡ ♡

Covered in paint and laughing, Grace waved goodbye to everyone as she ducked inside Seth's car and flashed him a smile. "I can't believe I'm saying this, but that was incredibly fun. Thank you."

"Thank *you* for telling me to ask you out."

Grace wagged a finger at him. "I didn't *tell* you to do it. I merely told you that I'd willingly go if you did."

"Thanks for coming so willingly then." Seth leaned in close enough for Grace to feel his breath on her face. Her heart raced as he glanced from her eyes to her lips and back to her eyes as though challenging her to tell him to kiss her as well.

Should she?

Just as she'd made up her mind to do just that—regardless of the fact that she was covered in paint—Seth smiled and backed away. Grace's heart sank.

When he shoved his key into the ignition and started the car, Grace forced her thoughts back to her earlier, less-than-willing feelings. How much they'd changed. The sight of Alec completely doused in paint and still having a good time, along with the fun camaraderie of the group, had made the experience one Grace wanted to repeat. Yes, several of the shots had stung, but not nearly as bad as she remembered. It was as if Seth's sweatshirt gave her an extra layer of protection that Grace was loath to part with. Maybe he wouldn't notice if she "forgot" to return it.

"Okay, so we have a couple of options," Seth said as he pulled from the parking lot. "One, go to dinner looking like an art project gone wrong. Or two, head home to change and go for a really late dinner someplace nice." He winked. "But only if you promise to change back into that fabulous red shirt."

Grace smiled, wondering what he'd say if she chose option one—not that she ever would. The thought of Seth leaning in to kiss her paint-splattered face didn't sound nearly as romantic as it did moments before. Maybe that's why he'd backed off. She sneaked a glance at him. He *was* planning to kiss her at some point, wasn't he? Because that part was non-negotiable.

"Two," she said.

Seth's face split into a grin. "I was hoping you'd choose that one."

Once Seth dropped her off, Grace quickly showered and changed then applied her makeup. When she pulled out her hair dryer, her favorite song came on the radio so she sang along, raising her voice to be heard above the sound of the whirring. A feeling of giddiness and anticipation swept through her as she sang and even danced.

Behind her, the bedroom lights flickered on and off as a deep voice rang out from what sounded like the hallway outside her bedroom door, "Grace?"

She simultaneously yelped and jumped, dropping the hair dryer. It clattered onto the granite vanity top with a loud bang. Grace stared at it for a moment before she had the presence of mind to turn it off.

"Sorry, did I do that?" Seth's voice came again. He didn't sound the least bit sorry.

"You could say that," Grace returned, trying to slow her racing heart at the same time she raked her fingers through her windblown hair.

"You decent?"

"Yeah, but I might strangle you, so I'd keep my distance if I were you."

Seth's head poked around the side of the door with a grin fixed on his face. "Hey, gorgeous."

How could she not smile at that? Grace shook her head, looking at him through the mirror. "You could have knocked, you know," she teased.

His handsome body came into full view as he leaned his shoulder against the doorjamb and folded his arms, still watching her. "I did. I also rang the doorbell. I even poked my head inside and called your name, but you didn't hear me. I thought it would freak you out if you walked into your front room and found me sitting there, so I was trying to let you know I was here. Didn't work so well, did it?"

Grace reached for her curling iron and turned it on. "Not so much. But I'll forgive you if you let me finish getting ready." When he didn't move, she raised an eyebrow. "You're going to stand there until I'm done, aren't you?"

"I can't seem to take my eyes off you."

Grace set down the curling iron and turned, placing her hand on his chest as she pushed him backwards. Over the years, she'd developed a fool-proof system that gave her hair those relaxed, beachy-looking curls. But in order to do it, she had to part her hair into sections and create a few haphazard-looking ponytails—sort of Pippi Longstocking meets Cindy Lou Who. She wasn't about to let Seth see her like that—not on their first official date.

"Why don't you go and make yourself comfortable on my couch? I'll be out in a few minutes."

"If I promise not to stare, can I stay?" Seth asked. When she started to shake her head, he added, "C'mon, I'll be bored sitting out there all alone. I can keep you company while you finish doing your hair."

Grace let out a breath and felt herself caving. Why hadn't she hurried faster in the shower and not taken quite so much time to do her makeup? Then she would have heard Seth's knock and been ready. "Fine, whatever. Just no jokes about how I curl my hair."

Seth raised an eyebrow. "How do you curl your hair, exactly?"

She pointed a finger and said, "No jokes," before grabbing her curling iron once again.

Seth gave her a half smile before disappearing from sight. With a sigh of relief, Grace quickly sectioned off her hair, creating four lopsided ponytails, and started curling away.

"Hey, is this you standing on The Great Wall of China?" Seth's voice sounded. Apparently he was examining the picture frames that lined the top of her dresser. The snoop.

"Yeah."

"Wow, you and Alec look so young. It's strange seeing him standing on two feet." He paused. "Are those your parents with you?"

"Yeah."

A clink and shuffling sounded before Seth's voice came again. "The Louvre, Sydney Opera House—and is that you sitting on the elephant? Talk about a well-traveled family."

Grace couldn't argue that. Her parents loved to travel. From the time she and Alec were little until the day of his accident, they'd vacationed at least two times a year. Iceland, New Zealand, a safari in Africa, a cruise in the Caribbean—you name it, Grace had probably been there at some point.

But then Alec's accident happened, and vacationing didn't seem as exciting to Grace as before, especially not when Alec refused to go. So she'd refused as well. At some point, their parents resumed vacationing without them, always issuing invitations to both her and Alec even though they knew they wouldn't be accepted.

The pictures covering her dresser now served as a bittersweet reminder of happier times and how much things had changed. Every time Grace looked at them, she couldn't decide if they should be displayed on her dresser or locked away in the attic.

Through the mirror's reflection, Seth appeared, holding one of Grace's favorite and most hated pictures—her and Alec, standing on top of a run at the Whistler Blackcomb ski resort in British Columbia. "This is my favorite," he said.

A stab of pain hit Grace in the chest. No matter how many times she'd wanted to throw that picture against the wall, break the glass and burn it, she'd never been able to bring herself to do it. That had been one of the most fun and memorable trips they'd taken, but the pain of loss was still as biting as the cold wind that had blown that day. Grace forced her eyes away from the reflection as she fought against the rising emotion.

"Nice hair," Seth said, smiling at her reflection in the mirror.

"Shut up." But Grace couldn't muster the teasing tone to go along with the words.

Seth's smile disappeared as he looked down at the picture. "This wasn't the day that Ale—"

"No," said Grace quickly. "It was the last trip we took before his accident—a day that will never happen again no matter how much I want it to."

Seth leaned his shoulder against the doorframe as he studied her, this time with a look of consideration. "No day can happen more than once. You know that, right?"

Grace nodded. She knew exactly what Seth was saying, and he was right. Even if Alec still had two working legs, that moment could never be repeated. That was life.

At least Alec still breathed, still talked, still smiled—unlike Lanna's brother, who was buried somewhere in the ground. Grace needed to remember how lucky she was to still have her brother around.

Two large hands landed on Grace's shoulders, and Seth turned her around to face him. "You okay?" he said.

She nodded again, meeting his gaze with a question in her eyes. More than ever, Grace wished for his strength and positive outlook on life. "How do you stay so happy and optimistic when your best friend's life was taken away?"

Seth blinked. "Wow, that's a pretty heavy question coming from someone with four pigtails."

With a laugh, Grace pushed him away and quickly tugged the elastic bands from her hair, letting it fall to her shoulders. "There. Better?" she said.

"Much." Seth tugged on one of her curls and gave her a look of appreciation. Then he shrugged and stuffed his hands into his pockets before clearing his throat. "I think the difference between me and you is that I don't blame myself for Mike's death. He got cancer. Yes, it sucked that I couldn't do anything to change that, but I never blamed myself. You, on the other hand, think that just because you coerced Alec into going skiing that makes his accident your fault. But you didn't force him to make that jump. He did it, and now he's living with the consequences of that decision. I wish you could believe that."

"I do—or, at least I'm starting to, thanks to you." Grace stepped toward him and placed her hands on his arms, running her fingers up and down his defined biceps. "Everything changed so drastically after his accident. All the happiness we shared as a family was sucked away, leaving us with no other option but to cope. But ever since that first wheelchair basketball game, I've seen snatches of the old Alec emerge. It's like you've opened a portal and allowed some of that happiness to return."

Grace paused, moving her fingers up to play with the collar of his shirt. "I know I've misjudged you and pushed you away again and again, but I'm really glad you didn't go far. The truth is, I'm falling for you." There, she'd said it. She'd laid her feelings out on the table for him to take or leave. Somehow, though, she wasn't worried.

Seth searched her eyes for a moment before interlacing his fingers with hers and slowly dipping his head. Their foreheads touched, and he placed her hands behind his neck before circling her waist with his own. Grace's heart sped up as he pulled her against him and dropped his head further to nuzzle her neck. Shivers ran down her spine and goose bumps broke out all over her body. Her breath caught in her throat as his lips slowly made their way from her neck to her mouth, landing there with a tentative touch. Her fingers brushed through his hair as he deepened the kiss, pinning her against the counter.

Grace could count on one hand all of the truly perfect moments in her life—the kind where her happiness peaked, when everything around her seemed to click into its rightful place. That day at Whistler Blackcomb had been one of those times. But this moment—this one perfect moment, as Seth's arms held her and his mouth explored hers—trumped them all. Only instead of everything around her fitting into place, Grace felt as though she was the one being snapped into place. And that place was with Seth—the only person who'd ever made her feel this alive, this happy.

"I think I need to stop kissing you now," Seth murmured against her lips.

"Why?" Grace complained, tightening her hold on him. She wanted to bask in this perfect moment for as long as possible.

"Because that bed behind me is way too much of a temptation."

"Oh." Grace pulled back just enough to see his face. Her lips drew into a smile even as her heart warmed. Why had Grace ever worried that she'd be just another conquest for him to cross off his list? He was a gentleman through and through.

"So . . . yeah," Seth finally said, filling the awkward silence.

The funny expression on his face made Grace giggle. As soon as the sound escaped, she couldn't stop, especially when she remembered they were standing in her bathroom. Who would have thought that such a perfect moment would happen here? The giggles erupted into full on laughter.

"Thanks," said Seth, drawing back. "I actually needed that."

More laughter followed—so much that Grace had to hold on to the counter for support.

Seth watched her with an amused expression. "Is this going to happen every time I kiss you?"

Grace shook her head, taking a deep calming breath to force the giggles away. Finally, when she felt like she could speak, she said, "What do you say we go get that dinner now?"

"Good idea."

Twenty-five

♡ ♡ ♡

$\mathcal{S}$eth was all about being different. It had taken so long to finally convince Grace to go out with him that when she placed the responsibility for planning the date on him, he immediately vetoed boring in lieu of something a little more memorable. Like paintballing and dinner at the Bizzarro Italian Café in downtown Seattle.

One glance at the wide-eyed look on her face when they entered the establishment, and Seth knew he'd chosen well. No one could enter this place and not gape at the eclectic, almost garish décor. Antique chandeliers hung next to old bicycles, and the walls were covered in mismatched frames that held everything from paintings to chalkboards to mirrors. For this particular restaurant, it worked.

Seth breathed in the tempting smells and wrapped his arm around Grace's shoulders. He tugged her closer, thrilled that he could do that without fear of her running away. He could hardly believe that she was here, with him. That he'd kissed her and she didn't run. Or that she'd admitted to falling for him. His heart still thumped with warmth and excitement every time he pictured her looking up at him, telling him that.

"What do you think?" he asked, glancing down at her.

She looked around, taking in the restaurant with her beautiful wide eyes. "I have to be honest. When you said a nice restaurant, I pictured something a little . . . different." She tilted her face up and smiled. "I should have known better."

"I've got to be different than the other guys."

Grace laughed. "Oh, you're definitely different, all right." She elbowed him lightly in the ribs. "But in a good way."

Seth smiled. In his book, a "nice" restaurant was a relative term. It meant great food and service—which this place had, as Grace would soon find out. The moment she tried a bite, she'd be hooked. Guaranteed. Seth's mouth watered just thinking about it.

In no time at all, they were seated and waiting for their order. One perk of taking Grace out for an insanely late dinner was the lack of a long wait. This place was usually packed.

"What's good here?" Grace said as she examined the menu.

"Everything." Seth had tried every dish they offered. "But the clam linguini and elk Bolognese are my favorite."

"Elk? As in . . . ?" Grace made a face over the top of her menu.

"As in the most incredible meat you've ever tasted in your life."

She lowered the menu and set it on the table, clasping her hands over the top of it. "You do realize we're talking about Bambi's uncle or cousin, right? Are you really okay with eating that?"

"Bambi was a deer, not an elk. Big difference."

"Like I said—cousins."

Seth grinned. "Cousins or not, elk tastes nothing like deer."

"You're impossible." Grace took another glance at the menu and sighed. "I'll try the linguini."

"Good choice."

Seth gave their order to the waitress then took Grace's hand in his, playing with her fingers while they waited. The entire night still felt so surreal. Grace. Here. With him. At Bizzarro's. He thought of the awkward phone conversation from a few days earlier and had to duck his head to hide his smile. Never before had a girl told him to ask her out.

Grace leaned closer and lowered her voice. "Mind if I ask you a personal question?"

"Shoot." Seth was all about asking and answering personal questions. It meant progress. It meant more distance from a term he'd come to hate—professional.

Grace bit on her lower lip the way she always did when weighing her words. Finally, she blurted, "Are you a trust-fund kid or something?"

The question caught Seth off guard, and he laughed. Only a few months before, Grace had said she didn't want to know the answer to that question, but here she was, acting as though curiosity had finally gotten the better of her. It was kind of adorable.

He shook his head. "No trust-funds for me. Far from it, actually. My parents were as middle-class as you could get."

Grace watched him, waiting. But when he said nothing more, she asked, "Did you win the lottery then? Publisher's Clearinghouse? A grand prize from some sort of contest?"

"None of the above."

She chewed on her lower lip once more before dropping her hand to the table. "Oh, I know. You played the stock market and won big."

"Isn't that about the same as winning the lottery?"

Grace frowned. "You're not going to make this easy on me, are you? Do I really have to beg?"

Seth continued to play with her fingers. They were long and soft and fit perfectly in his. "Once upon a time, you told me you didn't care if you knew or not."

"I lied."

Seth laughed again then pulled her fingers to his lips and kissed them lightly before setting her hand back down. "You crack me up."

"Don't you dare change the subject."

"Okay, okay." Seth shifted in his seat and leaned forward, resting his elbow on the table. "Way back in high school, I learned about an interesting invention called the internet. It blew my mind, and I found myself reading everything there was to know about it. The more I learned, the more I realized it could go places someday—big places. So I used my entire savings to buy every big domain name I could think of that was available—Walmart.com, Stockmarket.com, Pier1Imports.com—you name it, I bought thousands of them.

"Then I started to learn HTML and gradually created websites for some of the more generic ones. In time, I was able to recoup some of my initial investment through advertising, but it wasn't until one of the companies approached me about selling them a domain name that I really started making money. I sold enough to pay for my MBA then waited for the internet to gain even more momentum before agreeing to sell more. It was crazy how much the larger companies were willing to pay for a little domain name." He shrugged. "So I guess, in a way, I did play the lottery and won big, but I never really saw it that way. To me, it was a conservative investment opportunity. I just had no idea how big the returns would one day be."

Grace watched him with an unreadable expression. Her eyes weren't guarded or wary like they often were with him, but Seth had no idea what she was thinking. Did she chalk his fortune up to sheer dumb luck or did she understand all the time and effort Seth had invested into educating himself about the internet, learning HTML, developing websites, getting his MBA, and eventually negotiating some significant and intimidating deals as a fresh-out-of-college graduate?

For whatever reason, Grace's opinion of him really mattered.

"Now that's impressive," she said. "I didn't know anything about the internet until one of my teachers told me I could use it for research purposes. By then, it was pretty established."

Grace cocked her head to the side and studied him. "A lot of people in your situation would spend their days playing and lounging by the pool—not coaching soccer for underprivileged kids, buying them shoes, and turning their after-school building into a fun and safe haven."

Seth looked away, feeling undeserving of her praise. Before he met Grace, he'd been more the playing and lounging type. Yes, he'd donated money here and there to various charities or his alma mater, but only because they happened to call and he answered his phone. It wasn't until Grace came along and forced him to see beyond his own life that he now knew what it felt like to be a real contributor.

Seth shifted again in his seat. "Yeah, well, that was really all your doing."

Grace's lips tugged up into a smile. "Really? Because I don't recall telling you to buy shoes or stock a room with games or build a wall." She gave his hand a squeeze. "You're amazing, Seth Tuttle, and I feel very lucky to be here with you right now."

It was a rare thing for Seth to be at a loss for words, but he was now. He wanted to say "Likewise" or "Ditto" or "No, *I'm* the lucky one." But the words all lodged in the lump in his throat. With a few simple and candid words, Grace had reached into his heart and touched it. Seth suddenly found himself wanting to be the person she believed he was capable of being.

How could Seth possibly convey with words what he felt for Grace? It took massive self-control not to lean across the table and kiss her then and there.

The waitress interrupted the moment by setting steaming plates of food on their table.

Seth stabbed his fork into his food and lifted a bite-sized portion, wagging it at Grace. "Want to see what Bambi tastes like?"

Her eyes widened slightly before she rolled them. "I can't believe you just said that. You're terrible."

"Don't I know it." Seth put the fork in his mouth and smiled.

Grace took a bite of her own meal and started gushing about how amazing it was. After that, it didn't take much convincing for her to give Seth's elk a try—which she also loved.

After dinner, Seth left the car in the parking lot and interlaced his fingers with hers. They wandered through the city streets, taking in the sights, smells, and lights. They told stories about their youth, laughed at embarrassing moments, and shared their dreams for the future. Seth took every opportunity to pull her into the shadows to steal a kiss and hold her close. The hours passed like minutes, and Seth never wanted the night to end.

But when he caught her yawning for the fourth time, Seth finally led her back to his car and he reluctantly drove her home. Outside her front door, he held her close and kissed her long and hard, as though he were leaving on a year long voyage instead of merely going home to catch a few hours of sleep before seeing her again.

Seth always knew Grace would be worth the wait, but until he paused to reflect on their time together, he didn't know how worth it she really was.

Twenty-six

♡ ♡ ♡

The warm and beautiful summer days started speeding by, and Seth's therapy sessions became fewer and farther between. He used to dread the day that happened, but not anymore. Now that his evenings and weekends were filled with Grace, the time he spent in her clinic as a patient became a perk.

Seth took her paintballing again and again, and Grace attended all the games he coached. They helped to tutor those kids involved with summer school and doubled with Lanna and Alec. They jogged, hiked, sailed, kayaked, Grace cooked for him, and Seth cooked for her. Other than Seth's contract work and Grace's job, they were practically inseparable.

At the six-month post-surgery mark, Seth arrived home from a consulting session completely exhausted. He wanted nothing more than to snuggle with Grace on the couch and watch whatever movie she wanted to put on. But as Seth walked inside his house, shouts of "Congratulations!" greeted him. Surrounded by all their friends, Grace stood in the center, holding a cake shaped like a mountain. A tiny skier stood at the top of a run with the words, "Way to go, Seth! You made it!" Then she kissed him on the cheek and officially pronounced him all better. No more therapy sessions were needed.

Seth set the cake on the table, wrapped his arms around Grace, and hooted as he spun her around until they were both dizzy. His knee was healed, Grace was officially a part of his life, and the mountain biking season was still in full swing. Life couldn't get any better.

Later, after everyone but Grace had left, Seth came up behind her as she rinsed the dishes and turned her to face him, pulling her close.

She lifted bubble-covered hands and laughed. "I'm all wet."

"I don't care." Seth lowered his mouth to hers. In no time at all, her arms wound tightly around him, dampening the back of his shirt as she responded with the same enthusiasm she always did. Over the past couple of months, Seth had learned that when Grace opened her arms to someone, she did so whole-heartedly.

A raw and tender emotion tugged at Seth's heart. Her beauty, charm, kindness, humor, and goodness had thrust their way into his heart and took over. Seth found himself falling more in love with her every day.

"Marry me," he murmured against her lips.

Grace pulled back, her hands resting against his shoulders as she stared up at him with startled eyes. "What did you say?"

"I said marry me." Seth had never been more sure about anything. Grace had become part of him, and he didn't want a life without her in it. He wanted to come home to her every day, or be there when she came home. He wanted to see her wake up, watch her curl her hair with those haphazard ponytails, and go to sleep with her every night. He wanted to walk down the aisle and commit himself to her forever.

"Are you serious?" Grace breathed, still staring at him.

"I've never been more serious about anything," Seth said, his voice sounding hoarse and emotional. "I love you, Grace. More than I ever thought possible." His fingers closed over hers, and he moved her hand to cover his heart. "Like it or not, this belongs to you and always will."

Tears pooled in her eyes at the same time her mouth lifted into a smile. She bobbed her head up and down in quick, jerky movements.

"Is that a yes?" Seth asked.

"Yes, it's a yes." She laughed and sniffed, wiping her eyes with the back of her hand. "I love you, too."

Seth's smiling mouth lowered to hers, sealing their agreement with a long, drawn-out kiss. No matter how many times he kissed Grace, it was never enough. The warmth of her lips and the way her body felt against his was like an addictive drug.

"Want to go ring shopping?" Seth murmured against her lips.

She pulled back. "Right now?"

Of course right now. Seth wanted every current patient, future patient, or guy on the street to know that Grace was taken. "No time like the present."

Grace stood in her front room, half listening to the Today show on TV as she looked out her front window. The Saturday morning skies were bright and blue, promising a beautiful day. Seth would drive up any moment, and she couldn't wait to see him—or discover what he had in store that day. "It's a surprise," he'd said. "Dress in something comfortable that can get dirty."

So Grace had donned some old workout capris and a t-shirt. Then she'd carefully, and regretfully, slid off her beautiful new diamond ring and placed it back in its box in her top dresser drawer. She'd only had the ring two days, and her finger already felt naked without it. But she wasn't about to risk losing it during a hike or paintballing, or whatever Seth had planned.

Which was what?

Anticipation filled her stomach as she waited impatiently for his car to appear. When it finally rounded the corner, carrying two bikes strapped to the rack on top, Grace smiled. They were going biking—something she hadn't done in years. The prospect thrilled her. She could already feel the wind lifting her hair and smell crisp humid air as she pictured them cruising around on one of the many biking trails Seattle had to offer.

Seth had chosen well. This would be so much better than getting pounded with a bunch of paintballs.

But when his car pulled to a stop in front of her apartment, Grace took a closer look. The bikes weren't beach-type cruisers. They had large beefy tires, dual suspensions, and uncomfortable-looking seats. They were mountain bikes.

Grace should have known that Seth would try to convert her to the sport, especially now that she'd proclaimed him fully recovered. But in the back of her mind, she'd secretly hoped that his ACL tear would make him want to choose the less-dangerous paved or graded dirt trails. Looking at those bikes, Grace knew he was here to take her on a "real" mountain biking expedition—one involving large rocks and uneven ground.

A nervous pit filled Grace's stomach. How many patients had wound up in her office because of an injury resulting from falling off a mountain bike? Whether it was recovering from a broken leg, arm, or torn meniscus, she'd treated too many to count. It was a dangerous sport.

Too bad Seth happened to love it.

"Surprise," Seth said when she opened the door for him. "We're going mountain biking."

"Yeah, got that." Grace hesitated, not wanting to pull the plug on his enthusiasm. "Um, you do know I've never done it before, right? I'm not sure I'll be any good."

Seth pulled her in for a quick kiss then said, "You'll be a natural, trust me. And don't worry. I'm starting you off with the easiest trail around. One ride, and I guarantee you'll be hooked."

Grace wasn't so sure about that. But she hadn't been sure about paintballing either, and now she loved it. Maybe she'd feel the same about mountain biking. Maybe she might even come away with a better attitude about her brother wanting to give it a try.

"Okay," she reluctantly agreed. "Let me grab my shoes, and we can go."

Less than an hour later, Grace stood next to her bike while Seth tightened the strap on her helmet.

"These are duel-suspension bikes," Seth explained, "so they'll absorb pretty much every bump you come across and keep the ride pretty smooth—even the large bumps. So don't be afraid to take them head on." He gave her a few additional pointers before mounting his own bike and clicking one of his shoes to the pedal.

"Your feet are locked to the pedals?" Grace stared at his feet, horrified. She knew a lot of street bikes had pedals like that, but had no idea mountain bikes did too. It seemed so wrong. Possibly even suicidal. No wonder people broke or tore so many of their body parts.

"It makes riding easier, but I definitely wouldn't recommend it for a beginner."

Grace wouldn't recommend it for anyone. "What if you hit something and lose your balance?"

He grinned. "You either get out of the binding fast or you go down with the bike."

The nervous pit that had come and gone since Grace had first seen the bikes returned with a vengeance. What had she gotten herself into?

"Ready?" he asked.

No. Not now. Probably not ever. She swallowed. "As ready as I'll ever be."

Seth pushed off and locked his second shoe into the pedal. Grace tentatively followed. The trail turned out to be pretty smooth, and before long, she found herself relaxing. The peace and beauty of the surrounding mountains breathed new life into her. It was nothing like riding on a trail through a crowded park. No wonder Seth loved this sport so much.

They rounded a bend, and the terrain suddenly changed. It sloped downhill, and the once-smooth and flat trail became rough. Ruts, tree roots, and large rocks invaded the path and slowed their progress—or at least Grace's progress. Her body tensed as she maneuvered her way through them, stopping every so often to walk her bike over a particularly large obstacle. Seth, on the other hand, only stopped to wait for her to catch up. He seemed so at ease, taking each bump with the fluidity of an expert.

During one particularly tricky patch, Grace hopped off her bike yet again and lifted it over the large, protruding root of a massive pine. Before mounting again, she watched Seth with both admiration and envy as he surged ahead, climbing a steeper section of the trail with what looked like very little effort.

His front tire suddenly jerked to the left, and Seth pitched forward over the handlebars, taking the bike with him. He hit the ground hard on his right shoulder before his bike finally broke free from the bindings. It bounced down the hill like a ping pong ball then clattered to the ground near Grace's feet.

"Seth!" she screamed. She dropped her bike and stumbled forward, leaping over his as she ran toward him. She was suddenly at the bottom of the ski run again, watching Alec over-rotate his jump and land on his back. Had Seth injured his spinal cord? Had he broken his neck? Back? The worries collided in her mind as she dropped down beside him.

"Please tell me you're okay," she said with a shaky voice.

Seth started to sit up, and Grace immediately pushed him back down. "Don't move."

"Relax," he breathed. "I just got the wind knocked out of me, that's all. Look." Seth raised one foot and wiggled it in the air. "I can move it just fine. My arms work too." He grabbed Grace around the waist and tried to pull her toward him, but she resisted.

"Oh c'mon," he joked. "Don't you want to kiss me better?"

How could Seth joke at a time like this? Was he hiding some pain or injury that he didn't want Grace to know about? "You promise you're okay?"

"Promise." He rolled to a sitting position with a groan. "Just a little bruised, that's all. No biggie. This isn't the first time I've fallen, and I always walked away just fine."

Grace didn't feel the least bit comforted. After all, Alec could have said the same thing before the day of his skiing accident. But not anymore. Grace couldn't help but worry if the day would come when Seth couldn't say the same either.

She wanted to tell him to stop mountain biking, that he couldn't do this anymore, no matter how much he enjoyed it. But the words lodged in her throat as if they knew they had no right to be spoken.

"I'm okay, Grace, really." Seth's hand rubbed up and down her arm as his eyes pleaded with her to not worry.

From the looks of things, he *was* okay—this time. But that didn't mean Grace could turn off the worry, especially now that she'd witnessed firsthand what could happen on a mountain bike. And Seth had called this trail "easy." What were the more difficult trails like? She shuddered at the thought.

"Would it be okay if we turned back now?" she finally said, more than a little shaken. Suddenly, a crowded park trail seemed like a wonderful thing.

With concern etched across his brow, Seth nodded slowly. "Yeah, okay. You've already seen the best part of this trail anyway."

It was then that Grace realized something. Once the terrain had become more challenging, she hadn't noticed the scenery at all. She'd been too focused on not falling, and where was the fun in that? Nowhere.

Keeping the thought to herself, Grace stood and held out her hand to help Seth up. In no time, they were back on the trail with Grace taking the lead. Their progress was even slower than before, with more uphill climbs, but they eventually made their way back to the car. As Seth finished strapping the bikes to the roof of his car, Grace sat in the passenger seat and stared through the windshield at a cluster of dark green pines. While the beauty still surrounded her, the peace was absent, replaced by an almost haunting foreboding. What if something bad happened to Seth? How would she handle it?

When Seth slid in next to her, he reached over and laced his fingers through hers, inadvertently reminding her of how well they fit together. Grace squeezed his hand and pushed the worries to the back of her mind.

Twenty-seven

♡ ♡ ♡

Grace rapped lightly on her brother's door and stood back, tapping her foot against his concrete front porch as she waited impatiently for someone to answer. Normally, she'd let herself in, but Lanna's car was parked out front, and Grace wasn't about to barge in on them.

Only thirty minutes earlier, Seth had dropped her off at her apartment, where she'd quickly cleaned herself up before jumping in her car and driving straight here. She had a small window of time before Seth returned to pick her up for dinner, so she needed to get back soon. They planned to take the ferry over to Bainbridge Island in a few hours.

Grace should have waited until the next day, but she couldn't bring herself to be patient. She needed to talk to someone. Now. Although she'd originally come for Alec, seeing Lanna's car made Grace realize that the person she really needed was Lanna.

The door opened, and Lanna appeared. She wore an apron, held a wooden mixing spoon, and had a smudge of something gooey on her cheek. "It's Grace," Lanna called over her shoulder before turning back to Grace with a bright smile. "So glad you're here. You're just in time for caramel popcorn."

Grace laughed. "Who eats caramel popcorn at three o'clock in the afternoon?" Her stomach growled as she said it, and Grace realized she hadn't eaten lunch. Only a couple of granola bars Seth had given her after their mountain biking fiasco.

"We do." Lanna pulled Grace inside and shut the door. "Just wait until you try it. It's my own special mixture of marshmallows, brown sugar, and butter. You'll love it."

Grace's stomach growled again, louder this time, and Lanna pointed a finger. "See? You know you want some."

Alec sat on the couch, watching a How It's Made episode on TV. A large machine pressed down, cutting circles from large black leather sheets for who knew what. Grace shook her head. Her brother had always loved that show.

"Hey, Grace, long time no see," Alec said dryly. He still came to her clinic twice a week to work out, so it had only been two days since she'd seen him.

"I'm here for Lanna, not you," Grace quipped, biting her tongue so she wouldn't add, "so there."

"Really? You came to see me?" Lanna grinned as she drew Grace into the kitchen and filled a bowl with delicious-smelling caramel popcorn. She pushed it toward Grace. "I know we just saw each other at Seth's party the other day, but we didn't really get to talk much. How are the wedding plans coming along?"

"Slow." Grace pulled up a chair and sat down, eating a handful of some of the best caramel corn she'd ever had. "You know Seth. Deciding on invitations, food, and photographers isn't his thing. If it were up to him, he'd take me to the courthouse tomorrow and seal the deal."

"Don't you dare," said Lanna. "You need a proper wedding so I can be a proper bridesmaid. Speaking of which, we're still on for shopping Monday night, right? I've already told Seth and Alec that they're on their own for the night."

"Definitely." With her mom living across the country, Grace would have had to shop for wedding dresses alone if it weren't for Lanna. Besides, a girls' night out with Lanna was exactly what Grace needed right now. No extreme sports, no stress about her future husband—just a fun evening out.

"Have you scheduled the church yet?" Lanna asked.

"Yeah. For October seventeenth."

"So soon?" Lanna's smile widened. She clapped her hands and gave an excited hop. "Yay! But oh my goodness, we have so much to do before then. Order flowers, schedule a caterer and a band, pick invitations, find a good photographer . . ."

Lanna continued with her list while Grace fought to push away the unsettled feelings in her gut. When the scheduler for the church had said the soonest available date was mid October, Grace thought it sounded too far away. But not anymore. Now, two months felt more like a blink of an eye. Was Grace ready to walk down the aisle toward a guy who loved to risk his neck on a daily basis? After this morning, she wasn't so sure.

"Earth to Grace," Lanna cooed, her eyes sharp and speculative. "What's wrong?"

"Nothing, I, uh—" Grace stopped. This was why she'd come, wasn't it? To lay her fears on the table and pray that someone could smash them to pieces? "Actually, I need to talk to you."

Lanna's eyes filled with worry. "Oh no, what's wrong?"

Grace went on to explain about the morning's events—how Seth had taken her on a "mild" ride then proceeded to pitch himself over his handlebars. Grace explained her fears, worries, and reasons behind her hesitation. With each sentence, the pit in her stomach grew.

"I just don't understand why Seth likes mountain biking, heli-skiing, or any other sport that could land him in the hospital with a broken neck or worse," Grace finished, her eyes pleading with Lanna to make the pit go away.

Lanna let out a breath and offered a sympathetic smile. She pulled up a barstool next to Grace and sat down, leaning her elbow on the counter. "There's a reason he's like that, you know."

"Why?" Maybe if Grace understood that aspect of him a little better, she'd come to accept him for who he was and not worry so much.

"He's told you about my brother, Mike, right?"

"Yeah."

Lanna nodded. "The two of them were so close, like brothers. When Mike found out he had an advanced form of stomach cancer and there was nothing to be done but try to slow it down, they decided to live life to the fullest for whatever time Mike had left. They went sky-diving, heli-skiing, got into mountain biking and bungee jumping, and even flew to Myrtle Beach to race cars. You name it, they tried it. It was almost like Mike wanted something else to get him first, and Seth went along with it because he's incredibly loyal—almost to a fault.

Lanna let out a breath and dropped her gaze to the table. "After Mike finally passed away, I thought Seth would tone it down, but he didn't. Instead, he found new friends— ones that loved the adrenaline rush as much as him. At first I was angry, because it seemed like he didn't mourn at all for my brother, but then I realized he was just mourning in his own way, by doing those things that reminded him of Mike. I think that's partly why he still loves that kind of stuff. In a way, it keeps Mike alive."

Lanna leaned closer and placed her hand over Grace's. "When Seth loves, he loves deeply. Look at the way he never gave up trying to help me with my program or the way he never gave up with you. He's there for the people he loves and always will be." She paused, meeting Grace's eyes once again. "He adores you, Grace. He's always had a pretty upbeat personality, but I've never seen him as happy as he's been these past couple of months. If anyone can tone him down, it's you."

As Lanna talked, the pit in Grace's stomach gradually dissolved, leaving her feeling relieved. Lanna's honest and heartfelt words not only soothed Grace's worries, but it made her see Seth in a new light. She understood him better and admired him even more. And with that understanding came the knowledge that she needed to embrace the adventurous side of him because it was part of what made Seth Seth. A big part.

Grace pulled her hand free and wrapped her arms around Lanna. "Thank you," she said. "For being such a great sister to Seth and to me. You have no idea how much I needed to hear that."

When Lanna pulled back there were tears in her eyes. "I've never had a sister before."

Grace smiled and hugged her one last time. "You do now."

Twenty-eight

♡ ♡ ♡

Following her talk with Lanna, Grace's doubts all but vanished. On Monday, they went shopping as planned and found the perfect wedding dress: A Bateau sheath gown that hugged Grace's body from its elegant capped sleeves to her waist. But her favorite part was the way it fanned out in a beautiful A-line skirt that swished as she moved. Grace fell in love with it instantly and looked forward to the wedding more than ever, especially after Lanna introduced her to an incredibly talented photographer.

Everything was back on track.

Saturday morning, Seth took her wakeboarding. Normally Grace loved riding on the boat and waterskiing, but every time Seth dove in the water to take his turn, she felt the stirrings of another pit in her stomach. He pulled stunt after stunt after stunt—everything from something he called a *heelside raley* to a back roll. Grace stiffened when his board left the water then let out a breath when he landed safely or came up for air. But then he attempted something called The Whirlybird, lost his balance mid-air, and landed hard on the side of his head. Even above the noise of the engine Grace could still hear the thwack. Her heart beat a million times a second until he resurfaced and slowly made his way toward the boat with a bleeding nose.

Owen joked and teased, Seth joked back, and Grace remained tense and worried for the duration of the ride. And a doubt crept back in.

A few days later, Seth took her to a rock gym. As she tightened her harness, Seth explained that it was the perfect place to learn the basics before they went for a "real" climb in the mountains. Grace pictured the IMAX movie she'd once seen of some crazy climber scaling a two-hundred foot cliff in Zion National Park, and the doubts came rushing back like a wave breaking on the beach.

But when she and Seth took a walk through the park, taste-tested food for their wedding, started coaching fall soccer, and went kayaking, the doubts subsided, and Grace was never more sure that Seth was the person she wanted to spend the rest of her life with. Why couldn't all their dates be like that—fun, adventurous, and romantic?

If only.

About a month before their wedding, Seth drove Grace to an unknown destination, telling her it was a surprise. Normally, she loved surprises, but with Seth, they'd sort of lost their appeal. Would today be the day they climbed a real mountain? She hoped not, although Seth was headed away from the mountains, not toward them, so that couldn't be it. Her stomach twisted into knots as they continued to drive.

This is who Seth is. You can't change him, nor do you want to. Which was true. His loyalty and love of life were two of the reasons Grace had fallen for him in the first place. She needed to remember that.

Seth finally turned into a parking lot with a sign that read *Harvey's Airfield* and cut the engine. He twisted toward her and grinned. "Ready?"

Butterflies whipped around in Grace's stomach. An airfield. Somehow, she knew they weren't here to take a nice, calm scenic flight over the beautiful Seattle area.

"For what?" she mustered. *Don't say skydiving. Please don't say skydiving.*

"We're going skydiving."

The butterflies turned into large angry bats, beating against her insides. Lanna's once-comforting words dissolved into a pile of ash as the pit returned with a vengeance. If Seth wanted to jump out of a plane at who knew what altitude to careen through the skies so he could keep Mike's memory alive, he'd have to do it without her.

Grace stared at the small airplane hanger, still not moving to release her seatbelt. "Correction," she finally said. "*You're* going skydiving. *I'm* staying right here."

Silence. Grace could practically feel his eyes burning into her profile.

"You don't want to go?" he asked.

Wasn't it obvious? Of course she didn't. All of her pent-up emotions that had been slowly building for the past several weeks broke loose. Grace clenched her fingers into fists as she turned to face him. "No, I don't. Just like I don't want to rock climb for real, and I don't want to go mountain biking again. Or heli-skiing, for that matter, just in case you get any ideas come winter. Seth, this is getting out of control. Actually, it *got* out of control the day your surgeon and I said you could resume normal activity. Then suddenly it's like you have a death wish or something. I mean, you don't, do you?"

At some point during her speech, Seth's smile vanished, replaced with a mixture of confusion and worry. "No, I don't have a death wish."

"Then why all of this?" Grace threw up her hands then gestured toward the airplane hanger. "Is it really to keep Mike's memory alive? Because there are a whole lot of other ways to do that."

Now Seth looked really confused, not to mention upset. "What are you talking about?"

Realizing she'd probably sounded incredibly callous and rude—not to mention presumptuous—Grace bit her lip. She suddenly felt like she didn't know anything—about him or anything else. Why were relationships so hard sometimes? Why couldn't you just find the right person and automatically be on the same wavelength?

Grace sighed and glanced out the passenger window, unable to look at Seth any longer. "Lanna told me about you and Mike and how this extreme sports thing all got started. I just assumed that's why you kept at it—to keep his memory alive." The words sounded so wrong now, as though Grace had forced herself into a deeply personal part of his life that he might not be ready to share with her.

Seth closed his eyes and let his head flop against the back of his headrest, saying nothing. Moments passed as an uncomfortable silence engulfed the car and sucked some of the oxygen from it. Grace suddenly felt the need to roll down a window, but her fingers stayed clasped tightly together on her lap.

"Yes, Mike's diagnosis was how it all got started," Seth finally said. "And I'll admit that after he died, I kept it up partly because of him. But I also do 'these things' as you call them because I like them. Because I love the feeling that comes from staring fear in the face and saying, 'Bring it on.' Life has so much to offer, and I want to experience it all."

Grace swallowed, still staring out the window. When he said nothing more, she asked, "And if I don't?"

"Then you don't." Seth shifted positions and reached for her hand, holding it between them and coercing her to

211

look at him. "Grace, if you didn't want to do all of this stuff, why didn't you say so?"

"Because it's who you are, and I—" She really had no idea how to finish that sentence.

"Exactly," said Seth. "It's who *I* am. But it doesn't have to be who you are. You're beautiful, strong, independent, and intelligent. You make me laugh, you're incredibly fun to tease, and you're adventurous. Those are all reasons that I love you—reasons that aren't going away because you don't want to launch yourself out of a plane or scale a mountain. We have plenty of other things in common."

"I know," Grace said, not feeling at all appeased. While she appreciated his words, she also felt like he'd sort of missed the point. It wasn't about embracing each other's differences or Grace not wanting to participate in extreme sports. It was about her not wanting *him* to keep risking his neck. Although he said he didn't have a death wish, his actions proved otherwise.

But was it fair to ask Seth to change? If he didn't like that Grace stayed up way too late researching new studies and therapies or that she loved apples and peanut butter—something Seth detested—would it be fair for him to ask her to give those things up? Would he even consider it?

No, because Seth accepted her as is, lock, stock, and barrel. He didn't want to change Grace any more than he wanted to change himself.

Grace laced her fingers through his, reminding herself yet again that she and Seth were a good match. She loved him, and he loved her. In only a month, they would be married, and if Grace wanted to walk down that aisle with complete confidence, she needed to learn to be as accepting of him as he was of her.

Maybe if Grace wasn't with him when he jumped out of planes or scaled rocky cliffs, she wouldn't worry.

Maybe.

Twenty-nine
♡ ♡ ♡

"Invitations sealed, addressed, and stamped," Lanna announced, sliding the last one into the box Grace would drop off at the post office on her way back home from the after school center. Lanna had offered the space so they could spread out and stay organized, and Grace had gratefully accepted. They'd met earlier that Saturday morning, and were able to pound out the invitations in only a matter of hours.

Seth had planned on helping, but Grace let him off the hook with a "thanks, but no thanks." His handwriting was deplorable, so she wasn't about to let him anywhere near the envelopes. Not the least bit put out, Seth didn't waste any time rounding up some friends to go mountain biking. Alec included. Her brother had finally purchased a wheelchair mountain bike and couldn't wait to try it out.

As Grace stuffed the extra invitations and envelopes in a box, her mind wandered in Seth's direction. Had Seth gone over his handlebars again? Had Alec? What about Owen and Garrett? Were they as care-for-nothing as Seth could be?

An anxious feeling settled in Grace's stomach. Hopefully, Seth would call soon to let her know they were okay so she could stop worrying about them.

She glanced at Lanna, who didn't look the least bit concerned. It wasn't fair. "Aren't you worried?" Grace blurted. "About Alec mountain biking, I mean?"

Lanna tossed the last of the pens in her drawer and shut it. She shook her head. "I'm actually excited for him. Every time he tries something new that's out of his comfort zone, something good happens to him. He's happier, which makes me happier." She shrugged and leaned against her desk. "Besides, his skiing accident made him realize he's human, so I know he'll be careful. Seth, on the other hand . . ." Lanna wiggled her eyebrows in a teasing way.

"Which is exactly why I'm worried." Grace didn't see the humor. Lanna was right. Seth wasn't nearly as cautious, and the reminder only made her more anxious. She frowned. "He's so reckless sometimes, and I keep picturing him getting thrown from his bike and hurting himself. I wish I could be more like you and not let it get to me, but I can't make myself stop."

Lanna's expression turned sympathetic. "When I was younger, my mom had this saying framed on our wall. It said, 'Worry is like a rocking chair. It gives you something to do, but doesn't get you anywhere.' For some reason, even as a little girl, I liked it. After they passed away in a car accident, whenever I'd start to worry about what would happen to me and Mike, I'd remember that. It's helped me so many times."

Lanna looked like she was about to say something more, but the ringing of Grace's phone interrupted them. Grace snatched it from her purse and answered without looking at the caller ID.

"Seth?" she said, needing to hear his voice.

"Grace, it's Alec."

"Alec?" Grace's forehead crinkled. What was he doing calling her? Had he meant to call Lanna instead?

"Something's happened," Alec said. "There was this jump, and Seth took it, and—Grace, he's hurt. I'm not sure how bad. We're waiting for the ambulance now."

"Ambulance?" The word came out as a hoarse whisper. They'd called an ambulance, which meant that no one dared to move Seth. Which also meant they had to be worried about a serious injury.

Once again, it was as if Grace was transported to the bottom of that ski run, watching Alec get loaded onto a bright orange sled because he wasn't allowed to move either.

"Tell me he's okay, Alec. Please," Grace pleaded.

"He took a bad fall," said Alec. "He's unconscious right now, which is why we don't want to move him."

Grace's stomach tied itself into knot after knot after knot. Seth was supposed to be on his way home. Safe. Not injured and unconscious. "Where are you? I'm coming right now."

"The ambulance will get here before you." He paused. "I think I hear the siren now. I'll call you as soon as I know which hospital they're taking him to."

"Alec . . ." Grace couldn't hang up, not until she knew Seth would be okay. Not until she heard his voice.

"I'm sorry," Alec said. "I've gotta go. I'll promise I'll call you soon."

The line went dead. Not knowing what else to do, Grace dropped to the nearest seat, clutching the phone with shaking hands. Unconscious. Ambulance. Hospital. The words boomed in her mind like a loud thunderstorm.

Lanna sank down beside her and grabbed hold of her hands. "What happened?"

"Seth's hurt and unconscious," Grace managed to say. "They had to call an ambulance."

Worry knitted Lanna's brow as her fingers tightened around Grace's. "He's going to be okay."

Don't say that! she wanted to shout. But it was too late. The words were already out and now hung in the air like a bad omen.

Grace's mother had told her the same thing that day in the hospital when they were waiting for news of Alec. But her brother had been far from okay, and now anytime Grace heard those words, it did everything *but* comfort her.

Grace shot Lanna a frustrated look, as though she'd just jinxed Seth. "You don't know that. Nobody does." Lanna could tell Grace over and over again that it was useless to worry, but how could she not when Seth was lying on some mountain somewhere, broken and bleeding?

Lanna sighed and tilted her head to the side. "You're right, I don't. Maybe he'll walk away from today just fine, or maybe he'll end up in a wheelchair like Alec." She placed her hand on Grace's. "Either way, he's still breathing and still alive. In that respect, he *will* be okay."

The words sounded like fingernails on a chalkboard. She pulled her hand free. "You don't get it," she said. "You've only seen the better side of Alec. You weren't there after his accident. You didn't have to be the girlfriend who got dumped or the family he tried and tried to push away. For ten years I had to stand by and watch him shrink away from life, knowing there was nothing I could do about it. Ten years! Do you have any idea what that's like?"

Grace crumpled, dropping her forehead to her palms as the worst of her fears came to the forefront. Seth, no longer smiling. Seth, shutting the blinds on the world and on life. Seth, pushing her away the way Alec had done to his high-school girlfriend. The most difficult times during the past ten years came rushing back, torturing her mind with one painful reminder after another.

Grace couldn't do it again, especially not with Seth. She wasn't strong enough to stand by and watch him go through that.

A sob escaped, and Lanna's arm came around her, rubbing up and down her back. "I'm so sorry, Grace. I didn't realize."

Grace's phone rang again, making her jump. Like a hot potato, she tossed it at Lanna, knowing she was too much of a basket case to take the call.

A short conversation later, Lanna hung up and tugged Grace's arm. "He's awake now. They're taking him to Valley General on the other side of town. Let's go."

A car ride had never lasted so long—not even the cross-country trip Grace had taken when she'd moved to Seattle. Every stop light turned red at the wrong time and every car ahead of them drove too slow. What was going on with Seth? Why hadn't Alec called again? They had to be at the hospital by now. They had to know *something*.

Please let him be okay, please let him be okay. Over and over she prayed.

Finally, when Grace couldn't stand it anymore, she grabbed her phone and dialed Alec's number. He didn't answer.

"They'll call when they know something," Lanna said quietly. "Alec knows how worried we are."

We. The word served as a rude awakening. Of course Lanna would be just as anxious as Grace. How could she have been so rude before? Fighting back more tears, Grace glanced out the window and watched the buildings pass slowly by.

"I'm sorry," she said finally. "About before. I'm just such a mess right now, and I didn't mean to take it out on you."

"I know." Lanna squeezed her hand, showing she wasn't upset or offended. "We're going to get through this."

Grace nodded, wishing the driver in front of them would learn how to use his gas pedal.

By the time they arrived at the hospital, the sun was high overhead. Grace slammed the car door shut and raced for the emergency room doors. They still hadn't heard anything from Alec.

Inside, the receptionist asked them to take a seat while she checked Seth's records to see where he was and if he was allowed visitors. Grace paced the waiting room and dialed Alec's phone once again. This time he answered.

"I still don't have much to tell you," Alec said without preamble. "Seth's awake and coherent. He wants to talk to you, but he's speaking with a nurse right now. We're in one of the ER rooms, but I'm not sure which one. The doctor says he can't move until they've read the results of the x-rays. Oh wait, here's the doctor now. Gotta go."

"Alec?" But he'd already hung up. Grace shoved her phone into her purse and walked straight to the receptionist, who'd finally looked up the information and directed them through two swinging doors.

"Well?" Lanna rushed after her. "What did he say?"

"They're talking to the doctor now." Grace rushed down the hallway, walking as fast as she could. Lanna's footsteps echoed behind her. When they arrived at the right room, the door was open, but Garrett and Owen blocked the way. Grace stopped behind them, straining to hear the doctor's words.

"Looks like you got off lucky this time," the doctor said. "Other than a concussion, you're going to be just fine."

Relief poured over Grace, making her lightheaded and weak. Seth was okay. Really okay. Lanna had been right after all.

Maybe this was a good thing. Maybe Seth would now see that he was human and breakable and—

"Take care of yourself, and no more crazy stunts, got it?" the doctor added.

"Sorry, but I make no such promises, doc," Seth's said with the usual teasing lilt in his voice. "I was that close to landing it, and next time, I will."

The doctor chuckled while Grace took a small step back, shaking her head. Next time? Why wasn't Seth treating this more seriously? Didn't he understand what could have happened? What almost *did* happen? It was like he didn't even care that he'd nearly hurt his body beyond repair.

Lanna cleared her throat, giving them away. Garrett glanced over his shoulder and moved aside, opening a path to Seth's bed.

One foot in front of the other, Grace walked slowly forward as conflicting emotions ping-ponged around inside her head, battling for control. She should feel only joy and relief. She should throw her arms around Seth, kiss him, and tell him how thrilled she was that he was okay. But doubt and fear kept her at the foot of his bed, unable to do anything but stare at the bruises and tape covering the cuts on his once-perfect face.

"About time you got here," Seth teased, lifting his arms to welcome her into what would be a warm and wonderful hug. She wanted so badly to walk into his arms and accept it, but something held her back.

Seth looked so handsome, so strong, so *human*—a human that seemed to think he was invincible no matter how many near misses he had. In that moment, Grace realized something. She couldn't live her life this way—with someone like him. It was too hard, too painful, too much.

Grace couldn't force herself to go to him and feign relief and joy when she was falling apart inside. Oxygen suddenly seemed hard to come by and the room way too crowded. Grace needed to get out of the room and as far away from the hospital and Seth as possible.

"I'm sorry," she choked out. "But I can't do this anymore." He deserved more of an explanation than that, but Grace couldn't say anything more—especially not in front of all their friends.

The bed creaked as Seth moved forward, reaching for her. "Grace—"

Prying the engagement ring from her finger, she dropped it on his bed. "I'm so sorry." With a strangled sob, she took a step back and bumped into someone. Without apologizing, Grace spun around and fled the room. Down the hall she ran, not caring that she didn't have a ride home. She'd call a cab later.

Once outside in the warm September afternoon, Grace gasped for air, feeling like her happy little world had just been torn apart.

Seth grabbed the bag containing his street clothes and began yanking at the ties on his hospital gown. Every movement had his body protesting the pain, but he didn't care.

"Unless everyone wants a show, I suggest you leave." The words came out harsh, but all Seth saw was Grace's ring—the one she should be wearing—sitting on some lousy hospital bed. He needed to find her and talk some sense into her. Now.

With the exception of Alec, everyone filed out of the room. Alec, on the other hand, merely turned his wheelchair away and stared out the window as Seth dressed.

"Don't go after her just yet," Alec said quietly.

Seth pulled his t-shirt over his head and grabbed his shoes, plopping down on the bed to put them on. "Why?" Nothing Alec could say would make him not go after Grace.

Alec twisted around to face him, looking worn out, tired, and dirty. "What you did today was stupid."

"Excuse me?" Seth paused, holding his shoelaces in his hands as he glared at Alec. He'd just lost Grace, and now her brother was calling him stupid? He didn't need this right now.

"The doctor was right—you did luck out." Alec wheeled himself closer and glared. "Seth, you attempted a back flip on bike. That's something you try a hundred times into a pool first. Any sane person would tell you that."

Seth's bruised body was saying the same thing, but he wasn't in the mood to hear it. Not when Grace was getting farther and farther away.

Ignoring Alec, Seth tied the last of his laces and stood, heading for the door.

"She's right, you know," Alec's voice rang out.

Seth stopped and stiffened, knowing he wouldn't like what Alec had to say. But he couldn't force himself to walk away either.

Alec approached from behind. "She shouldn't have to live her life always worrying you'll pull something stupid like you did today. You can't ask her to do that, not after all she's been through already." He paused and let out a breath. "A few months ago, you told me that my accident doesn't just affect me, it affects the people close to me as well. And you were right. I think you'd do well to remember that now."

With that, Alec wheeled himself past Seth and out of the small, barren hospital room. Seth watched him go, making no move to follow or find Grace.

Alec's words cut straight through as the full extent of what Seth had done to Grace sank in. Although his body felt bruised and beaten, his heart ached.

Thirty
♡ ♡ ♡

Grace went through the motions at work, but everything around her felt dull and lifeless, as if someone had erased all the color in the world. She smiled and joked with her patients, but her heart wasn't in it. It was broken.

Four days earlier, she'd given her ring back. She hadn't spoken to Seth since and didn't feel any better now than she had then. If anything, Grace felt worse. Seth hadn't tried to call or stop by. He hadn't even sent a text. It was like he'd accepted the fact that Grace was no longer a part of his life without so much as an argument.

That hurt more than anything.

Grace said goodbye to her last patient and walked into the break room, grabbing an apple from the fridge even though she had no appetite. She took a large bite and chewed, letting the juices run down her dry throat. From here on out, every day would get a little easier. It had to. In time, her heart would mend. She'd find a guy who liked to sit on his couch and play video games. A guy who thought an adventurous date was watching an action film. A guy who preferred strolling through the park to mountain biking and jumping out of airplanes.

But would he have Seth's energy, his ability to find joy and humor in pretty much everything? Would he be playful and fun and zap away all the gloominess in the world?

Grace frowned, missing Seth more than ever and wanting him to walk through the door right now.

If she were on the outside looking in, she'd probably want to yell at herself for being stupid, that Seth was perfect for her, and she needed to take one day at a time and not worry about what could happen. But she wasn't on the outside. She was on the inside, with a heart too vulnerable and scared to watch Seth leave every day and wonder if he'd come back in one piece.

"Hey, something wrong?" Cameron pulled out the chair across from her, flipped it around, and sat down. "You look like you just went through a bad breakup." He paused, searching her face before recognition dawned. "Wait, did you?"

Grace frowned. Cameron was the last person she wanted to have this conversation with. He was about as deep and sympathetic as an earthworm. But she couldn't outright lie to him either. "Maybe."

"Why?" His forehead wrinkled in confusion. "From what I could tell, you and Seth are great together."

Grace studied him. The fact that he'd figured all that out from observing her might mean that he had a little more depth to him than she thought. If Grace opened up to him, would he surprise her? Had she given Cameron too little credit?

Reluctantly, Grace gave him the Cliff's notes version of what had happened and waited anxiously for him to say something—anything—that would set her world straight once again.

Cameron cast a sidelong glance at the door, as though he felt in over his head and now wanted to make a break for it. When his attention returned to Grace, he cleared his throat. "How is that different from being married to a cop? Or anyone, for that matter? I mean who's to say Seth won't die in a car accident tomorrow? You can't protect him from everything."

"It *is* different," Grace argued. "Yes, police officers willingly put themselves in danger, but it's for a greater good. And yes, freak accidents happen all the time, but they're just that—freak accidents. Seth, on the other hand, willingly puts himself in harm's way, and for what? Because it's fun. It's an adventure. What about when kids come along? What then? How could I possibly tell our future child that something bad happened to his daddy because he wanted to experience an adrenalin rush?"

Cameron glanced longingly at the door once more and sighed. "Maybe you're right. Maybe it's for the best." With that, he patted her knee and walked away.

Grace frowned at his retreating back. It was all for the best? Did he really consider that a good pep talk? Apparently Cameron wasn't mentor material after all—not that she really expected otherwise.

"Knock, knock," said a deep voice from the doorway.

Grace jumped before realizing it was just Alec, sitting in a wheelchair and watching her. What was he doing here?

"Don't tell me you forgot about our training session."

Grace let out a breath of frustration. She had forgotten. Normally Tuesdays were the days she trained with Alec during her lunch break. But today it only meant four days since she'd walked away from Seth.

Tossing her half-eaten apple in the garbage, Grace left the break room behind and headed toward the bench press. She watched as Alec slid himself from his chair to the bench, swung his legs up, and laid down. Although he'd gotten better at doing that, the dead weight of his legs still made the movement look awkward.

This is why you gave the ring back and walked away—so you don't ever have to watch Seth go through something similar.

"Earth to Grace," Alec said.

Her eyes flew to his, and she realized Alec was waiting for her to change the weights out. What was he benching again? She stared at the weights, but couldn't make her foggy brain recall. Last week seemed like months ago.

Alec sighed. "Add fifty-five pounds to each side," he said patiently.

"I was just about to do that," Grace lied.

He rolled his eyes. "Yeah, and I was just about to walk."

Grace ignored him as she loaded the weights to one side. Twenty, forty, forty-five, fifty, done.

Alec watched her with a contemplative expression. After a few moments, he raised an eyebrow. "So . . . did you cancel the church?"

The question came out of nowhere. Grace blinked at him in surprise. "What?"

"The church—the one you're supposed to walk down the aisle at in three weeks. Did you cancel your reservation? What about the caterer, the flowers, the band?"

Grace suddenly felt weak, and she sank onto a nearby chair. *Cancel* seemed like such a final word, as though her emotional breakdown in the hospital somehow constituted a done deal—the kind you couldn't take back or say, "Hey, I've changed my mind." More than anything, Grace *wanted* to change her mind. She wanted to call Seth up, apologize for freaking out, promise to never do that again, and beg him to forgive her. She wanted the ring back on her finger and wanted to walk down that aisle in three weeks.

What she didn't want was a life filled with fear and worry.

Alec stared at her, waiting for an answer. She blinked. What had he asked again? Oh right, the church. "Um, no," she said. "I haven't gotten around to cancelling it yet."

"Why?"

Wasn't it obvious? Because she couldn't bring herself to do it. Just like she couldn't bring herself to do anything about the invitations that still sat on her kitchen counter. Instead, they remained where they were, serving as a reminder that Grace's life was currently in limbo-land—at least until she and Seth had the chance to really talk things through and figure it all out. Problem was, Grace wasn't sure she was ready for that kind of conversation yet.

Alec sighed, grabbed hold of the bar with only half of the weight loaded, and hoisted himself up to a sitting position. He glanced around the room briefly, as if to make sure no one was listening, then met Grace's eyes. "I tried to break up with Lanna."

What? Twice now he'd totally caught her off guard. Why would Alec possibly want to break up with Lanna? They were perfect for each other. "When?" she finally asked.

"About a month ago," said Alec.

"Oh." Grace let out a sigh of relief. Since they were still together that meant Lanna had somehow talked him out of it—something that Seth had yet to attempt with Grace. She suddenly felt envious of her brother. At least Lanna had put up a fight.

Alec leaned forward, resting his elbows on his knees. Then he snickered and shook his head. "You know what she said to me? After she sat on top of me and pinned me to my chair, that is."

Grace's mouth pulled into a smile at the image. "What?"

"She looked me straight in the eye and said, 'What are you afraid of? That one day I'll decide you're too much work and leave? Because that will never happen. What *could* happen is that I could die tomorrow from a brain aneurism or some other random thing. So could you. No one knows how long their time in this life will last. You just have to embrace every day and hope and pray that you'll get another and another. And I hope I get lots of days with you, because I want way more memories than I have right now, Alec Warren. So unless you tell me you don't care about me, I'm not going anywhere, and neither are you.'"

Grace nearly laughed. It was such a Lanna thing to say, and Grace wished she could have been a fly on the wall for that conversation. She could only imagine the look on Alec's face.

"She was right, you know," Alec continued. "Today could be it, so we may as well make the most of it."

If only it were as easy to apply the words as it was to understand them. "I'm glad to hear she talked you down," Grace said. "Breaking up with Lanna would have been the dumbest thing you could've done."

Alec raised an eyebrow. "Hypocrite."

"What? No." Grace frowned. "My situation's different."

He shrugged. "What worries you the most? That Seth will one day end up in a wheelchair like me?"

"No, that he'll end up in a coffin."

Alec cracked a smile at that. "There is that."

Grace glanced out the window. "Besides, what I worry about the most is the aftermath. What if something bad happens and he tries to push me out of his life the way you tried to do? What if he changes, too? I just don't have it in me to relive the last ten years all over again."

Alec didn't answer right away. He let the silence grow denser and denser until it felt like a heavy weight around Grace's shoulders. When she didn't think she could bear it any longer, he said, "You're forgetting one thing."

Grace's eyes flew to his. "What's that?"

"That Seth isn't me." He held up his hand as if to ward

off any arguments. "I'm not saying I condone his recklessness, although I think he'll tone it down from here on out. But look what happened when he tore his ACL. Did he hole up in his house and wallow? No. He got out, rented a bunch of wheelchairs, and convinced his friends to play wheelchair ball. He's the type of guy to make the most of any situation. Yes, he'd probably mourn for a little while, but then he'd pick himself up, get that sit-ski and that wheelchair mountain bike, and he'd keep doing what he loves to do. Because that's who Seth is—the type of person who really *will* make the most of it."

Alec let his words sink in then grabbed the bar and lowered himself down once more. "You're miserable without him, Grace, and I'm sure he's just as miserable as you. Go talk to him. Tell him to grow up and stop pulling crazy stunts, mail those invitations, and walk down that aisle. You'll always regret it if you don't. Take it from someone who knows all about regrets."

The words seeped into Grace's heart, warming it and filling it with hope. This was what she'd wanted to hear ever since she'd taken that ring off her finger—a reason to put it back on. Her brother was right. Seth was different.

Grace looked down at her brother with new respect and appreciation. "Regret is a funny thing, isn't it? It's such a heavy, yucky feeling, and no one likes to have it hanging around. But at the same time, it has the power to turn people into something wiser and stronger than they were before. Like you. Thank you."

Tears glistened in Alec's eyes as he nodded. Then he quickly blinked them away and tightened his fingers around the bar. "Are you ever going to add the rest of the weight? I'm beginning to think that I'm *your* therapist instead of the other way around."

Thirty-one

♡ ♡ ♡

The rest of the day, Grace felt lighter and happier—more at peace than she'd felt in four days. As she met with the rest of her patients, her smile was genuine and her focus right where it needed to be. On them.

At the end of the day, as she gathered her things together, Cameron poked his head into her office. "Glad to see our little chat made you feel better. I was thinking you should come clubbing with me and Talia tonight and get your mind off things." He shrugged. "Who knows, maybe you'll meet someone interesting. What do you say?"

It was nice of Cameron to think of her—not that Grace would ever be interested in the type of guy who hung out at a club—but she had something else in mind for tonight. Something that included a guy she was already very much interested in. "Thanks, but I'm going to pass."

He pointed a finger at her. "Just don't go and load up on ice cream or something stupid like that. No one's worth losing that nice figure for."

Grace nodded, thinking of the pint of Rocky Road ice cream she'd ingested the night before. If only Cameron knew how many times she'd turned to that treat for comfort over the years. "I'll keep that in mind."

"You do that." With another point of his finger, Cameron backed out of her office. Once he'd disappeared, Grace grabbed her keys and headed out. A smile played on her lips at the prospect of having Seth's ring on her finger by the night's end—assuming he still wanted it there.

But before she could find and talk to Seth, Grace had a few things to do. She needed to finally get those invitations off her counter and in the mail and make a quick stop at the nearest bike shop. It was time to get a bike of her own.

The stranger inspected Seth's mountain bike with the eyes of a novice. In his button-down, collared shirt, the man looked like he belonged more in an accounting office than on a mountain bike. He squatted down, studied the derailleur then glanced at Seth through wire-rimmed glasses. "Does Shimano make a good derailleur? I was told that's the most important thing to look for on a bike."

Seth tried to hide his annoyance. Good brakes and shocks were what? Just a perk? From the moment this guy had opened his mouth, it was clear he was a mountain-bike wannabe who knew nothing about the sport and couldn't tell a high end bike from a Mongoose purchased at Walmart.

"It's pronounced Shim-*aw*-no, not Shim-*a*-no," Seth clarified. "And yes, they do. The XTR is top of the line. As are the brakes, shocks, wheels, and frame."

"Why are these pedals so small?" he asked next.

Seth resisted the impulse to pry his bike from the guy's fingers. Who didn't know what a click pedal was? A guy who didn't deserve to own Seth's bike, no matter how much he was willing to pay. "They're designed to be used with cleats so your feet stay on the pedals. I have the originals somewhere in my garage and will switch them out."

The man fiddled with the brakes and even tried to switch the gears. "And you say the brakes and tires are top of the line as well?"

"I upgraded them myself," Seth mustered. He should have priced his bike what it was worth instead of discounting it for a quick sale. Then maybe someone who actually knew something about mountain biking would have shown up instead of this moron.

"Yourself?" The guy frowned. "Why would you mess with a bike that's supposedly top of the line?"

"To make it even better," Seth said. Did he really have to explain that? He grasped his bike by the handlebars, ready to put it safely back inside his garage. He'd find another, more deserving buyer. "Listen, I really don't think this is the right bike for you. Maybe you should try Baylor Bikes. They're not far from here and could hook you up with something you'd probably trust a little more."

The man grabbed the handlebars on the opposite side, as if afraid Seth would take it from him. "No, that's okay. I think I'll take it."

He *thought*? Seth's patience was about up.

A car drove by, slowed, and pulled into Seth's driveway. His glance flickered from his bike to the car, then immediately back to the car, where Seth zeroed in on the driver. Grace. Their eyes met through the window, and Seth's heartbeat sped up. Suddenly, he didn't care about his bike or who bought it. In fact, he was ready to thrust it at the man and say, "Here, take it. It's yours."

Grace left her car behind and was now walking toward him, looking beautiful and kissable and wonderful. She wore the red shirt from their first date—a shirt Seth had come to love—and her hair hung in soft curls around her face. He wanted to crush her to him and kiss her long and hard to make up for all the days he hadn't been able to.

"What are you doing?" she asked, glancing from the bike to the idiot man.

"Selling my bike."

"Why?"

Did she really have to ask? "Because it's dangerous, and I don't do dangerous things anymore."

The corners of Grace's mouth twitched up. "That's too bad because I'm here to ask for mountain-biking lessons. How are you going to teach me if you don't have a bike?"

"What?" Seth had never felt more confused. She wanted lessons? Why? She hated the sport.

Grace stuffed her hands into her pockets and shrugged. "I just bought a bike and figured it would be a good idea to learn how to ride better. I was hoping you could be the one to teach me."

"I'm sorry, you did what?" Seth asked, his forehead crinkling in confusion. Grace had given her ring back on account of a mountain-bike accident, and now she'd gone out and bought a bike on purpose? Nothing was making sense right now.

"I. Bought. A. Mountain. Bike." Grace emphasized each word. "I'm here to borrow your car so I can go pick it up. Mine doesn't have a bike rack." She paused. "Yet."

Seth felt as though he'd entered a surreal universe where everything was the opposite of what it was supposed to be. He was selling his bike. Grace just bought one. Even the potential buyer of his bike was acting smarter, based on the fact that he was finally scribbling out a check for a bike worth much more than the asking price.

Grace eyed the man. "Sorry, sir, but the bike's no longer for sale."

"What?" He shot Grace a confused, blank stare—one that brought Seth back to reality.

Without a second thought, Seth pulled the bike—*his* bike—toward him. "She's right. It isn't for sale anymore."

"But I drove all the way from North Gate," the man protested. "And I have the check already made out."

Seth dug in his pocket and pulled out two twenty-dollar bills then slapped them into the guy's hand. "That should more than cover your gas."

The man frowned and glared at Grace before shoving his checkbook back inside his pocket. With a huff, he turned and stalked to his car. Seth had never been more glad to see anyone go.

Slowly, he lowered his bike to the ground and left it there. His heart hammered as his eyes met Grace's. "Did you really just buy a bike?"

"Were you really just about to sell yours?" She walked toward him, stopping right in front of him.

"Yeah," said Seth.

"Why?" she asked again, her beautiful green eyes focused on him.

"Because I'd rather have you." Seth paused, wanting to pull her to him, but not daring to touch her just yet. "I actually listed it Saturday night, but no one came to look at it until today. I figured I couldn't ask you back until I had proof that I'm willing to change."

Her lips drew into her mouth as her eyes glistened with unshed tears. She blinked them away and smiled. "That's ironic, because I bought a bike for the exact same reason." She took a tentative step toward him and interlocked her fingers with his. "I came here with a compromise: I'll learn to mountain bike the mild runs if you promise to stay away from x-game-ish stunts. I can't stand the thought of anything bad happening to you."

Seth brought his hands to her shoulders and rubbed them up and down as he looked her in the eye. "Grace, what I said back in the hospital to the doctor—about making no promises to tone it down—that was only a pathetic attempt to lighten the mood. The truth is, I underestimated the angle on that jump and never meant to attempt a back roll. But it threw my front tire up, and I had to try to get it all the way around or I would have landed flat on my back. In those few seconds, I'd never been more scared in my life." He paused. "At least not until you gave my ring back and walked out on me. That was worse than anything." His fingers gripped her shoulders tighter, willing her to understand. "Please, believe me when I say that I will never do anything like that again. I don't want anything bad happening to me either and would never want to hurt you in any way."

Grace continued to fight back her tears, then nodded. "You have no idea how good it is to hear you say that."

A smile played on Seth's face as he finally brought his hand to her collarbone, just below her chin. She swallowed as his fingers trailed to the back of her neck. Tentatively, he pulled her closer. His mouth met hers slowly and carefully at first, then much more eagerly. Grace had never felt or tasted so good, and Seth couldn't get enough. Four days had been way too long to be apart from her. She belonged here, with him.

When her arms wrapped around his neck, Seth lifted her off the ground, pulling her tight against him as he deepened the kiss.

A loud whistle sounded from a car passing by, and Grace broke away, laughing and blushing. "Maybe we should continue this in a less public place."

Seth reached for her hand to pull her inside his house, but she resisted, tugging him toward the garage instead.

"*After* we pick up my bike," she said. "The store closes at seven."

Seth groaned, feeling starved for more of her affection. "We can always get it tomorrow."

She shook her head. "I want to see what you think of it

now. It's green and gray and a little sparkly. I fell in love with it the second I saw it."

Seth stopped, pulling her to a stop as well. "Please tell me you didn't buy a mountain bike based on looks."

Grace bit her lip briefly before glancing up at him. "What's wrong with that? I mean, a mountain bike's a mountain bike, right?"

Seth groaned again, then laughed, wrapping an arm around her shoulders as he guided her toward his car. With a shake of his head, he said, "No, sweetie, it's not. How much did you pay for it anyway?"

"Way too much. The thing cost six hundred dollars."

Seth laughed again, harder this time. As he opened the door for her, Grace looked at him in confusion, probably the same way the wannabe mountain-bike buyer had looked at him earlier. Only on Grace, the expression was adorable rather than annoying.

Seth would take her back to the store, get a refund, and show her how to pick out a *real* mountain bike. Then he'd bring her back here and continue the kiss where they'd left off.

"What's so funny?" Grace said.

"You are." Seth couldn't resist giving her a quick kiss before closing the door. Then he jogged inside his house, grabbed a box off his dresser, and slid into the car next to her. With shaking hands, he held the ring out to her, feeling like he was proposing all over again. "I found this somewhere it didn't belong. You wouldn't happen to want it back, would you?"

She grabbed the ring from him and slid it onto her finger. Then she leaned over and kissed his cheek, murmuring, "Only if I get you back with it."

Thirty-two

♡ ♡ ♡

About four months later

Over 8,000 acres of skiable terrain stretched out beneath Grace as she and Seth rode the Harmony Express lift to the top of the Whistler side of Whistler Blackcomb in British Colombia. The sun shone down from a clear blue sky, making the nippy thirty-degree temperature feel not quite as cold. Grace raised her face to the sun and smiled.

It had been exactly eleven years to the day since the last time she'd been here and ridden this same lift to the top of the run. Only then, Alec had sat next to her with alpine skis strapped to his feet. Today, Seth sat next to her with Alec and Lanna on the chair behind them. After weeks of lessons so he could figure out his new sit-skis, Alec finally felt confident enough to face the slopes on his own—well, with Lanna, Seth, and Grace, anyway.

Grace looked over her shoulder at her brother and Lanna. The two of them had officially gotten engaged a month earlier and were eagerly planning an early summer wedding. Grace couldn't be happier. Only a year before, this

236

day had seemed like an impossible dream. But then Seth and Lanna came along, and that dream was now a reality.

Just as Seth had promised, he toned it down. There was no more sky-diving, no more extreme mountain biking, and no more dangerous stunts. As the weeks passed, Grace found herself worrying less and trusting more. She even started to enjoy mountain biking.

In early January, Seth had surprised her, Lanna, and Alec with this trip to Whistler Blackcomb. He'd called Grace's parents to make sure the date was right, booked hotel rooms, and purchased lift tickets for the four of them. Then he'd pointed to the bittersweet picture of Grace and Alec standing at the top of the Harmony Express lift.

"We're going to that exact same spot and snapping a picture," he'd said. "It will be like a before and after shot, reminding you both of how far you've come."

Tears had prickled Grace's eyes the same way they did every time she recalled Seth's words and reflected on how wonderful her husband was. She scooted closer and laid her head against his shoulder, feeling the wind nip at her face and loving every second of it.

"You ready for this?" Seth asked with a teasing tone. The statement had become an inside joke between them. Every time Seth took her on some new adventure—be it mountain biking, wakeboarding, or kayaking—he asked her that same question. The day of their wedding, she'd turned the tables and had asked him.

"Bring it on," he'd answered, making Grace laugh.

Ever since that memorable moment, any time the question was asked by either one of them, the response was the same.

"Bring it on." Grace smiled, snuggling closer.

Seth's arm tightened around her, and he rested his chin on the top of her head. "That's my girl," he said.

237

At the top of the lift, neither Grace nor Alec could remember the exact place they'd stood all those years before. Seth pulled out the picture and studied it.

Grace laughed. "I can't believe you brought that with you. Isn't it enough that we're at the top of the same lift? We can stand anywhere."

Seth shot her a look. "Apparently you don't understand the concept of before and after pictures. The background and camera angle have to be the same."

"But we could spend all day trying to find that exact same spot," Grace argued, not wanting to stand in the cold for any longer than necessary. The wind was always more bitter at the top of the lifts.

"Then we're going to spend all day," came his response. "And tomorrow, too, if we have to."

Grace looked to Alec and Lanna for help, but Lanna only offered a sympathetic smile while Alec shrugged, balancing himself with poles that looked like mini skis. "Don't look at us," Alec said. "You married him."

Seth lifted his camera to his face, glanced at the screen, then back at the picture. A few steps to the right and he did it again. He looked ridiculous dodging other skiers as he tromped through the snow with a camera in one hand and an old picture in the other.

After a few minutes, Grace had enough. She walked over to him and lifted the camera strap over his head, taking it from him. Then she waved at a nearby skier. "Mind taking a picture for us?"

"Sure," the teenager said.

"But I haven't found the right spot yet," Seth protested. "This is the whole reason we came here."

Grace handed the camera off and pulled Seth toward Lanna and Alec. "Over here," she said to the kid. "There's four of us."

"Fine," Seth said. "We'll take one of all of us, then I'll take one of you and Alec in the right spot."

Grace stopped and placed her gloved fingers on his chest. She looked into his eyes at a face she'd come to trust and love more than she'd ever imagined possible. "This picture is all I want," Grace said. "It's like you said before. No moment can ever be repeated, and I'm more than okay with that. You and Lanna are now in our lives for good, and you're both a part of what makes today so special." Grace pointed to the picture from the past that Seth still gripped in one of his gloved hands. "That was my before." She patted his chest. "You're my after. Got it?"

A smile spread across Seth's face as he shoved the picture back into his pocket. "I like being your after," he said. Then he dipped his head, gave her a quick kiss, and put his arm around her as they walked to where Alec sat and Lanna stood. Facing the camera, he pulled Grace tight against him.

"Bring it on, Whistler Blackcomb!" he hollered, making everyone laugh as the snapshot was taken.

Later, the picture was framed and placed on Seth and Grace's mantle, right next to the one of her and Alec. Every time she paused to look at them and reflect on the befores and afters of her life, Grace came to realize that sometimes bad things happened, and there was nothing she could do about it. But like a seedling from a large oak tree, out of the bad could grow a good so big and beautiful that it overshadowed everything else.

Seth had taught her that. Just like he taught her about life, about adventure, and about love. Although he would always tease and wreak chaos and try Grace's patience, there was no one else she would rather live her afters with.

Dear Reader,

Thank you so much for carving time out of your life to read one of my books. I hope it took you out of reality for awhile and into a world of escape and rejuvenation because everyone deserves that once in awhile.

If you enjoyed this book, I'd really appreciate a review from you on Goodreads or Amazon or wherever else you'd be willing to post one. Word of mouth is the best kind of advertising there is, and I could definitely use your help to get the word out.

I also love to hear from readers, and if you're so inclined, you can find me at www.rachaelreneeanderson.com.

Thanks again, and happy reading!

Rachael

An excerpt from Karey White's

MY OWN MR. DARCY

Chapter One

The theater was nearly empty. It might have been because of the late hour but I suspected it was because this movie was going to be a snoozefest.

"Darn, they got the best seats," Mom said, tilting her head toward a row of silver-haired women.

"Mom, there are plenty of seats," I said.

"I know, I know. I just wanted to be right in the center." Mom started up the dimly lit stairs. We lagged a few steps behind her.

"What have we gotten ourselves into?" I whispered to Janessa.

She gave me a stern, best-friend glare and an elbow jab. "Your mom's excited. Don't spoil it for her." I rolled my eyes.

Janessa and I were the only teenagers in the room. Everyone else was even older than Mom. The five silver-haired women were talking loudly and giggling. They probably didn't get out much. One of the women held a handbag the size of carryon luggage in her lap and another had a scarf with a jeweled pin that sparkled even in the near darkness.

There wasn't a man in sight. No wonder Dad had refused to come.

"How about here?" Mom said, indicating seats two rows in front of the senior citizen contingency. I looked at Janessa and she shrugged her shoulders. We followed Mom into the row and I planted myself with a sigh into the plush seat. At least the theater was nice—new enough that my seat still had spring and my feet didn't stick to the floor.

Mom linked her arm through mine. "Lizzie, you could at least pretend to be having fun. I'm letting you go to a late movie on a school night. Do you think you could muster up a teeny tiny smile?"

I gave my mom a cheesy, fake smile. She shook her head and laughed and I caved and smiled a real smile. "I don't understand why you wouldn't want to come," Mom said. "You know you were named after the main character."

"I thought I was named after Dad's aunt," I said.

Mom waved me off. "Her, too. I wanted to name you Elizabeth after Elizabeth Bennet because she's strong and smart and confident. All the things I wanted you to become. Dad thought it was silly to name you after a character in a book, especially since our last name is Barrett. I finally got him to agree by reminding him he could tell everyone you were named after his aunt."

"Just because I'm named after her doesn't mean this movie won't be boring."

Janessa elbowed me again. "Come on, Lizzie. This is better than homework. Or being in bed. Thanks for convincing my mom to let me come, Mrs. Barrett."

"I'm glad you could join us," Mom said.

"You'll have to tell us how closely it follows the book," I said.

Mom looked at me with suspicion. "Just remember, you

girls are seeing this movie in addition to reading the book. Not instead of reading it."

"Of course, we'll read it," Janessa said.

The truth was I had no intention of reading the book. I'd started it three times since Mr. Malloy gave us the reading list and I just didn't get it. The words made no sense and by the third page, I was lost. I was depending on this movie and the Internet to give me all the information I'd need to ace this unit.

"I'm serious. Lizzie? You girls promise me you're going to read the book or we'll leave right now. I won't help you cheat." I stared at a woman with an unusually large smile on the screen. I guess her oversized white teeth were supposed to entice us to visit Dr. Stonesmith's office for free teeth whitening. "Are you going to read the book, Lizzie?" The screen changed to a lawyer with perfect helmet-hair who could defend my rights if I was hurt in an auto accident. "Lizzie?"

"You know I always end up reading the books, Mom. I'm a good student. That's why I'm in Honors English."

"We'll read it together, Mrs. Barrett," Janessa said.

Satisfied, Mom settled back into her seat. "You're going to love it. I've read it every few years since I was your age. And I've seen the 6-hour mini-series at least three times," Mom said. "This is going to be fun."

I enjoy a good romance and Mom assured me this was, but I preferred romances that took place in the twenty-first century. I'd seen a couple of movies made in the eighties and nineties that I liked, but only a couple. Mr. Malloy had told us Pride and Prejudice was a classic romance from the early nineteenth century.

That was two-hundred years ago!

Jane Austen may have been a talented writer, but what did anyone from two-hundred years ago know about romance? And Mom. Sitting here in her mom-jeans and a pale blue polo shirt, Mom didn't exactly inspire romantic confidence. She couldn't even convince Dad to come with her. If this was a romance for the ages, it shouldn't have been difficult to persuade the love of her life to sit beside her in a dark theater for an hour and a half.

When Dad had refused for the tenth time, Mom turned to me. Lucky for her, Pride and Prejudice was next on our reading list or it would have taken a hefty bribe to get me here, whether I was named after this Elizabeth or not. Thank goodness for Janessa. At least sitting through the movie would give us something we could laugh about later.

The lights dimmed and the previews began. I nestled down in my seat and propped my feet up in front of me.

I have a theory about previews. I think you can tell a lot about a movie by the previews they show before it and if my theory held up, we were in trouble. The first trailer was for a movie about a Scottish cyclist with bi-polar disorder. Fun! The star was cute but the movie looked dismal. The second starred Russell Crowe as a greedy businessman who learns the meaning of life when he travels to Europe to sell a vineyard. Ugh. Riveting stuff.

The movie opened with some pretty scenes of the English countryside and a piano song so gentle and lilting, it could have put me to sleep. Elizabeth walked across the meadow reading. I'd seen Keira Knightley in Bend it Like Beckham and she looked even prettier here. There was a houseful of girls and a silly mother. There was a father that liked to tease the mother. And woo hoo! The new guy was single and rich and he was going to be at the dance.

Soon a crowd of poorly dressed country folk was dancing to some lively music. It was crowded and noisy and I could imagine the room probably smelled bad.

And then something happened—both on the screen and inside me. I took my feet off the seat in front of me and leaned forward. The new guy and his friend had just walked into the dance. Mr. Bingley was smiley and charming and cute in a goofy way, but I hardly noticed him. His friend was Mr. Darcy.

And Mr. Darcy was magnificent.

Sure, he was surly and dour. But he was tall and imposing. He looked around the room with contempt and while his mouth said boorish things about the local girls, his eyes were drawn toward Elizabeth.

Blue eyes.Interesting eyes.Expressive eyes.

The rest of the movie I was enchanted. I ached for it to go on and on and dreaded the moment it would end. Every time Mr. Darcy was on the screen, I melted. When he looked at Elizabeth, I couldn't breathe. When he helped her into the carriage, I gripped the armrest a little tighter. When he danced with her my heart stopped beating for a second. He was the most intriguing man I'd ever seen.

Did I mention Mr. Darcy's eyes?

And then they argued in the rain and they were so passionate and the place was so beautiful. I knew every daydream I'd ever dreamed would have to be re-imagined to include those giant, mossy pillars and that vast, green countryside. Even the rain was romantic.

I wondered if they'd kiss. I wanted them to kiss. The anticipation of it all was killing me and I considered asking mom how it would end just to ease my mind, but I couldn't let her know how much I was enjoying this movie she'd had to drag me to. Mr. Darcy leaned in so close I don't know how they didn't kiss. His feelings were so obvious in his eyes I don't know how Elizabeth could stand it.

And then Elizabeth refused him. How could she? Just kiss her! She'd be putty in his hands if he'd just kiss her. But he didn't and when he left and she collapsed against the wall, I wanted to cry.

Oh no! I was going to cry. I couldn't cry at this movie. That would be far too embarrassing. I blinked hard and fast.

It took much too long for Mr. Darcy to reappear on the screen. Okay fine. It wasn't that long, but it felt much too long. He was so quiet and hard to read, but when he was with his sister, he was happy and he smiled.

Oh my goodness. That smile. And I wanted to float away in his eyes.

I loved this movie and it was going to end much too quickly. Finally Mr. Bingley, who turned out to be more adorable than goofy proposed to beautiful Jane. And then there was the hateful aunt. Rich snob! No wonder Mr. Darcy was so arrogant. And then Elizabeth couldn't sleep because she knew she was in love with Mr. Darcy, so she went for an early morning walk in the meadow.

The meadow.

During the forty-five seconds that Mr. Darcy walked across the meadow, my life changed. Each long stride he took toward me—I mean Elizabeth—lodged itself in my heart and I would never be the same. The mist, the sunrise, the trench coat, and the sweet declaration of his love melded into the most beautiful few minutes I'd ever seen and I was bewitched body and soul.

I felt a terrible emptiness when the movie ended. Mom and Janessa started talking almost immediately but I didn't listen to them. I sat perfectly still, listening as the piano music filled my soul.

When the lights came up, I followed Mom and Janessa out of the theater to the chilly, almost-empty parking lot. "Did you like it?" Mom asked. I nodded. "What about you, Janessa?"

"It was much better than I thought it would be," she said. "At least I'm not dreading the book so much now."

"You'll love the book," Mom said.

"I'll understand it better now that I've seen the movie," Janessa said. "Lizzie? Are you okay?"

"I'm fine."

"You have a funny look on your face."

I shook myself back to the present. "No, you have a funny look on your face." Maybe sarcasm could rescue me. I couldn't let them know how utterly transformed I was.

Janessa shook her head. "Whatever."

That night I couldn't fall asleep. Something had happened to me. I was no longer the person I'd been just a few short hours ago. I didn't think about Jake from the soccer team, the boy who'd been my crush for the last six months. I no longer cared if he noticed me or not. He was just a boy, after all.

That night a dream was born. I'd discovered what I wanted, what I knew someday I must have. I knew I could never be satisfied until I found it.

I wanted my own Mr. Darcy.

Two

SIX YEARS LATER

Janessa walked into the kitchen stretching like a cat awakened after a century of slumber. Even in the morning, with her short, dark hair sticking up in all directions, she was beautiful. Janessa was the much prettier half of our best-friends duo. Her blue eyes and fair skin seemed lit from within, ethereal almost. My light, wavy hair and the freckles across my nose and cheeks would never inspire people to call me beautiful. Cute was the word most often used, if anyone commented on my looks at all.

"Oh, you're still here," she said. "I thought you'd be gone to work already." Janessa was a manager at Urban

Elegance, a boutique women's clothing store in the mall. She didn't have to be to work until nearly ten so I was usually gone before she got up.

"I needed a good breakfast this morning. There's a teller meeting during lunch and Delia always orders the worst food. I may not get anything decent to eat until tonight."

"How was your big date yesterday? I wanted a full report but you were already asleep when I came in." Janessa pulled out a bowl and rattled through the spoons. Everything she did in the kitchen made noise. Even by herself, she sounded like an entire staff of energetic sous chefs. She loudly shuffled through a half dozen boxes of cereal before settling on Cheerios.

"It was fine but it wasn't a big date. It was lunch."

"Was there potential?"

"I don't think so."

"What was wrong with this one?"

"Who said there was anything wrong with him?"

"You don't have a list of objections for me?" Janessa raised one eyebrow, a talent I couldn't master no matter how hard I tried.

"I don't have objections about everyone I date," I said.

"So when are you going out again?"

"Probably never."

"So there was something wrong with him." Janessa said.

"No, there wasn't. He was a perfect gentleman," I said.

"Then why don't you want to go out with him again?" I shrugged. "Listen Lizzie. Any guy who gets up the courage to ask a girl out at the grocery store should get a few bonus points. Go out with him again."

Last week I'd been standing in the Asian aisle of the grocery store picking up some curry paste and coconut milk. "Do you actually drink coconut milk?" a tall, cute guy asked.

"I suppose you could but I don't know anyone who does. I use it for chicken curry."

"Sounds interesting. You like Indian food?"

"It's actually Thai."

"I haven't had Thai food for years. I don't know why. I think I liked it."

"I start craving it at least once a month. Sometimes I get it from PokPok and sometimes I make it myself."

"PokPok?" he'd asked.

"It's over on Division Street. If you like Thai, you should try it. The food is amazing."

"I'll keep that in mind. I'm Chad, by the way." I shook his outstretched hand. I couldn't help but smile. It was cute that he'd shake my hand in the grocery store.

"I'm Lizzie."

"Nice to meet you, Lizzie. I'm just stocking up on ramen." He waved a little plastic pouch of ramen and put it back in his basket.

"Ramen has its place," I said.

"Sure." I watched as he walked away. When he reached the end of the aisle, he turned around and walked back to me.

"I just have to ask. Would you mind if I called you sometime? Maybe we could meet for lunch or something?"

"Oh, um . . ." He was cute and earnest but I could already tell there was no future.

"Unless you're not available. You probably have a boyfriend, right?"

I shook my head. "I don't have a boyfriend."

"Then can I call you?"

"Uh, sure. I guess so."

"Great." Chad handed me his cell phone and I punched in my number. "Thanks. I'll be in touch." He put his phone back in his pocket and shook my hand again before he left.

He'd called me two nights ago. We'd met for lunch yesterday.

"I just wasn't interested," I said to Janessa. "Can we leave it at that?"

Janessa folded her arms and looked at me for so long I started to squirm. "What?"

"I wish you'd look at yourself. You're ruining your life with this stupid obsession."

"I'm not obsessed." I stood up quickly, nearly tipping my chair over. I rinsed my plate and put it in the dishwasher. I could feel Janessa's eyes on me the entire time, but I refused to look at her. "And just because I'm not interested in this guy doesn't mean my life is ruined."

"Let me guess. Was he blond?"

"Knock it off."

"Too short?"

"He wasn't short. I've got to go." I left the kitchen with Janessa on my heels.

"Was he too cheerful?"

"Oh brother. I'm not having this conversation with you."

Janessa grabbed my arm and turned me toward her. "Yes, you are."

"I'm going to be late for work."

"Then we'd better talk fast."

"I don't have anything to say," I said.

"Then I'll talk. You listen. You have to start giving these guys a chance."

I folded my arms tightly. "I give them a chance."

"You give them one date, two at the most. But you're not really giving them a chance because your mind's already made up before you even go out."

I was getting annoyed. "I don't have time for this conversation again." Janessa was practically reciting word for word what she'd said after my last date. And the one before that.

"Lizzie. If you don't want to have the same conversation, do something different. Shake things up a little." She smiled and did a little shimmy. I refused to smile no matter how silly she looked.

"How do you suggest I do that?"

"If this guy . . . What's his name?"

"Chad."

"If Chad calls you back, go out with him again."

I sighed. "I don't see the point."

"Did you get a serial killer vibe from him?"

"No, I got a nice-guy-that-doesn't-deserve-to-be-led-on vibe from him."

"Nice guys are good. So you'll say yes, right?"

"If I'm not interested, it wouldn't be fair to say yes."

"Oh knock off the baloney. You haven't been fair to a guy since high school. You're just afraid if you get to know a guy, you might like him. And wouldn't that be awful? Was Chad funny?"

"Yes, he was funny."

"Handsome?"

I sighed. "I don't know if I'd call him handsome, but he was cute."

"Cute is good. Especially if he was funny. So go out with him again."

"You act like it's all up to me." I walked to the closet and collected my purse. Like a tiger leaping on her prey, Janessa pounced at the bowl on the entry table and grabbed my car keys. "This isn't funny, Janessa. I'm going to be late for work."

"Then let's make a deal. You agree to go out with him ten times before you toss him aside and I'll give you your keys."

"Ten times?No way."

"That'll give you time to get to know him."

"You've got to be kidding."

"I'm serious, Lizzie. Ten is a good number. In that amount of time, you can make a real decision. Instead of one based on a stupid movie."

Now Janessa was skipping through a minefield. "It's not a stupid movie and I've got to go."

"It's the stupidest movie in the world if it ruins your life."

"Nothing's ruining my life and I'm going to be late. Give me my keys and we'll talk about this later." A little tussle ensued as I tried to rescue my keys from her clutches. I almost had them when she darted to the bathroom and shut the door hard and fast, locking it behind her. "This is real mature."

"I don't care about mature. You're my best friend, Lizzie. I love you and I'm trying to save you from yourself."

I banged on the door. "Give me the keys. Now." My voice had become shrieky.

"I'll give you the keys as soon as you promise you'll go out with him ten times."

"I doubt he'll ask me out again."

"Why? Were you a jerk?"

"No."

"Are you sure?"

I hesitated, knowing I hadn't been very good company. "I'm pretty sure."

"If he doesn't ask you out, you have to ask him."

"No way am I asking out a guy ten times. No way!"

"You just have to ask him out once. If he doesn't return the favor you can move on. But you have to be nice to him and give him a reason to want to ask you out again."

"This is the dumbest idea you've ever had."

"Listen Liz, I'm doing this for you. Give a guy a chance before you give him the old heave-ho."

I leaned my head on the door. "Just give me the keys. Please." Now I was whining.

"You're the one keeping yourself from your keys. And probably true love."

I looked at my watch. Now I'd have to risk a speeding ticket or get to work five minutes late. I wasn't sure which was worse—a ticket from a police officer or a tongue-lashing from Delia.

"Fine. I'll go out with him again if he asks me."

"And?"

"If he doesn't ask me, I'll ask him?"

"Right. And how many times will you go out with him?"

"Way too many," I said under my breath.

"I can't hear you."

"Ten times.If he asks me."

The door cracked open. "And you'll be nice to him?"

"Whatever you say. Now give me the keys."

Janessa emerged from the bathroom and triumphantly dropped my keys into my outstretched hand.

"You're an idiot," I said.

"An idiot that loves you and wants you to be happy," she said. She turned and headed down the hall. "Someday you'll thank me," she sang.

"If I don't kill you first." I slammed the door behind me.

If you enjoyed this excerpt and would like to read more, you can find this book on Amazon or read more about Karey and her books at www.KareyWhite.com.

Acknowledgements

A hundred-million thanks to Braden Bell, for his amazing critique skills. To Karey White and Annette Lyon, for their keen eyes and editing genius. To Julie Bellon, for her talented way with words and willingness to help me with the blurb for this book. To my mom, Linda Marks, for always being ready and excited to read anything I write. To my children, for being patient and supportive. And to my husband, Jeff, for being the wonderful person you are.

About the Author

ℛachael Anderson is the author of five books and two anthologies. She's the mother of four and is pretty good at breaking up fights, or at least sending guilty parties to their rooms. She can't sing, doesn't dance, and despises tragedies. But she recently figured out how yeast works and can now make homemade bread, which she is really good at eating. You can read more about her and her books online at www.rachaelreneeanderson.com.